Harriet Elizabeth Prescott Spofford

Sir Rohan's Ghost

A romance

Harriet Elizabeth Prescott Spofford

Sir Rohan's Ghost
A romance

ISBN/EAN: 9783337048952

Printed in Europe, USA, Canada, Australia, Japan

Cover: Foto ©Andreas Hilbeck / pixelio.de

More available books at **www.hansebooks.com**

Sir Rohan's Ghost.

A ROMANCE.

BOSTON:

J. E. TILTON AND COMPANY,

161 WASHINGTON STREET.

1860.

University Press, Cambridge :
Electrotyped and Printed by Welch, Bigelow, & Co.

At her feet he bowed, he fell, he lay down; at her feet he bowed, he fell: where he bowed, there he fell down dead.

" Si l'on entendoit bien la différence qu'il y a entre l'impossible et l'inusité, et entre ce qui est contre l'ordre du
cours de nature, et contre la commune opinion des hommes;
en ne croyant pas temerairement, ny aussi ne descroyant
pas facilement, on observeroit la reigle de *Rien trop*, com-
mandée par Chilon."

MONTAIGNE.

CONTENTS.

CONTENTS.

Sir Rohan's Ghost.

I.

SIR ROHAN.

THERE is a Ghost in all aristocratic families, and therefore it is not to be presumed that the great house of Belvidere was destitute. But though it had dragged on a miserable existence some three hundred years without one, at last that distinction was to arrive. Sir Rohan had a Ghost. Not by any means a common ghost that appeared at midnight on the striking of a bell, and trailed its winding-sheet through the upper halls nearest the roof, but a Ghost that, sleeping or waking, never left him, a Ghost whose long hair coiled round and stifled the fair creations of his dreams, and whose white garments swept leprously into his sunshine.

Sir Rohan had left his home in the northeast of England, and had refurnished one more cheerful, on the opposite extremity of the island, in

Cornwall. Pleasant fields extended on either hand, a woody mountain climbed behind, and the long swells of the Atlantic rolled in front. Fine pictures adorned the galleries, soft draperies shrouded the apartments, and delicate sculptures confronted you at every turn. But something else confronted Sir Rohan; the Ghost had flitted too, and even here he found no rest. If he galloped up the lawns from his morning ride, the sad, pale face looked earnestly from door or window on him and faded; and if he rowed homeward in the sunset, with his listless spray-washed sail, the same face gazed from a balcony dreamily out to sea.

In determined attempts to lay this Ghost, Sir Rohan threw himself into the heat of foray and battle. Braver knight there was not in the kingdom; but he left the army, for the shape glided perpetually between his sword and his foe, charged breathless and with glistening eyes beside him, rode with the same glitter as earnestly in retreat, covered him with its oppressive vacancy when he fell, till sense ebbed away with his blood. Then Sir Rohan essayed oratory and statesmanship; but the shape, so distinct that it seemed as if others too must see it, swayed its long arm beside him as he spoke, and sobbed Banshee-like, with a rustling inspiration, in his pauses. Sir Rohan left the bench and bar. Dissipation opened its arms to receive him, midnight drawing-rooms were proud to hold him, gay dances wreathed themselves to his motions, rosy cheeks flushed at his approach. But a pale cheek was beside the rosy ones, an airier form glided through the dancers and did not disturb the set; and, with the red wine before him, a long white finger plunged down the glass and brought up the glittering trophy of a golden ring. Sir Rohan reformed. Yet perhaps in the dry recesses of old libraries he might be alone, and so he delved deep among musty tomes, striving to bury his heart with the dust of ages that he found there; but another hand shifted the leaves as he read, and eyes devoid of speculation met his as he unconsciously turned for sympathy in the page. When on some rude map he traced the route of conquerors, another finger followed his, pointing out spots at which he did not glance, and resting wearily on places he would gladly have blotted from existence;

and as his eye wandered in quest of some desired volume on higher shelves, the Ghost fluttered up and down below it. Sir Rohan left literature.

Was there, then, nothing in which this haunted man could bury himself? He, who was in no wise else a coward, here followed the beck and call of a nameless fear, a shrouded and indistinct influence, that forbade adventure and exploit, and with a cold, bold hand played jarring discords on his heart-strings, and fought perpetually with the strong heroic ambition that opposed it. To the lustre of a great name Sir Rohan would fain have added further brilliance, but to good deeds and the gentle sway of charity and pity he never once thought of applying this impulsive and superfluous energy; and since the Ghost stood at every other avenue, (and mayhap at this as well,) his life bade fair to vapor itself away into visions as idle as those of the early fog. For him the earth had lost its beauty, the shade of mystical woods no longer allured, nor did the dash of free waters exhilarate; the sky was robbed of its slanting sunshine, down whose beams had once slid glorious forces of young life and strength to join his own aspirations; a dark miasma seemed to have risen and blotted out the blue, and with the upspringing of its fathomless arch his soul never once rose, for he carried his eyes on the ground, as one who gropes darkly step by step.

Was Sir Rohan hypochondriac? Was his Ghost but the indigestion of numerous rich dinners? Was it some unwhisperable remorse that clothed him, still living, in a pall? Or was it any restless honor that glamoured ceaselessly across his straining sight?

Be that as it may, he consulted neither priest nor leech; for disease is to be cured only by those who know its seat and cause, and how many in the world — or out of it — that number might include, Sir Rohan himself best knew.

In rare, cool evenings, when peace fell with the dew, and the flute of the crickets sweetened silence, what had this man but his Ghost? When the snows folded earth and sky in plumy whiteness, what fell with the flakes, changing and wavering at every gusty flock, but always the Ghost? What pleasure was for him, though Nature took him by the hand and led him through her flowery labyrinths, unrolling her arcana gorgeous with scutcheons of purpose and performance, and filling him with the lore of her mystic ways, when the Ghost also had the keys, turned them softly in the wards, and entered with him, diffusing her dark effluence over all things, like a blot? What cup ever brimmed at his lips, but the Ghost had first distilled her drop of refined poison there? He was a man into whose composition large passion and quick resolution had entered; but now, like a cloud borrowing shape from the underlying promontory, as if she were real, he fleeting and false, he forsook all choice, assumed her shifting habit, and veered with the veering Ghost.

II.

OVER THE HILLS AND FAR AWAY.

ONE summer day, buried in the deep ferns of a high common, the warm, sweet breeze streaming in long wafts above him, many hours he lay fingering restlessly at the little mosses and dainty violets,—face downward, lest glancing up he should see the Ghost where she sat, so white and thin that the sunshine fell through her delicate texture upon the flowers he touched, her fingers lying wearily also upon the violets, while her sad eyes weighed him down with their flickering but tireless gaze. The hum of innumerable insects rose around him, and the long emerald lances of strange flies hurtled beyond; now and then a lark dropped a strain of song down from some covert in the skies, or a nightingale in its low nest twittered faintly through the noon a breath of melody, and hushed itself again. Sir Rohan's

2 *

heart, which had been so long torpid, opened anew, and became warmed and filled with the sweet influences of nature; the richness of the matured year, in the gorgeous pageant of its summer, defiled across his senses; all the beauty to which he had been insensible unsheathed itself and flashed through his soul; the growth of a weary while at last accomplished itself, and in the long hours of that balmy day he believed the artist to have been born. Years seemed to have passed since he wandered out upon the common, and the early morning, with its dew and fragrance, loomed as far off as the purple inlands do to sea-coast mariners; again he had a purpose.

Refusing to give credence to the doubt that the Ghost could not thus be laid, he rose and pursued his way with uplifted head and elastic step; nor was he conscious how steadily he gazed before him, turning neither to right nor left, lest the accursed object should meet his eyes, nor how unequal the quick beatings of his heart made the chant he hummed, and, lest any rustle and flow of drapery beside him should fill its intervals, that he hummed unbrokenly. Under his doorway, he paused and turned back a glance on the gathering twilight. A cold touch fell upon his wrist, growing bolder till the long fingers closed their icy grasp around it; constrained, he met the shadowy eyes that hovered and grew still close before his own. A bale-fire for a moment glowed within them, fading to a dead glare and then sinking into obscurity, while the appalling grasp loosened, the touch ceased, and through the darkness of the night nothing was to be seen but the evening star hanging and trembling just above the gray horizon. Perhaps it was the Ghost's farewell. A new sense of freedom suffused his being, and he laughed a long and bitter laugh as he leaned scornfully against the wall. Could the Ghost have left a companionship such as that? Perhaps by absence she renewed her power, or peradventure she was journeying.

That night Sir Rohan slept well, and as if bathed in rejuvenescence he met the morning light, full of fresh strength and courage. A tedious initiation lay before him, but he had patience for it, since true genius is well content to wear the harness for a while, that its strength may be made available,—and so at first he groped that he at last might soar.

Time was valueless to him; and whatever hours elapsed ere he had mastered his art, he did not count them, but in his freedom, and as he would say, drawing in his breath exultingly, in his solitude, he began and pursued his task. Day by day found him before his easel. The first song of dawn spread softest shades of unattainable color before his thought, the vertical rays of noon toned his visions down to subdued splendor, and sunset found and gave him those brilliant dyes in which few artists have dipped the brush. Sir Rohan's reach was high indeed; what he brought down and spread upon his canvas he hardly dared hope would prove commensurate with his conceptions, nor that he could make others see what to him had such distinct and beautiful reality.

It was merely an ideal, allegoric in its nature, on which he at last expended the mature flow of his skill and imagination. Through it he designed to illustrate a truth, although he had not sufficiently freed his mind—unbiased enough generally—from the puerile conceits of fancy-

sketches, and thus his outline was neither original nor spirited; and while acknowledging this,
he triumphed in the power he found to suffuse
and impregnate it with an indescribable pomp
and lustre. His whole heart was in his work.
The Ghost had apparently vanished, or if her
spell, so long his death in life, ever entered his
memory, he laughed joyously at the present and
most mockingly at the past, thoroughly despising
his old and pitiable weakness. He toiled constantly, and no thought not inspired by his painting possessed him. He seemed to have wrung
the hues he used from the very heart of Nature.
Sunsets, concentrating their glow, rendered more
radiant by the prismatic dews of sunrise, deepened, softened, and mellowed by the purple tenderness of twilight tints, could not be more
gorgeous than the ineffable magic he evoked.
Magic? Once or twice Sir Rohan almost trembled at mysterious moments when, after producing any great effect, he felt the silent air of
his room pulsate, as it were, around him, drawing
away and contracting again as if a vacuum had
been there created, while after every such occur-
rence a pressure of which he had frequently been

conscious was removed. Often prolonging his delight till the place was filled with shadows, he discerned a brighter atmosphere around himself, in whose pale, uncertain illumination he worked, while jets of white light, like little tongues of flame, gathered and flowed from his brush into the picture. Something in his own performance, unfinished though it was, appalled him; and at such moments he wrought only more vehemently and unshrinkingly,—never in the morning, however, undoing what he felt to be the inspiration of the twilight before.

And yet he was not quite free of the Ghost. Perhaps it was not possible thus violently to pass from one such state to another not less peculiar and intense, or perhaps his imagination now and then conjured up a semblance, languid and wan indeed, of what had been a weary fact of his existence. Still more likely it is that the sharpness of his distress had become dulled by use, and he felt it as a part of himself; so much so, that, having fallen to a stagnant depression, relief from this incubus would result in a bewildering buoyancy. He endeavored ceaselessly to forget.

Truly precious things, in art as in nature, are

seldom spontaneous, but require growth and deliberation beyond the germ; and thus Sir Rohan, who carried his method into all this, had once laid aside his implements, and was considering the law of combinations and equivalents, when he felt what at first was a stream of cool breath across his closed eyelids, slowly increasing to a cold but almost imperceptible finger-touch. If this were the old shadow, how much of its power was lost!

Frequently, while at his work, he had a perception of certain harmonious properties of the universe, and more particularly of those particles composing the atmosphere, which seemed to emit one vast gentle accord as they moved interfluently among themselves. So perfect and integral must this harmony be, Sir Rohan reasoned, that unless when disturbed by some extraneous or adverse influence it is imperceptible to mortal ears; and thus, whenever heard by him, he knew that the vibrations were audible only by means of this dissonant and divulsive presence, as hostile, it appeared, to the kind forces of nature as to him. At the time when his eyes felt these cold finger-tips, he became aware also of this outer harmony throbbing in long rhythmical waves of finest sound, as if drawn from silver wires by a low, hot wind. This was unapproachable, almost infinite; on all sides of him he heard a chord produced perhaps millions of cycles away, but on its bosom and overtopping it like the foam on a long sea-swell, the atoms of air immediately in contact with himself seemed each to drop a golden note of full music down, till a distinct melody, bursting with tune and modulated by this grand spheric accompaniment, panted along the hot summer noon.

Opening his eyes, Sir Rohan saw nothing but the vacant room, the great vases of blossoms drooping in the sultry heat, which he constantly kept for the rich tints and suggestions of coloring they afforded, the wide-open window with the distantly russet hills through it drawing down veils of paler mist to the valleys in their bosom, and the cloudless sky that bent its ardent arch and with fiery languors kissed the nearer summits till they smoked. No wind stirred any little branch; no actual murmur broke the spell, if spell it was; but still the mighty music surged on, blending with his breath, with his heart-beat, and neither ceasing suddenly nor dying away; perhaps it touched the key-note of sleep, for over his perturbation a drowsiness wrapped itself, and erelong he slept. Sleeping, Sir Rohan naturally dreamed.

To his artistic eye, so long exercised upon material form, the dream assumed the distinct peopling of a series of vivid views, rather than the vague and edgeless fantasies of usual sleep, although during the first few moments of its duration he saw only five fine, black lines or wires drawn across a gray profound, and bearing, in a certain order, musical characters of fire, each one of which, as he read its tone, grew brighter an instant, imparting its blaze to the next, until he read the perfect score of the melody to which he was listening but a moment before. Some strange words, long lost, hummed along his memory; and as he delivered himself further to the guidance of his dream, they also became as audible as the music which they joined.

> In the summer even
> While yet the dew was hoar,
> I went plucking purple pansies
> Till my love should come to shore.

3

The fishing lights their dances
  Were keeping out at sea,
And come, I sung, my true love!
  Come hasten home to 'me.

But the sea it fell a-moaning,
  And the white gulls rocked thereon,
And the young moon dropt from heaven,
  And the lights hid one by one.
All silently their glances
  Slipt down the cruel sea,
And wait! cried the night and wind and storm,
  Wait, till I come to thee!

By what sudden change accomplished he knew not, nor was he at all astonished thereat, when instead of the bars of music he was aware of a still picture of low-country life. A canal sweeping its umberous waters slowly onward through banks lined with the green sunshine of early willows, and down toward a low stone bridge whose twin arches spanned the turbid flow and broke it, ere reaching the narrow pier, into numerous long ripples. Beyond, the country was one level expanse, clothed in the vivid pestilential green of fens and marshes, and above, a calm sky belted at the horizon with a low, brilliant west. Leaning over the bridge, a female figure tall and lithe, clad in some sober gray, her white cap hanging by its ribbons down one shoulder, and her dark unbraided hair blowing in long tresses against the zone of sunset; in her hand a bunch of reeds, which she trailed in the broken ripples. So exact the lines of this Flemish picture, that Sir Rohan saw clearly defined the black shadow which fine separate lashes threw over large gray eyes, and the delicate confusion of palest olive and ruddiest peach upon the oval cheek. The presence at a distance of another person, a dark, slender youth with arrested attention, Sir Rohan felt rather than saw, although he caught the glitter of a ring of curious device upon the latter's hand, and felt certain that the eyes of the two had met, when through her parted lips he heard, as if for the first time, the tune dreamily trilling, —

> I went plucking purple pansies
> Till my love should come to shore.

And the long gray ripples, growing fainter and darker, seemed to murmur responsively, as they swept onward with divided currents, —

> Wait! cried the night and wind and storm,
> Wait, till I come to thee!

How quickly the night fell on this scene, nor by what means the low-country canal became a narrow rural lane winding between high stone walls, over which luxuriant hops clambered and hung their blossoming sprays and bunches of greenery on the other side, Sir Rohan did not pause to consider. Nor did he wonder at seeing the soberly-clad girl wandering lingeringly down its avenue, arm in arm with the shadowy youth, till some great bars opposed their progress; nor, as she mounted the stile beside them, did he wonder at seeing the ring of curious device shining, this time, on her hand, nor at the utterly happy gleam from her loving eyes as she turned to him standing below and holding a little bunch of violets and rue that had lain in her breast. An indistinct sorrow stole over Sir Rohan as he saw the head crowned with its royal braid, the face with its sunshine and beauty, the whole vignette, recede and fade away to somberest mist, leaving nothing but the bars growing more and more distant, while gigantic notes of light started into flashes on their surface and thundered the old melody through his bewildered ears. There succeeded an interval of serenest rest, ere into

Sir Rohan's dream quietly stole the same figures again,—the same, yet different. The quiet gown, the simple cap, were gone; the lady trailed rustling satins over whose majestic folds the gloss of golden intricacies of needlework sparkled and deadened as she walked. Jewels, which might be the heirlooms of untainted ancestry, lay on her bare white bosom and encircled her brow, and the ring of curious device still flashed on her snowy hand. Her eyes, glowing with passion, bent on the face of her companion as they wound slowly up the outer turret stair in a broad dash of moonlight, his arm supporting her waist and his eyes meeting her own. Around them lay a different landscape. Long sweeps of moors, dun and dark, like petrified sea-swells; mountains distantly grand and shadowy; a mighty river lapsing down to meet its bridge of a hundred arches, and its flickering silver masts; the ocean clamoring his eternal sorrow from wine-dark depths, and with white, speechless lips of angry froth forever lapping the cliffs and crags far up along the northward. But the dreamer feels that the lovers see none but each other, and as the old tune creeps up from gulfs of silence, he sees the youth gaze for a moment inland over those dim hills, and hum, half to himself : —

> " En un verde prado
> De rosas e flores,
> Guardando ganado
> Con otros pastores,
> La vi tan fermosa
> Que apenas creyera
> Que fuese vaquera
> De la Finojosa ! "

A breathless, silent rapture seemed stealing over this part of Sir Rohan's dream, as if he himself were an actor of its wordless drama, — an inner intense glee, to which he had perhaps been alien for many years. Let us believe that in the dream, as in life, this moment of joy found its equivalent of pain. While he paused to turn it over in his thought, and extract the last sweet relish of its flavor, the illusive phantasmagoria existed no longer ; and when next the tide of sleep thinned itself, he saw a long, low-browed room, wainscoted in oak, uncarpeted, and fitted with furniture of an antique pattern. One only window lighted it, — a Gothic oval, and unglazed, so that the vines and sweet-briers, climbing without, twisted their tendrils into the crevices, and tossed their tempting garniture within. Midway of the room, and in the broad beam of yellow sunshine that thus fell through, sat the female figure of his dream. Garments of dark purple wrapped and swept around her, the masses of her purple black hair were looped heavily in their hateful weight, her eyes were larger and more hollow by reason of their purple rims; she sat half bent forward, her white hands, still sparkling with that single ring, clasped across her knee, and a dead despair settling slowly like a pall above her. If there were any other in that room, gloomy in spite of its sunshine, Sir Rohan's dream obstinately refused to recognize him. It seemed a weary age that, fascinated by the mute tragedy, he recalled and gazed upon its action; but while he gazed, the thick palpitations of his heart so shook and disordered him that the air wavered and trembled around him, bright specks danced in the shadows, a mist crept between him and herself, the room opened and spread its dark sides indefinitely into duskiness, the rush of great waters was in his ears, and when he recovered his vision he saw only long black hair sweeping headlong down the current, a ghastly face whose eyes, hard as pebbles in a brook, reflected no light as they sunk beneath the hurrying stream, a white arm clinging round a floating branch, a hand gleaming with the ring of curious device, obscurely, as it washed downward through the roar and eddy of this river of the North. How it seemed only the low canal, hundreds of miles away, flowing on to meet its bridge, while the voice of the ripples, setting in black angry swirls round the single pier, seemed to repeat the words with a harsh sudden cadence; nor why, when with a dreadful start it all vanished, and he knew only the Ghost, his own Ghost, standing before him and singing from the score, loud and clear, while her hard eyes transfixed him.

> Wait! cried the night and wind and storm,
> Wait, till I come to thee!

Sir Rohan never wondered, — but with a groan grew faint and dizzy in his sleep, and suffered this dreamy sense to reel away from him. What a shiver seized him then! what a noise was in his brain! how thunderously his weary heart beat forward on its way! with what a fierce quaking he sprung into the centre of the room, nor felt relief at finding it a dream! The sun had hardly declined a degree, the noon was not less sultry, no softer shade enveloped any object; he had whirled through the great eddy of his youth, he had ploughed and reaped the seed whose fruit he was never to exhaust, and he had slept ten minutes.

Doggedly he examined his pencils, ground more oil into his browns, and again feverishly busied himself over what was now his solace. Glancing upward, he noticed with a thrill of horror that the eyes of the picture — for it was no landscape — emitted such a green, hard glare as had lately pierced him. Indeed, he had painted them gray. Without pausing to regret the care he had bestowed on their finish, the artist raised his brush with one stroke to obliterate them, when he reflected that such procedure would utterly ruin any chance of obtaining succeeding transparency and brilliance, besides fouling the delicacy of touch which his after work should wear. Perhaps scraping would answer as well. But the palette-knife and even sharper instruments were of no avail, for he remembered what powerful siccatives had been employed, and the impenetrable varnish of sandarach and poppy-oil with which, in order to preserve the primal freshness and bloom of the tints, he had early overlaid this portion of his work. Neither acid nor alkali weakened the unendurable stare; and still throbbing from his dream, perplexed and baffled, he felt as if reason would desert him did he fail in effacing its chance. Had the Ghost almost left him free, that he should perpetuate her eyes upon his canvas? Exasperated, he seized a vial of inflammable oil, intending by its means to burn off the obnoxious surface, thus endangering the blossom of many years' labor, when the lazily ascending smoke of a distant lime-kiln caught his eye and suggested a new remedy. He hesitated a moment, half fearing to leave those eyes alone, and then, laughing at himself, went out quickly and closed the door.

Intent on his moody thoughts, and regardless of the heat, he walked swiftly forward, meeting in his way but one face,—and that a handsome one, flashing on him from a travelling-chariot that lumbered along the rarely frequented highway,—till he reached his destination; when having obtained a small quantity of lime, and wasting no words on the burners, he betook himself homeward. It was a half-hour's rapid walk; on one side, across some sterile fields, the sea running in long, low lines up a yellow beach, and filling the air with an unbroken drowsy drone. But the sea did not attract Sir Rohan's regard; indeed, lest its advancing wash should throw some rejected secret from its bosom, he turned his eyes on the other hand, where, across the neglected lands and luxuriant woods of his own estate, rose the chimney-stacks of the lonely house. No living thing, it seemed to him, ever crossed his path; he suspected that the grass ceased growing in his footsteps, yet did not marvel why beneath the fervors of the noon, the Ghost, alone unwearied, refused to join the universal spell of rest and hush. At last, re-entering at a postern door, he again sought his work.

Having slaked and mixed the lime with a strong mineral alkali, he plastered it upon the part to be destroyed, not heeding a faint rap on the door, and turned to other details yet unfinished. But till success in this was assured, he found it impossible to proceed, and threw down his implements in anger. It would then be many hours ere he could resume his task, and, having generally employed the strong meridian light, he found himself suddenly at a loss for occupation. Accordingly, remembering the timid rap of the old steward whose application had met with usual success, and designing afterward to employ himself in the greenhouse, so called, which alone of all his former luxuries he retained, Sir Rohan opened his door, and traversing the hall, partially descended a broad, winding staircase.

III.

IT was a long time since he had entered these
grand districts of the house, and, closed and
deserted, the walls had gathered damp, the
panels dust, the whole region a funereal gloom.
As he looked down, he saw without surprise,
since he had grown incapable of such emotion,
that the gay curtains and carpets were dim and
faded, the ornaments fallen from their brackets,
and thick, silvery, shaking webs woven from cornice to cornice of the long drawing-room. He
saw without a shudder the rare cast of some
antique statue staring sad and forlorn from its
nook of tarnished tapestry, like a corpse risen
with the mould and mire of the grave upon it;
and no question arose in his mind at the wide-
open hall door, and the sweet, fresh draught bearing thence through the close rooms. Still look-

4

ing down, as if under the influence of another dream that made him motionless, his eye rested on a figure standing by the old clavichord, and he waited till the dream should pass and the spell loosen its chain. A girl, tall and in the gloom, standing by the old clavichord and noiselessly moving her fingers over the stained keys. Had he seen her before?

A singular face, totally destitute of any roseate glow, but by no means wan,—rather, one would say, a soft, creamy skin that should not be otherwise. The chin extremely short and upturned; the mouth compensating for some width by rich, velvet curves and handsome teeth, the upper lip a haughty, disdainful feature; the nose well moulded, with thin nostrils, and occupying more than its classical third in length. A face whose first impression was one of peculiar loveliness, the next, a captious sentiment that it was greatly too wide; but few, perhaps, saw it without recurring to the first. The forehead was low and wide, the dark masses of hair sweeping off it in a long line, till, dropping with a sudden wave below the cheek, they were looped up again, as Sir Rohan had seen other hair, into a kind of crown-like comb. Eyebrows fine, feuille-morte, and without arch, nearly met across this face; and beneath, the long-cut waxen lids were heavily fringed. A gleam of sunlight stole timidly through an open shutter, and then in a broad sheet athwart the face, as Sir Rohan observed it. The girl raised her lids in the abrupt illumination. Square as the outline might be, albeit without the high cheekbones which characterize this class of countenance, it was well worth while if that were necessary to give such purport and range and large magnificence to the eyes, — soft, dark, lustrous, and bearing a dazzled splendor at the light, through the golden warmth it imparted to them. Ah, well! Sir Rohan was to paint other eyes to-morrow.

It pleases me to think that that face, now so fair and soft, never lost the smooth, olive skin, even through the season of a long life, nor sowed its cares in wrinkles when they grew too many for the heart to bear alone; nor that those eyes lost their brilliant kindliness, though wearing forever the frightened aspect which one cruel day was to give them, — though never, when the snow of weary years lay between age and youth, daring to look back and sun themselves in the gleam of any lost happiness, — though borrowing all their joy from those Beulah hill-tops which only the old have in certain prospect. Yet there was something in the face which led you not so much to its owner as its authors, till you lost yourself conjecturing under what conditions and circumstances it had obtained life. A peculiar face, — had Sir Rohan seen it before? Was it his Ghost, come in tangible form — but was it tangible? Pshaw! did it not flash on him from the travelling-chariot? Did ghosts wear long cloaks half untied and pulling apart from the confining cord; or gowns, just seen beneath, of a fawn brocade, to harmonize with the other brown shades; or antique jewels and a moonstone carcanet? Did ghosts touch the uncompliant keys of clavichords, and entice thence sweet, unfamiliar sounds? Unfamiliar, — only too well known, indeed! Could it be anything but his persistent enemy who played, with the long, slender fingers of her left hand, the very melody to whose tune the sorrow of his life had been this day set? The sunshine that had been creeping along the once gorgeous pattern of the floor, nestling and mingling with the yellow tinges there, stole up across the foot, the tall figure whose drapery fluttered in the increasing draft, the queenly neck, and withdrew behind a cloud, while the girl began humming the same tune and beating a gentle time with her head.

Sir Rohan recovered himself, concluding that the supernatural was not an agent in this apparition. It was a tune common enough in Kent, —he had first heard it there; she was probably a Kentish girl, too charming a piece of flesh and blood ever to throw off for filmy, impalpable essence. If his Ghost came in that shape, she might stay while she pleased. But was not his Ghost a fairer shape, whose dead eclipsed this living, breathing beauty? Why think of it? It was pleasure enough, for one revelling in form and color, only to gaze, as he did, on the picture to which the drawing-room door below was frame; to ask by what means she had entered his house did not occur to him. Before Sir Rohan began to reason, the tune had ceased, and while he gazed, the girl, glancing round, glided up the apartment out of sight. He remained a moment, and then, half doubting himself, stole back upon his steps. Two questioning eyes in every darker shadow sought his own, and a long-drawn sob was audible beside him, as, quickening his motions, he sprang up the stairs and confronted two men on the upper landing; one was his gray-haired steward.

"I have been seeking your worship," said he, timorously, but without reply, for the other had seized Sir Rohan's hands, and was pouring forth rapid question and answer over a long-lost friend.

"I am not dreaming, then!" said Sir Rohan unsteadily, at last. "This is you, St. Denys, and your daughter below?"

"I, certainly," was the cheery response, "and my ward below. God give me long life! for the name and fame of St. Denys flow to a rascal when I die."

"We won't talk of dying," said Sir Rohan, looking behind him quickly, "and while we live will grasp what we may. How did you find me?"

"In the simplest way conceivable. We lunched at an inn yclept the Belvidere Arms, and, remembering that you buried yourself at one time in

Cornwall, I inquired for its patron. Still, I had difficulty in recognizing our gay youth in one taciturn, possessed gentleman, till mine host christened him Sir Rohan!"

The old man had withdrawn. "Something ails you, Rohan," said his friend. "You are in trouble!"

"The weather and a walk," was the hurried answer, "and — and dyspepsia!"

"Parent of all blue devils! Come down to this dungeon of yours, into which I have taken the liberty of inviting some sky, alias light and air."

"My friend can take no liberty in my house."

A merry bow from the friend prefaced a prescription for good health and spirits, which closed by recommending good company. "For which purpose — "

"The sky has fallen and dropped you here."

"And consequently I shall see a rapid improvement in Monsieur le Cadavre!"

Sir Rohan shuddered again. "I am better," he said directly, "already better." And indeed his friend would have been like a bracing wind blowing through sultry fever regions, did not his unfortunate choice of words act as a series of electric shocks, constantly thrilling his patient. By this time they were in the drawing-room.

"This is a drawing-room of the Belvidere estate in Cornwall, Sir Rohan," said his friend. "Probably a place unfamiliar to you."

"I should be, perhaps, ashamed to say that a quinquenniad has passed since I have stood in it," replied he whose Ghost had at least taught him to discriminate delicate shades of truth.

"And this is Miriam, my child."

As the girl turned to receive his salutation, he extended his hand. Shy as a bird, her own dropped into it an instant, and brushed away again. Yet there was something positive in that slight touch; most different in its soft, warm sense from the gelid grasp that had so often met his palm,—more real it could not be.

"I am very happy," said he, with a grave courtesy which had lost nothing from disuse, "in welcoming the child of St. Denys to my house, although but a dreary place to shelter youth and beauty."

"Well, well," laughed his friend, "a candle would not be brilliant in sunny windows."

"But she has brought the sun in with her."

Miriam raised her large, wary eyes, and, throwing back the haughty head, surveyed her host with quick displeasure, — motions which did not escape Sir Rohan.

"I am at a loss as to what title —" he began, turning to St. Denys, who interrupted him, saying, as he laid his hand caressingly upon her shoulder, —

"No need! Since the morning she had been sixteen years my darling, this child has been afflicted with a whim, and throws off my name and protection and love —"

"Not your love or your protection, father," she murmured, quickly.

"And chooses," he added, "to be known only as Miss Miriam."

"And why?" escaped Sir Rohan's lips before he could recall it. Yet he had been waiting to hear that voice address him, and now it came, low, clear, and full of inflections.

"Because I have no other name," she replied instantly, and with a proud gesture which the possession of sixty titles could not have enhanced. He seemed to have heard it elsewhere.

"Pardon! I was born for mistakes on this afternoon, I think."

"Sir Rohan, Miriam, was my friend before you knew the light, and seeing less and less of him as years passed, I soon saw nothing. In a while wondrous rumors reached us from the corners of the earth, then all sounds were lost,— and here he is. Where is your housekeeper, Rohan?" with a quizzical look at the existing neglect.

"I have none. My steward's maid attends to my necessities."

"I doubt if she can do so much for me!"

"As exacting as ever," returned the other, with an absent smile. "We will soon find servants enough."

"A sorry day for them, if spiders can make it," exclaimed St. Denys, tossing off a tawny Arachne who danced, on a long-spun thread from the dusky ceiling, across his face.

"And if I confess that this is the best room I have, what will my guests think?"

"That the drawing-room generally occupies that rank among apartments, and that the little feminine element so bustling in my home may effect, by your permission, a slight revolution in the shape of two sleeping-rooms here! What say you, Miriam?"

"If Sir Rohan desire it—"

"By no means," said Sir Rohan. "The young lady is wearied with her journey. It will be unnecessary;" and excusing himself, he soon found the old steward, who was awaiting him in anxiety of mind.

"Let your wife, Redruth, move herself and maids up here, at what salary you please," said his master. "Procure other servants from the village at once. We will dine at six, and let two bedchambers be cleansed and aired by twelve." Having received which orders, and it being now nearly four, the steward scrambled away to perform impossibilities, and Sir Rohan ascended to his own room. Without bestowing a glance on his painting, he wheeled the great chair out upon the landing, and, in a moment after, descended and deposited it inside the drawing-room. The young lady was walking up and down, with her skirts gathered in one hand from the floor, and her brow wearing an expression of combined amusement and annoyance, as Sir Rohan opened a casement, and shoved it over the smooth terrace.

"You will find it less dusty and sufficiently cool, Miss Miriam, without," he said, and in order to conduct her there, he again offered his hand. She looked round, however, for his friend, and stepping across the sill, lightly planted St. Denys in the chair, and took her own seat upon the turf at his feet. "She's tired," she said as St. Denys laid her head against the cushions of the chair, and, dropping the lids from her first gaze that crept across the woods, then up the distant fields to the lawn below, and finally rested on the smooth cheek, she slept the deep sleep of a healthy child.

"I do not understand," said Sir Rohan, leaning against the window. "Is this your daughter who says father to you?"

"You are very slow, then! We make believe, as children do. Seriously, though, you know I do not hold in chance, and thus I take my accidents as commissions from God. So when we heard of this child, then some five weeks old, a foundling in the house of a tenant, we took her home; and the woman, an old dame who had found and sheltered the babe on some tramp or journey, we judged would be the best nurse. And she has been God's gift to sweeten a bitter draught he poured out for me not long after. So, she is my daughter."

"It is many years since we met."

"That, indeed. Nearly a score."

"You married?"

"Yes."

"And your wife?"

His friend paused as if heaving the weighty words from some painful depth. "I lost her."

"Still unfound?"

"One day I hope to find her. She is dead."

It did not seem so sorrowful a thing to Sir Rohan; or if he had the pity, he was compelled to probe the wound.

"She died suddenly?" he asked.

"By a long illness, a year after Miriam came."

"And has never returned,—you have never seen her since?"

"Rohan!"

"I am vexed to have occasioned an unpleasant thought. And who named the child, Miriam?"

"My wife."

"It is strange to know no more about her."

"Yes. We met with no clew. Her nurse died some five years since; I often wondered if she had no information, but she denied with genuine surprise when questioned once. Yet on dying, she called Miriam and whispered to her."

"What?"

"I never asked."

"You are very simple, then," said his interlocutor.

"Changing parts," said St. Denys. "You, Rohan! have you married?"

A sudden spasm of pain darted through Sir Rohan. The happy humble-bee, swimming homeward honey-laden through the air, could not have stung so savagely, nor have caused him to spring, like one shot, from his station. However, immediately resuming his self-possession, "No," he answered.

"Ah? There was a legend among us, I remember, just after we parted with you, that you were buried with some sweetheart, some beautiful peasant-girl, now in the depths of these Cornish haunts, and then in that forlorn tower of yours at the North."

"A legend, like most others, more pretty than

true," returned Sir Rohan, with a shade more pallor on his face.

"You wear proof-armor, then?"

"Not at all. I adopt bolder tactics, and wear none. A noble archer does not strike the defenceless."

"Never doubt but your turn will come."

Sir Rohan did not reply, and it was some time before St. Denys spoke again.

"And how do you pass your time?" said he, at last.

"As you see; at the last profession I have adopted — painting — and in deadly self-introspection."

"Ah! and you see no company?"

"You are the first."

"Have you exhibited any paintings yet?"

"None. I have never finished any of sufficient worth to look on myself."

"But you intend it?"

"Hardly."

"Great goodness, Rohan! What a wretched life! No wonder you are sad as a masque of tragedy! Why don't you kill yourself?"

Another spasm of pain. "Then I also should be a Ghost!" he exclaimed vehemently.

The guest sprang up in alarm, but Sir Rohan relapsed to his former stern reticence, with his eyes bent fixedly upon the distance. A momentary doubt of the sanity of this recluse overpowered St. Denys, and he may have trembled lest he had brought his treasure into the den of a madman. But the tenderness of his nature soon regained its balance, and he reflected, with pity, that the unhappy man's loneliness was ruinous. Nevertheless, his sudden movement had roused the girl from her convenient nap, who looked round amazed an instant, and then rose laughingly. No flush of sleep stained her cheek; her haughty coolness seemed as involuntary as her breath. Just stepping from the footprints of the child into the sadder ways of womanhood, she walked almost as if conscious of fate, with a quick, impetuous gait, to meet it.

"Mistress Miriam wears the air of a Spartan," said St. Denys.

"Rather like the Brown Girl of the Ballad," Sir Rohan returned.

"Alas for fair Elinor if I confront her with my bodkin!" laughed the Brown Girl.

The image of an Elinor who might, instead,

meet her, glimmered before Sir Rohan, blotting out the young face that laughed without dimples, and he turned away to evade it.

Miriam stooped over the chair. "He is very strange, this friend of yours, papa, with his sudden ways and mouldy house. Don't stay here long," she whispered.

"He is too unhappy, and perhaps ill, to be left longer in this state. Entertain him while here, and perhaps he will go with us."

Miriam raised her eyebrows and her shoulders as if the prospect did not charm her.

"Do you suppose he means to starve us?" she said.

"Young ladies who take naps in company should have courage —"

"But I was so tired!"

"Here he comes, — if you should ask him!"

"O no, no, papa!"

"Miriam has a question to propose," said he, as Sir Rohan drew near again.

"Hush!" she whispered.

"Can I answer it?"

"By the help of all your formulas and statistics," said the other.

She turned with a pretty mixture of defiance and shame. "I am hungry," she said.

"An extraordinary question, which I hope dinner will answer. Let us hunt some up."

"I wonder," thought she, "if we shall have to eat it, standing, from the shelves of the larder."

"I wonder," thought he, "if there is anything in the house to eat." And he led the way back through the drawing-room and hall, to what had once been a sumptuous dining-room.

Less out of repair than the other apartments, it was yet large, gloomy, and from its solitary occupant, almost out of use. Nevertheless, since noon it had experienced a slight rearrangement; the glass doors of the cabinets and buffet had been washed, the walnut floor swept and polished, and curious pieces of furniture had been ransacked from other rooms. The table was laid with bountiful folds of snowy linen, ancient plate, and costly china; for wherein Sir Rohan, during these desolate years, had suffered himself to be served at all, he had caused himself to be served well; and, frugal as he was, had insisted on a certain table etiquette, though the equipage were untouched by him from day till dusk.

It was a dark room, and the glittering table occupied but a small corner of it. As Miriam entered, she swept forward and threw open the heavy shutters of the window behind it, and sent a glad burst of light through the place. Looking out, she disappeared, and in a moment returned with an armful of white raspberry-blossoms, and long wreaths of the purple night-shade, and heaped them in a large vase upon the sideboard.

"A bush for the wine," she said.

"And good wine needs no bush," returned Sir Rohan.

A white rose overlaced the window, and hastily gathering a few stems, they were placed in a glass upon the table; but not one was perfect, every rose bearing a small, brown taint, — observing which, she as quickly dashed them away.

"Perhaps Sir Rohan does not like flowers at dinner," said St. Denys.

"Excuse me," she cried, turning tartly. "We have them always, they are so cheerful."

"A new ornament. I like them," responded

Sir Rohan, and, absently tearing off a spray of the nightshade, he presented it to her, saying, "It agrees well with the Carthaginian hair."

"I seldom wear flowers," she exclaimed; adding instantly, "Yet these gorgeous stars, with their gold-drops at centre, tempt too much," and she hung them in the heavily festooned tress next Sir Rohan. A moment afterward the dishes were brought in by amazed waiters, and a stately servant stationed himself behind the host's chair. All formality was banished at the onset, when Miriam, to avoid spilling her soup, overset a decanter whose contents ran down the table in a red stream, just as, from his sudden movement, Sir Rohan's soup probably burned his mouth. Whereupon, hiding her embarrassment, she broke forth into merry quip and sally, till the room rung with her gay voice, and long before they rose, the pale Sir Rohan paused confounded at the sound of his own laughter.

Meanwhile a great noise and hurry had been holding high carnival in the region of the guest-chambers. Long since, large fires had been roaring up the chimneys notwithstanding the heat, beds had been airing, carpets spread, and coarse, clean linen from Mrs. Redruth's laundry waving in lavendered folds across bedposts and wardrobes. The maids were bustling about sufficiently for enjoyment, and the general racket was such as had not scared the echoes of this dead old house for half a century. But only an intermittent buzz reached the remote dining-room, where, dinner being concluded and the gentlemen not caring to sit over their wine, it was decided to remain, rather than adjourn to the dingy drawing-room; for through some fine sense, Sir Rohan felt an approaching danger, and this was a more familiar place than the other.

"How dark it is!" said Miriam. "An odd day of odd adventures. I smell thunder." And looking out, they all saw a large, brassy cloud driving swiftly over the paling sunset, and sphering the sky with ominous splendor. Miriam had taken a seat directly before the open window, and neither of the others were far off. Recalling old times, the two gentlemen had long conducted the conversation, when gradually silence fell, gathering an increasing awe as loud thunders broke close above them, letting sharp lightning slip piercingly down.

"When we were descending the Alps, last summer," said Miriam, "riding through a thunder-storm, the lightnings came and played round our feet."

"But I hardly think it rained so, there," said St. Denys, as one vast sheet gushed in torrents from the low bosom of the impending cloud, appearing, in the uninterrupted flashes that illuminated every drop, like a rain of fire. Sir Rohan sat leaning his head upon one hand, but with a singular alertness and vigilance apparent in his whole figure. Electric thrills had been coursing through his blood, till his fingers tingled and his eyes sparkled.

"Sir Rohan," exclaimed Miriam, "I believe if I should touch you, you would flash!"

"Try, Miss Miriam."

The same delicate, airy finger-touch met his a second.

"Ah, well!" laughed she; "you did n't, but it 's because you are cold as death." The word made him wince.

"Are you afraid?" she continued.

"No. It is a constitutional weakness, I fancy, something involuntary, so that in every thunder-storm an unwelcome force and intelligence of life crowds down, and is as suddenly wrung away, leaving me with an unaccountable depression, limp and wilted."

"We heard a fanatic preacher, yesterday," said Miriam, after a short pause, "who, I should think, was fulfilling the promise of his text, to-day. A strange-looking man, with long, white hair, pale face, and glittering eyes, and dressed in a dusty gray gown as if just off a long journey. He looked like some old shade. His text was, 'To-morrow I will stand on the top of the hill, with the rod of God in my hand.'"

As she spoke, a more dreadful crash than had yet been heard split the heavy air, and a bolt of flame fell at not a dozen paces' distance, while the withered branches of an old poplar shot forth simultaneously a hundred sparks, and a tower of fire streamed up in defiance.

"The chariot of Israel, and the horsemen thereof," ejaculated St. Denys; but almost before he ceased, the light went out, leaving only the charred trunk standing boldly against the low gleam of the horizon.

A throstle shook the rose-vines over the window, and whistled clearly a sweet charm against the rain.

"And behold the Lord passed by," said Miriam, "and a great and strong wind rent the mountains, and brake in pieces the rocks before the Lord; but the Lord was not in the wind: and after the wind, an earthquake; but the Lord was not in the earthquake: and after the earthquake, a fire; but the Lord was not in the fire: and after the fire a still, small voice."

Sir Rohan's head fell forward into his hands, and no one broke the stillness.

The storm had spent its violence, and was rolling away to the north. The rain still pattered from leaf to leaf, and poured off in plenteous streams down deserted alleys and ruined garden-walks. Darkness crept up from the distant corners, and brooded round them; but blacker shadows had already wrapt Sir Rohan, and he silently warred with them.

Still sitting there, a light, timid pressure was laid upon his shoulder, growing bold enough to remain. He knew it was Miriam, and did not turn. A sweet, strong influence seemed to flow to him from this gentle imposition of hands, a sense of peace to envelop him; and long, rejoicing under the delicious consciousness of reviving strength and vigor, he would have sat, had the touch long continued. But as if aware of his desire, she perversely flitted away, and opening the door into the lighted hall, suffered its gleam to irradiate the gloom.

"You are too sudden in your movements, child," said St. Denys, as she swept over a clattering chair in her way.

"And I was growing dainty as a lady with my fingers," she rejoined. "It's not my fault; but something about the house, some sprite twitches them."

"Do you think the miraculous would stoop into Sir Rohan's dining-room?"

"I don't care, papa. I want to hear that ghost-story. I came for that. It's just the house to be haunted, — unless the fragrance of paints and oils does not agree with their honors, — and just the hour. We have a ghost at the Castle, but he has been quiet so long as to afford no amusement. We were brought here, too, in a miraculous manner."

"You are absurd, Miriam," said St. Denys, with a smile. "Be quiet."

"Don't you know, Sir Rohan," she continued disregardfully, "that animals — brutes, of course — are said to perceive apparitions more quickly than men? Last night we were on the road very late, and going smoothly, when suddenly the horses began to caper from side to side, dashed into a lane, and then through a broken hedge, racing over the moor like hounds till they pulled up near another highway, and to-day that road took us to the village below here, where we had not intended to stop, and which was, you know, quite out of our way. It's a wonder our necks were n't broken. The coachman told me that he knew the creatures met the Swairth, — that he himself saw something swinging, white and shining, before them, and nothing could have tempted him to proceed. He told of it at the inn, and they said very likely it belonged up here; that it was the wraith of some forlorn woman of your house, and that, if papa had a tourist's curiosity, we should find some pictures here, and might see the wraith for ourselves. So you perceive the

Thing brought us here, and I wait for the story. Have n't you a ghost, Sir Rohan ? "

A class of words which Sir Rohan had grown to avoid even in his thought, was now perpetually dropping from the lips of his guests, and he expended his energy nerving himself against the abrupt attacks.

" No ghost ? " persisted Miriam.

" My ancestors never had one," he replied, in a low, distinct tone, the volume of his voice compressed from trembling.

" But you ! have you no phantom, no spectre ? "

" Pardon me if I say that you confound the terms."

" Have you, then, found any difference between ghosts and spectres ? " questioned St. Denys, gayly.

" There should be a distinction. A spectre seems rather to have risen from the grave, to own a glimmering shroud, to carry with it the smell of the dead and the air of vaults and coffins. But a ghost ! — A ghost," said Sir Rohan, " is a very different thing."

" Then you have nothing to tell us ? "

" Nothing."

"And I am positively cheated?"

"You must forgive the rural superstition."

"Well. If one opening fails, I can try another. I am a meteoromant, you know, an inheritance of certain people. I know a charm to ward off the Evil Eye."

"And that surprises no one, Miss Miriam."

"Nonsense! I tell papa's fortune often enough, and it comes true often enough."

"And what is St. Denys's fortune?"

"He was born to trouble and much peace. Begin as I will, these words always come and I must say them,— trouble, yet much peace."

"You divine by thunder and lightning, and, having called your imps around you, would now tell me my fate,— is it so?" and he extended his hand.

"Yes," poring over the hand gingerly, without taking it. "But there's no fortune for you, good or bad. I should think your life had been wiped out; there's not a line on the palm. Alackaday, kind gentleman," said she, assuming the sing-song gypsy tone, "great evil have you waded through, and greater is to come. Small pleasure will you know in life, and in sorrow will you die."

"A fortune not at all new," said Sir Rohan, dismally.

"Was it true?" she asked.

"You should know best."

" Papa says I don't know at all. But the fact is, that once when I was a child I fell in with some gypsies wandering through Kent, who fancied me strangely like themselves, taught me half their singular words and ways, and never come by the Castle now but they leave me a cake of rich and costly condiments;—so the housekeeper wrote. An odd life, that of the woods,—with a relish that no other life possesses. One would feel, I should think, living an outlaw in those deep recesses, like all the rest of the wild growth there,—the lichen on the trees, the little wood-pigeons, the six-striped snakes that shoot from under one brown leaf to another like darts of poison,—feel as if life ceased with death, if indeed death ever came there. I wonder why you never followed it, Sir Rohan, among your other adventures."

Sir Rohan did not think it necessary to tell her of the solitary days and nights he had spent housed with ' the cold-crowned snake,' and meet-

6 *

ing no response, she commenced pacing the long room, humming in a low key to herself. As she walked, the nightshade in her hair emitted a heavy fragrance, and having flung it down, she stole from the room. In a short time Sir Rohan heard a sweet strain wafting along, and recognized the tones of the old clavichord, softened by distance and winding toward them with a gentle insinuation. Trifles were now indeed the sum of his life, and he waited in horrified suspense till the indistinct prelude should unravel into the tune that so powerfully affected him. But when the voice joined the instrument, there rose, instead, the solemnly chanted opening of the song of Deborah.

"A voice as sweet as wild honey in the crevices of rocks," said Sir Rohan.

St. Denys had fallen into a doze, but awakened by the music, saw Sir Rohan bending forward, his hands upon his knees, spell-bound, like some old Egyptian statue. Still the voice, a rich mezzo-soprano of great compass, sang sweetly on, thrilling the hearers through the warlike spirit clashing and chiming with its melody. A pastoral simplicity was reigning over this portion of her chant, sinking gradually into quick, hurrying lower notes, till the earthly allies of the Israelites were numbered, when a lofty chord rolled up in a succession of broad flashes, announcing the helps which Nature sent to the battle.

"They fought from heaven," she sang. "The stars in their courses fought against Sisera."

A deep groan escaped Sir Rohan, and he grew rigid as iron. "The stars in their courses fought against Sisera!" he repeated.

"The river of Kishon, that ancient river, the river Kishon swept them away," proclaimed the victorious voice. "O my soul, thou hast trodden down strength!"

Sir Rohan would gladly have laid aside that vigilance which he had worn for years, had it been possible; but no oblivion came to his aid, no confusion of sound or sense would drown the words.

"Curse ye Meroz, said the angel of the Lord," she sang, clear as a clarion across the fray. "Curse ye bitterly —" when the loud snap of a rusty wire broke the burden suddenly. Sir Rohan rose and stood in the starlight, gazing out as if blindly protesting against the sentence. The summer night had slowly deepened, a gentle wind was lightly tossing fragrance from the rank flower-blooms without; rain dripped now and then with a low plash from the eaves.   A sudden meteor shot . across the sky, leaving a track of shining light where the eternal stars glowed coldly, untouched and unchanged in their places. What was the misery of one creature to them, he thought; but higher than they he dared not send a murmur.

Miriam speaking to Mrs. Redruth was now heard, and in a moment after, singing gently other verses of the chant, and armed with a taper, she came down the hall into the dining-room.   It was like the angel who, entering purgatory, struck the first dreadful letter from Dante's forehead, Sir Rohan thought.

"I have accomplished to-night what two generations have failed to do.   I have ruined your clavichord, Sir Rohan!" she said, gayly.

"To-morrow, then, we may hear that voice without a foil," he replied; "weak and thin, a strident griding foil, like the cricket three months hence."

Going to St. Denys, she received his good-night kiss, whispering, "Our rooms are in the same hall, papa, or I should be afraid."

"Good night, Miss Miriam."

"I wish you a good-night, Sir Rohan," was the demure response.

On the landing she paused to protect her candle from the draught, and as her happy unconscious voice fell downward, they heard her still singing from the chant of the Prophetess : —

"At her feet he bowed, he fell, he lay down; at her feet he bowed, he fell: where he bowed, there he fell down dead." A door slammed, the voice died, and all was still.

"And the evening and the morning were the first day," said Sir Rohan, as, when the clock struck one, he showed the remaining guest his room, and left him.

Seeking the steward, he gave some orders for cleansing and restoring the drawing-room next day. "You will remain for the present, Red-ruth," said he, "and I suppose it makes no difference to your wife."

"Lord bless you, no, sir! And right glad are we both at seeing your worship brighten a little.

For all these long years you 've been so dull and moping like, my woman says — "

Here, utterly confused and filled with abashment at the stern surprise with which his master regarded him, the steward hesitated, stammered an apology, and bowed himself away; whereon Sir Rohan sought his painting-room.

All things there were as he left them, — the brushes in the vase where they had been plunged, and the window open for the entrance of exhalations from the adjacent salt-marshes. Hastily closing it, he took the candle in his hand to look at his picture. It seemed to Sir Rohan as if he were becoming, since noon, more and more the master of himself, — all the past events of his life a dream, and nothing real but this day. What consternation overwhelmed him, then, when on approaching the canvas, with the light in his hand, every trace of the painting had disappeared, no glimpse was to be observed there, — nothing, in fact, but here and there a streak of some positive color, and the two staring patches of lime and soda! A cold perspiration beaded his forehead as he saw all this weary work absorbed and expunged. Did Destiny thus with one touch cancel the promise of years? Was it possible that, in drawing the Ghost's eyes from his picture, she had revenged herself by drawing after them the whole? Justice, not Vengeance, he said to himself; and with a sullen despair confessed that had the Ghost desired those cruel eyes to remain, no power of his could have effaced them. Again alone, his phantasms, and not he, ruled.

Setting down the candle, he stooped forward and searched the work eagerly. Low in one corner, a vermilion fillet close upon a mass of unspeakably precious ultra-marine; further up, some dim outline, obscured by a smoky air that curled across the whole. That was all. But as he searched atom by atom, he caught gleams of his former design, and, recalling by the help of memory line after line, the truth flashed upon his mind. His picture should have been full of purple shades; yellow, neutralized purple. As this idea seized him, the candle, which was flaring in its socket, dipt and fell into darkness, disclosing the moonlight that fell through the panes and overlay his easel. He waited for the effect. Slowly struggling in the beams, the dubious shades wrought themselves out upon his vision, till with ineffable satisfaction he saw every particle of his work, still undestroyed, resolve dimly in the uncertain light. He would have endured as much more pain for the sharp pleasure that now flushed and filled him. Purple, then, vanished by candle-light, he had discovered; and thus through his own suffering and failures he was instructed. Throwing himself upon the lounge, he slept his first unbroken slumber since he had endeavored to install art in the place of the Ghost.

IV.

THE WINE-CELLAR.

SIR ROHAN was awakened at morning by the sound of gay voices on the lawn so long consecrated to silence, and so frequently the battle-ground of the Ghost.

Having performed an unusually elaborate toilet, he paused at an open balcony window in the upper hall, and looked out. The lawn was not large, but, after descending a few terraces, quite even, green, and bordered with azalia-bushes, snowy camellias, purple rhododendrons in their glory, and, where the full wealth of a southern sun lay, a few superb ferns and rosy oleanders; the whole enclosed and sheltered from the Atlantic blasts by mighty firs, dropping their boughs with rings of shadow low upon the sward. A grape-vine clambered from branch to branch of these, weaving a natural trellis, and hanging great bunches of dewy beryl and emerald on the sombre green of its support. Here Sir Rohan had spent the prime of many mornings, striving to weary thought and seeking inspiration for his work while training blossom and tending root; and here the Ghost had always followed him, at first with gentle enticing and sad blandishments, and then with sudden intimations of terror and the whole armory of her ghastly array. Now, near the foot of the lawn, Miriam, having twisted a wreath of the flaming azalias in her black hair one long lock of which already streamed over her white dress, was throwing clusters of the unused blossoms at St. Denys, who repaid her warmly, while after every missile she tossed a laugh. Just as she had raised her hands both of them full of the blazing flowers, a sudden exclamation from St. Denys checked her, and turning swiftly, she saw Sir Rohan at the window above. Slightly abashed at proving herself a romp before this grave, quiet man, she dropped half her trophies and stood irresolute a second, winding the loose tress about her fingers; then, glancing up, she laughed again, threw the remainder of her brilliant store at Sir Rohan, and spreading her dress in either hand, swept him a broad courtesy.

How the face changes, thought Sir Rohan. What variety of expression! It is like a star on troubled waters when the tide comes in. "St. Denys deserves the happiness he finds in his child," he said, and returning her greeting, he soon joined them at the table.

After breakfast, St. Denys determining to walk to the post-town, Sir Rohan, wrapped in a long cloak, the invariable garb of his wanderings, accompanied him, — leaving Miriam, as she desired, in the tumult caused by the disarray of the drawing-room; where, on returning a few hours later, they found her, still revelling in the confusion, in close communion with Mrs. Redruth, and a bosom friend of half the maids. All the shutters were open, and floods of unwonted sunshine filled the room till every mote was alchemized to gold.

"Another Danaë!" said Sir Rohan, as she stood surrounded and transfigured in the radiance.

"A very dusty Jove," returned St. Denys. "It is the way of womankind, however, sir. Since they cannot revenge their wrongs by conquering and routing us from the face of creation, they wreak the exuberant spite on every unfortunate speck and grain of the grand primal element, dirt, in their domains; and an atmospherical stampede of dust, like the present, is their delight.   A savage onslaught on the unpleasant material supposed to have entered into the composition of man is instinct in the feminine nature!"

"And all the people shall say Amen," said Miriam, soberly.

"I thought you had important affairs to detain you, young woman."

"So I had, papa.   How could one go out when the noise and bustle inside had such attractions?   And besides —"

"Besides what?"

"I wanted to make friends with some women," after a pause and coaxingly.

"And have you succeeded?"

"Yes."

"By a primitive Freemasonry.   And have you had enough housework?"

"Not quite, papa."

"Satisfy yourself, by all means.   I shall lie

down, and as we ride this afternoon, perhaps two more strokes of a besom and one fling of a duster will be sufficient stimuli for a heartier banquet of scrubbing-brushes and mops, by and by."

"Take care, papa," she cried, sweeping threateningly down upon them. "The first stroke besoms you and Sir Rohan where the other nuisances go!" Upon which the two gentlemen beat a cowardly retreat, St. Denys to his apartment and Sir Rohan to his painting.

Shortly before luncheon, Mr. Redruth passed through the hall, with a large key in his hand.

"Where are you going, Mr. Redruth?" sang Miriam.

"To the wine-cellar, my lady."

"I am not my lady, remember. But may I go with you?" And without pausing for a reply, she followed him.

"It is a place hardly fit for ladies —"

"As fit for ladies as gentlemen," she retorted. "Is it so very much worse than the rest of the house?"

"Ah, Miss, it is a sad, sad house," said the old man, shaking his head. A sudden disposition to inquire about Sir Rohan seized Miriam, but, a nice honor restraining her, she followed Redruth silently along various steps and passages, till he unlocked a door at the head of one last flight, lighted a candle, and went down. Here, also, great cobwebs hung in flaunting sheets, the dampness had generated a blue mould upon the narrow walls of the stairway, and large fungi grew rankly in the interstices of the flags. As they proceeded, the roof vaulted above in massive arches hewn from the rock, with broad groins and a single row of immense pillars; they were under the main foundation of the house. Here lay a pile of broken bottles; there, a heap of puff-balls that Redruth had torn yesterday from the path; further along, the walls gave back a frosty glisten to the rush-light, covered as they were with crystalline incrustations that seemed to have exuded from the rock and settled from the air; and in the last recesses, behind doors heavy with chains, were bins full of curiously-shaped flasks bearing fantastic seals; and great casks, piled one upon another, whose heads, once cabalistically labelled in redolent warehouses, were now netted and wreathed in the dusty gossamer of the spider. It was a new place to Miriam, for in her well-ordered home she had never sought, nor would have found, one similar. If she had thought at all about it, she had fancied the wine on St. Denys's table was supplied in much the same manner as the three fish always to be found in St. Neot's well, or as some modern magician draws finest liquors from walls and tables where none ever existed before, and where we may suppose no great provision remains. On one side, in among the rarest Medoc, were hoards of claret that had long lost its mingled flavor and lay lifeless in dingy sarcophagi; while its fragrant kindred, exquisite Château Margaux, delicatest St. Emilion, and sweet wine of Roses from the Abbey of Ile, gathered a softer fire and richer purple in slumbering through the slow *feuilles* of their balmy dreams. Not far away lay the treasures of the Côte d'Or, and of Champagne.

"All these, Sir Rohan laid in nearly twenty years ago," said Redruth, "but they are losing now. Will you try them, Miss Miriam?"

"I came down to see, not to taste," she answered.

"Here is the most perfect wine in the world!" he said, drawing a bottle from its layer of white sand. "At least, they say it is. I'll show you one, soon, far finer, to my fancy. Yet none but that can equal the softness and strength of this. How racy it is, clearing the heart like a laugh, and yet how light, never leaving a fume in the brain; vinous, too, as if the very life and soul of the grape had been expressed into each vintage, and the vine would never blossom again. So full of perfume is it, that I wonder so small a space should contain such exhaustless odors, and half believe, at each bottle I uncork, that the King, upon his throne hundreds of miles away, will scent it slipping along the wind, and demand it! And what a crimson stain it has in the glass! — a glass as thin as air you should drink it from, Miss Miriam. If I were one of the heathen gods, I would turn the great hollow heavens into a drinking-cup, and wringing it full of the juices of the Côte d'Or, would sip and sleep through eternities."

"Perhaps that is what one of the Indian gods does do, — I think they call him Brahma," said Miriam. "But I've read that the ancients drank from murrhine cups, which shed an almost imperceptible fragrance through the draught."

"Ah! and these same ancients, I 've heard say, worshipped something called Bacchus. The poor things, I suppose, had never heard of Burgundy."

"Is that the name of this wine, Mr. Redruth?" asked Miriam, touching the little bundle of virtues daintily with her finger.

"That is one name, just as all the imperial family have a family name; but the Emperor himself has a name separate, and this is a very pretty one, — it is called Romanée Conti."

"All your wines have pretty names, I think. Do you know any that have n't?"

"Let me see. There is Schloss Johannisberger; that 's not so pretty."

"I don't know. Schloss is as pleasant as Castle, and the syllables jingle well. Yes, I think that is."

"There 's Marcobrunner — Montefiascone — Amontillado."

"No, indeed, Mr. Redruth, they are as musical as brooks."

"O, there 's Szeghi, a Tokay liqueur."

"And that has a savage sound which I like."

"Indeed then, Miss Miriam, they all must have sweet sounds. I hardly think so fine a thing could be ill-named," said the old connoisseur, with a sigh of pleasure, as he replaced the bottle.

On the other side were stored lively Rhenish, that might have been reposing unmoved some half-century; beyond them, dry Spanish and white wines; and in a still warmer nook, but half disclosed in the dim light, luscious liqueurs of the Levant, and rich muscadines of the south.

"Here," said Redruth, "is wine that I brought from Xeres myself, when Sir Rohan bought the French wines. You have been in Spain, Miss Miriam? No? Then you never saw the Tent grape, which is purple all through; nor the great vats, with steps to climb them, where they keep the Val de Peñas; nor the giant tanks at Alicant; nor yet the vine-dressers of Catalonia, swinging over precipices by slender cords, that they may tend the priceless vintage of some cranny no bigger than a grave. You would like the country where these Lagrimas come from. Tears, — they are not pressed from the unwilling bunches, but wept down by large white grapes that can well afford to be so bountiful. I do not know which were best, the laughing of Champagne, or the weeping of Malaga."

They were now in the last arch, whose thick draperies blinked through the unaccustomed rays, and swung heavily at the breath of the speaker while he busied himself in the ancient stores and stooping among the tressels, with the candle, sent fantastic shadows to dance up the dusky stone, still startling Miriam as the clinging webs now and then brushed her cheek.

"All the wine in this corner," said he, "could not be bought with gold. It keeps. There are a dozen kinds, placed here by another Sir Rohan, a hundred years ago. This is Rousillon, or Masdeu they call it up stairs, which means God's Farm; and it is that, indeed. Knights templar and monks have grown it. A color like a violet it owned, when new. Canary is this; it should have the smell of a pine-apple. Do you fancy pines, Miss Miriam? You shall have them at dessert to-day, for liking so well to hear about my wines."

"Virtue is its own reward, Mr. Redruth.

"Here is Madeira. If fire could be oily in the mouth and a cordial to the stomach, and yet have so delicious an odor that when swallowing it you felt like one prolonged nose down to your finger-tips, why, then fire were old Madeira."

Just above Mr. Redruth's head stood jars of sweet Cypress, and a carabas of Shiraz wine. "It is as sparkling and transparent as rock-water," said Mr. Redruth, pointing at the last. "I often wonder what kind of grape can have so clear a juice."

"I can tell you, Mr. Redruth, for I have seen it."

"Miss Miriam!" he exclaimed, with delight.

"O yes. They grow among some old ruins, and they are immense, gold-colored, and translucent, and are called royal grapes."

"Thank you, young lady. I did not think to learn anything of you, when you tripped down behind me, just now. I'm not very fond of young persons; but see! you said, a moment since, virtue was its own reward, and here it is. The wine I told you of is there; and after I have taken off the dinner wines, I shall come

back and toast your eyes, pretty one. That beside it is Johannisberger, whose name you like
so much; and next is Riesling, that grew at
Strasburg, where there is a fine spire, I think, —
the finest in the world, I think, — that tapers
off and lingers in the air as you will find the
aroma of White Hermitage linger in your
throat!" And taking a flask of Tokay from
beneath an anthiel of the same, he left it in her
hands as if in compensation for his absence
while going to decant the wines for which he
had come. "Some call this the king of wines,"
he said; "but it's not my king, as I told you."

As he went down the arches, followed by
his shadows, now bringing the rondure of big
empty tuns into light, and now filling the hollow
vaults with deeper gloom, Miriam's glances pursued him, and she puzzled herself fancying what
contentment he could find crawling in and out,
day after day, among barrels and bins, and
hoping to die no better. Then she remembered
the little flask of consolation that had been left
with her, and turned it idly in her hands, although in the darkness hardly to be seen.

Not a year before, in that delicious season

when October and November mingle their warm and cool hues in softest shading, making for us the Indian summer, she remembered to have wandered, one morning, through a vineyard of Tokay. The vines, somewhat shrivelled and brown, yet still bending with the affluent weight of their sumptuous and shining clusters, which nestled among the sere leaves as if in broad, golden salvers; the dews, not yet all exhaled, sliding from side to side, and as they hid in the heart of the bloom-bathed bunches, imparting to them one last flavor of morning, and sunshine, and sweet south winds; the lusty gatherers, with brimming corbeilles borne on their heads lightly as crowns and just supported by the caryatid curve of a sun-bronzed arm; the rosy faces of frolicsome girls, as they peered through alleys of the vintage treasures; the great, grooved tables, heaped like altars of Bacchus with purple abundance, even the pearly piles glowing in rich shadows; and the merry Hungarian peasants, whose white and naked feet vainly strove to conquer the exuberant and spirting crimson. She remembered the little brown thief, with his wide, sherry-colored eyes, his mouth and hands full of the gray stolen fruit; the scarlet-winged bird who swung in the sun beside her; the promise of distant snow, low in the air, that would soon lay its white morsels among the dark bunches left to gather the juice of the completed seasons; the stream braiding its remote banks with the light and gloom of creek and inlet; and the sailing shadow of a cloud sweeping over bending fields of yellow grain, and falling fainter and fainter, till between far blue hills that reared opposing relics of barbarous fastnesses it became only like the visible breath of the wind itself. All this was the tribute of the last vintage, but how many seasons had faded since that morning whose sunshine a hundred years ago had been clouded into the wine of the flask she held, drawing with them all the gay workers of that day! Grief and gray-haired winter and frosty death had succeeded their smiling summer, and they mouldered in mountain-graves, with the vintagers of the Cæsars, — yet their wine lived. An Emperor had supped from the kindred of this flask, lifting its silvery lustre to sway with an oily, indolent lusciousness between his eye and the sparkling lights, amidst ravishing music and beauty that made the night perfect, — and this had slept in what silent seclusion in the darkest recesses of a dismal cellar. What seas had rocked this wine till it clarified itself by tumult, what tropical fervors had filled it with spicy sweets, what large-starred Indian nights had wafted its ship through zones of frankincense and myrrh, with all the airs of Paradise, and in what tempestuous expanses had it ploughed when the waves rose like columns of green fire, knitting their white fans above the highest mast. Other flasks of the same growth might be lying on ocean-floors beside the drinking-cup of the gods; but this had ended all wandering, beneath the foundations of a forsaken manor. Still it amassed further richness, as the hair of the Enchanted Beauty grew to her feet. It had royal company, too, in its sleeping palace; and she recalled the names with which Redruth had entertained her. There was Homer's Nectar, still borne by rocky Scio as when the blind poet climbed its hills, feasting his grand eyes with the imagination of the sea. There was Vino d'Oro, made where the rustle of the cedars of Lebanon reached it, and through whose gardens perhaps Solomon himself had walked at cool of day. There was the wine of Hannibal's camp; and the wine of the Holy Spirit, such as mellowed in the great tun of Heidelberg, watched by grotesque sprites and demons perched atop, growing almost in the shadow of a Spire more perfect than the one which Redruth fancied, inasmuch as free offerings have a sweeter savor than extortions, and this rose and melted into heaven wreathed with a softer beauty than niche or pinnacle or buttress could bestow, bathed in the æsthetic adoration of that noble people who, without the aid of majesty or sanctity, could give farm and homestead and time to build up and complete this monument in air; and there was the Sang des Suisses,— the Wine of Blood,— a wine whose soil the life of heroes had moistened, and low on whose horizon lay the purple and silver phantoms of the Alps. She looked toward the obscure quarter of the creaming Ay, and thought of some possible rencontre of the famous sovereigns of the four great kingdoms of the world, who had each their vineyard on the hill-side there. There was the Lacryma Christi which alchemized the crust of a volcano

8*

into juices that, she had heard St. Denys say, the Roman Horace sipped as rare Falernian; and certainly Charlemagne had known the name and flavor of some among those Rhenish wines. Did not those Rhenish wines where now the candle flickered, make all beautiful landscapes possible in this dark and chilly cellar? Did they not bring the broad river and roll it through the gloom, between castle-crowned shores over whose sides clambered and tossed in sunny breezes multitudes of cool, whispering leaves, where feudal ruins, whose beacon-fires had once bounded from roof to roof, bright signals of incursion or attack, now crumbled amidst the eternal youth of luxuriant vegetation, hung their embrasures with imperial draperies, and housed in the cells of wall and corridor the purple swarms of harvest? Was not the chorus of the savage barons still to be heard, and the clang of their drinking-glasses? Were not the fair faces of sad-eyed nuns to be seen down the green vistas of tendril and vine? And under the palest moon did not the water-sprites weave misty fountains and long falls of spray in its arrowy middle current? Were they not the chrism of poetry and history and romance, and did not their names sing, as it were, to themselves? Fine company, too, were those island wines, that had exchanged their throne-like hill-sides rising on the far view of the mariner like clouds, and ever serenely taking the dash and turbulence of mid-ocean, for the wooden tressels beneath them now; their hedges of wild-rose and myrtle and pomegranate for the dust and films of this cellar; and for the darkness of this present shelter, the steep look-out from their island citadels, across boundless reaches of summer seas. If I drink of this Tokay, thought Miriam, I drink sunshine, and the grape, and Hungary and a certain wild freedom of its untamable atmosphere. What long voyages a-sea, and what silence and rest and perfect calm. But shall I taste them in it — if all these made a wine, would its flavor be that of Tokay? I would drink it then, indeed, but I may not like this — and while she mused, the flask, so lightly held, slipped from her hands and shivered on the flag. The costly liqueur ran slowly down the channels of the pavement, while Miriam stood aghast at the unpremeditated libation. Suddenly a strange perfume rose in clouds, wrapping her, and still curling upward and around. Softest summer and richest fragrance diffused through the damp and wintry vaults, and all the wealth of Araby the Blest seemed dripping from the air and lying at her feet. As she moved, her garments shook out sweetest gales, and the arches swelled to the pillared vastness of some incense-shrouded temple. While lamenting the catastrophe, she heard the voice of Redruth approaching.

"So it tempted you too much. You could n't wait for me!" he said.

Miriam was silent till he comprehended her misdeed. "I am so sorry!" she said then.

"O, it was priceless!" he exclaimed with a pang, stooping over the fragments.

"You should n't have bewitched me, then!" retorted Miriam, twice nettled.

"Well, well, Miss, you 're sorry, or you would n't be so sharp."

"I shall break everything in the house, if I don't go away soon."

"Better you should, than go away."

"Why, Mr. Redruth! I thought you would be provoked."

"It was yours, and if you like it better on

the floor, you're welcome. It's a shame to see good wine wasted, though, and this was the cream of the earth. Other wines are best grown on light sands from which they can draw no juice, or nourishment;—the sun and the air, the wind and the rain, feed them with pulp and sweetness: but the old Earth herself, Miss Miriam, gives its charm to Tokay,—draws its roots into her bosom, distils all her aromatic gums in pungent essences along its ducts, teaches it her secret. Yet I was not going to pledge you in it, but in a wine paler than amber, rarer than Tokay; in White Hermitage."

"Why in that, Mr. Redruth?"

"Because it has a sweet association in my mind with youth and beauty, and a love whose mystery I never learned. Shall I tell you?" He paused a moment, as if reflecting. Miriam's nice honor deserted. "It is not a score of years since Sir Rohan brought home with him, one day, a young lady handsome and stately-stepping as yourself," he continued. "Hardly my master's equal I might think,—though seeing her so little, and she so quiet before folk, it was not easy to judge. The noon they came—it was just about this season of the year — Sir Rohan passed down here with me; the great door yonder was open, and had filled the cellar with warm twilight. I was showing him the wines he had sent me to buy in Spain, when we heard a little rustle, and she had followed close behind him. I showed no more bargains that day, but at the mouth of this arch they pledged each other in White Hermitage. It was a pretty picture, — my young master, so tall and gallant, with all his glances on her, and she, tender and laughing and blushing — ah! I shall not see one like it again. They were here but a few days, and on one or two of those were gone from dawn to setting at some old ruins near, and then they went away to the North. She wore a curious ring that had been an heirloom in the family, and that he himself used to wear before her."

"Was this young lady Sir Rohan's wife?"

"I never heard that she was."

"Poor child! what became of her?"

"I never saw her again, and who would dare ask Sir Rohan a question?"

"I have asked him many."

"Yet I would not advise you to ask him this.

Since the day he came back alone, he has been what he is now."

Saying which things, Mr. Redruth brought up from a hidden recess a tiny bottle of White Hermitage. "There were three bottles then," he added; "after this there will be only one."

"But may we take it?"

"Of course we may! I never pass it but I think of the gray-bearded Hermit on his stony hill, setting the plants in every seam of the rocks. If he had ever been a bad man, he would have loathed the work that recalled hours of sin; and he must have been a good man, for he planted for posterity."

"Does that follow?"

"O, you don't agree with me, you 're for a quibble, you never drank Hermitage! But let us go out where the odor of the spilled wine will not mingle with it."

At the mouth of the arch he drew two glasses from the basket on his arm.

"Why do you bring them down here?" she asked saucily.

"Because when I am in the small wines, I sometimes get confused as to the kind I want, and am obliged to taste."

"I am afraid you have been down too long when you get confused."

"It may be, Miss Miriam, — it may be."

"O, I beg pardon, Mr. Redruth! I wasn't in earnest."

"No offence, young lady. But though I'm so fond of our wines, I seldom drink them, — not too often ; and no more does my master, or they would have been gone long since; and I do not think you were born when the last were laid in."

But it occurs to me here that, in the course of my observation, I have never met an individual who acknowledged that he had just been asleep, that he entertained the least curiosity concerning his acquaintance, that he was unfamiliar with the ways of the world, or whose irascibility was not to be highly excited by an allusion to the time when he should have gained more experience. How, then, could I find one who confesses that he takes wine too often?

Hanging his candle in a hook, Redruth drew the cork, and filled first Miriam's glass and then his own.

"Hold it up to the light, Miss, and see the

shiver that sparkles through it at the breath of the cold air. See how clear it is,—the chrysolite of the Bible is not clearer;—brighter than the gilding of the great mirrors up stairs, and fairer than the shine of straw. See the delicate topaz tint. It is the color of the sky just before an early winter's sunset,—palest, most pellucid gold. How thin and fine,—it looks as if the glass held only a splendid vapor that any wind might blow about in little flakes. Draw it nearer and take the perfume; what a rich and bounteous bouquet! You have the concentration of a whole garden of flowers, each one sweeter than the other. Taste it, and we need a word to say what the aroma is like. Here 's to your brown eyes, Miss Miriam!"

"And may you be cup-taster to Prester John, Mr. Redruth!"

It so happened that after he had been some time busy at his easel, it occurred to Sir Rohan to go on the same errand as Redruth, and see what store for choice palates yet remained in the cellar. In his preoccupied state of mind the open door was unnoticed, and he descended till he came to the heap of puff-balls which lay drying by the path. He had long contracted a habit of looking steadfastly ahead, and thus the scene, illuminated by the swinging taper, which had first been enacted in his own life, met his unobstructed view at the other end of the cellar. Amazed, he dropped his candle in the fungi, and paused to behold it. Miriam, white-gowned and with loosened hair, holding her sparkling glass to the light, like any Bacchante, while Redruth dim in shadow, as the dark figure of a cameo, projected her more brilliantly. As he gazed, the fallen candle kindled the withered growth beneath, which, flashing up, surrounded him for an instant with a pillar of fire, smothered again, and rolled on high a dense volume of smoke.

The intoxicating effects of the fumes of burning puff-balls are too well known to need comment ; and as Sir Rohan stood in a species of bewilderment, he inhaled their delirious vapor, still with his eyes on Miriam. Suddenly, while she yet extended her arm, he saw a little house-adder glide from a crevice of the stone, look about alertly, slip down and coil like a bracelet round her ivory wrist. He would have darted forward, but all power of volition was torpid, though he

beheld faintly through the smoke the white face
of Redruth paralyzed with fear, and he waited
in an agony of agitation and alarm. Miriam,
for the first moment ghastly enough, in the next,
bent curiously forward, and inspected the venomous little creature, that lifted its head till the
fangs danced before her eyes. Sir Rohan seemed
to see nothing that ensued; he only perceived
her in the instant of horror, for it was the very
device of the ring of his dream. In a breath he
comprehended that the Ghost had come to him
again; and as the little flames spread from the
fungi beneath him to those a step in advance, he
saw her, with her hard eyes piercing his, shaking
a web of fire betwixt him and Miriam. So, the
device of the ring his mother had worn, he had
worn, the Ghost had worn, Miriam was imperson-
ating. He felt the seconds of his delirament
stretching into hours, while the scene was as im-
movably fixed before him as if carved on the rock.
Could the Ghost by any subtle chymistry thus
have transformed and brought the ring back to
him in the gigantesque, planted at the foundations
of his house, as it was of his life, to send thrills
through every wall, and to be remembered at

every draught? It was in vain to call reason to
his aid, or to remember that the power of the
Ghost had been growing less and less for years;
the intoxication he had breathed ruled him as im-
periously as ever she had done, and he could not
but abandon himself to the wildest extravagances
of imagination, while counting the separate snails
that arched their yellow backs, and tracked the
stones around this device,—which was multiplied,
by the patches of light cast from the swinging
taper, into a thousand Miriams, each one fascinated by a glittering serpent,—counting the
bright-eyed toads who squatted above and gazed,
the white lizard and the gold beetle who emerged,
and stared, and hid themselves again. The current of fresh air blowing down from the open door
half roused him; broken reflections of the scene
floated away on the dissipating smoke; he wondered if men often lived so long as he was suffering;—the atmosphere became clear again, and
he saw Miriam take the snake by the tail, give
it a sudden twist and toss upon the distant flags,
where with a sharp hiss it slid from sight, while
she looked into Redruth's face and laughed. He
found his relief before he saw her action.

"How quickly you did it, Miss Miriam!" he heard Redruth say. "Why, I scarce saw the thing before it was gone!"

The effect of the puff-balls was passing off, and, tearing his limbs from their chain, he sped up the stairs again. In a few moments, with her slow, stately step, somewhat recalled from familiarity by the accident, Miriam followed, leaving Redruth, in astonishment that he could have dropped a spark, to set open the great door and cleanse the cellar, lest the smoke and spilled wine should corrupt and ferment his treasures. And had one looked in, a half-hour later, they had seen him staying himself, in Sybaritic composure, with flagons, and because there were no apples, comforting himself again with flagons.

V.

THE RINGS.

THE next day, Miriam told St. Denys of her experience in the cellar, and asked him if what Redruth had told her concerning Sir Rohan were true.

"You should not attend the gossip of servants," was his response.

"But Mr. Redruth assumed such a quiet patronage, that he seemed to have lost that capacity."

"He is old, and generally faithful; but perhaps his heart was warmed with the wines over which he was, as you say, so enthusiastic, when he spoke too freely of his master. Forget it, my dear."

"I suppose every one has his faculties concentrated on some particular point," said Miriam, after a little while; "and so with this man, every other beautiful thing only tends to illustrate and adorn his wines. He was something like a poet, only, papa, I don't think I like poets. And Sir Rohan — his point is his painting."

" Just now it is, but he 's as good at anything, as the melancholy Jaques has it."

" I wonder, after all, if he knows so much about any of his businesses as Redruth does about his one. Well, I 'm glad, papa, you 're not a poet, nor artist, nor any of those disagreeable things. You neither run nor halt, but do you know, I think you have an even gait, something too princely to stoop for trifles. There 's a compliment from your big baby! " and she twined her arms coaxingly round his neck.

" Compliment, indeed! Who gave you leave to flatter me? " he said, fondly putting back her disordered hair.

"Why, you see if you 've so fine a gait, the best thing you can do with it is to walk home! I want to be at home. Only think, it is ever and ever so long since we saw the Castle! "

" Ah, Miss Miriam! " said Sir Rohan, entering just then, " are you so impatient to get away? "

"Not impatient, sir," she answered, rearranging herself. " Only when one has been three years away, home has gained a kind of enchantment."

" I revolved various schemes for your entertainment, during my illness yesterday evening," said Sir Rohan ; "but so lonely is the vicinity that society is impossible. My only neighbor is Marc Arundel — at least he was —— "

" Marc Arundel ! God bless me ! have I escaped that man abroad, to hear of him first at home ? " exclaimed St. Denys.

" Ah ? He is your heir ? I had quite forgotten. Yes, his estate is about twenty miles away, — a small one. I have no doubt that there are other families between us, but unfortunately I do not know them."

" Pshaw ! what matter ? We did not come to see them, Rohan."

" Thank you. But, lest too much even of so good a thing as your humble servant should tire, the monotony must be varied. There are a thousand curiosities in the county which might interest Miss Miriam: cromlechs, old British fortresses, fabled abodes of Gog-Magog, and even some available mines —— "

" O, a mine ! a mine ! I should delight, of all

things, in going down a mine!" exclaimed Miriam.

"Perhaps you would not find it so delightful in practice as in fancy," said St. Denys.

"O, Sir Rohan!" cried Miriam, "is there one near here?"

"There was," he replied; "but it may be forsaken now; I will ask Redruth."

In a few moments, during which Miriam beat impatient tattoos with her foot, Mr. Redruth answered his summons.

"Yes, sir," he replied; "they work a lode of the great mine still, and that is on your own land. The other veins took a start some years ago, and are quite dead now."

"Can we enter it, Mr. Redruth?" cried Miriam.

"Why, Miss, I do not know as to yourself; but the gentlemen can, if ——"

"O, then, we will certainly go. I will get ready at once. Is it far?"

"Seven or eight miles, Miss."

"Then we had best have the coach, Miriam; your riding-dress might embarrass you."

"You will have to dress differently, for convenience in climbing," said Sir Rohan. "Perhaps Mrs. Redruth can accommodate you."

"Yes, papa. Thank you, Sir Rohan, I will ask her. I will be back in a minute," and she ran quickly from the room.

"Order the coach, Redruth," said Sir Rohan, "and accompany us, if you like."

"I will drive you with pleasure, sir," he replied, disappearing.

"How comes it, Rohan," asked St. Denys, while they waited alone, "that you dropped your acquaintances so entirely?"

"You refer to Arundel? O, I never knew him at all. Some time ago Redruth told me he had come into his property, by which I judged his father, whom I once knew, to be dead; but for himself, — he is little more than a boy."

"A very troublesome boy, — a scoundrel of some thirty years' growth, thoroughly possessed of evil. He has given me infinite trouble for Miriam. She is only eighteen now, but three years ago I had to take her abroad to avoid his pertinacity. It is best that it was so, for I had always found it impossible to have Miriam taught. She has learned little or nothing from books, nothing of use, yet adapted herself surprisingly to the languages of such countries as we lived in, and by a continual companionship with me has gained, orally, what all the types of Europe would have failed to impart."

"Did you free yourselves from Arundel?"

"Marc? O no; he followed us for a time so closely as to seem ubiquitous. But at last we escaped him. You know the greater part of my possessions are entailed on him."

"And yet I believe he is not of your blood."

"I wish I could say no drop, and thank God! But he is my only relative in the male line, though distant."

"Ah,—I thought it had been some indirect way, or unforeseen chance, that made him inherit from an uncle who was father and heir to your dead sister's child."

"To be sure. He has some small sum in the funds through that luck, and he knew that Miriam will have more there,—all the personal property. I would give half my remaining years to break that entail. Unless I should lose it, though, which is unlikely, Miriam will have a fortune fair enough; I hasten to reach home and lawyers, that my will and these settlements may be made."

"Why hasten? You are young yet."

"I am young, truly, but have no elixir for remaining so."

Redruth and Miriam returned now together; Miriam, with her travelling-cloak wrapped closely round her, revealing, notwithstanding, the well-booted foot and handsomely turned ankle, and with a singular cap tied over her ears, looking in the odd disguise, amid her pretty blushes and laughter, like the ladies on the stage who become pages as circumstance and the author command, or like some bashful impersonation of Rosalind. Lifting her hand to knock the cap jauntily on one side, she displayed, with a quaint coquetry, the neat miner's suit which she adorned.

"Mrs. Redruth has lent me some flannel clothes of her son's, who sometimes works in the mine," she said. "Do you mind, papa? You two will look infinitely worse when lost in the corners of some burly stone-cutter's raiment!" And they were soon bowling forward to the mine.

After an hour's drive, the road, which had been sheltered and pleasant, opened on a bleak level

bordering the sea and exhibiting few signs of cul-
tivation. Here the coach stopped, and having
alighted, they followed Redruth through one of
the various footpaths that tracked the moor. At
no great distance the smoke of the blowing-house
rolled up continual volumes, staining the faultless
blue of the sky, and poisoning all the sunny air
beyond; old shafts, that had been sunk and abandoned years since, lay on either side,—deserted
pits, round whose black abysses long grasses bent
with their own coarse weight; tall rushes, planted
to impede the progress of the sand inland from
along the coast, edged the horizon and tipped
themselves with the sparkle of the sea; and at the
root of a single tall and ragged pine-tree, the great
shaft yawned amidst heaps of rubble, long lines of
conduits and gigantic whirling wheels, enormous
frames of scaffolding and cables through which
the wind whistled hoarse tunes, and all its black,
terrible enginery and uncouth paraphernalia.
Miriam left her cloak in the coach, when St.
Denys returned for her, already arrayed for the
descent.

"Is 't a lass going down?" asked one of the
winze-men.

"As good wenches," replied his sullen companion, "have stayed down."

St. Denys was the first to enter the shaft, and having been safely lowered through the close, wet sides of the hewn rock to the first platform, the kibbul reascended for Miriam, Sir Rohan and Redruth speedily following. Then came the cautious clambering down steep, ruinous ladders, flight after flight, with dim perspectives into black galleries winding away like inquisitorial vaults,— far above, the fair sky now dark and blue as twilight,— far below, the twinkle of lanterns on yet lower platforms. The broken slats that might precipitate their lifeless bodies a thousand feet, the great, half-rotten beams that partially upheld the roofs, the monstrous gaps of the landing-places, just made visible by the candles they carried, filled Miriam with no manner of dread; she experienced, instead, a wild exhilaration. To Sir Rohan it was neither pleasure nor pain. All things aroused in him only the sentiment of endurance, and he went along with the same silent stoicism that he would have manifested if eternity had been a treadmill.

"How easy it is!" said Miriam.

"In the winter," replied the man who led them, "the ladders are so covered with ice, rain and sleet beating in with sharp flaws of the storm, that the way is full enough of dangers. Poor Dick fell down from here, a dozen years ago, when his hands were numbed and his feet slipped from the run-dle."

"Dick who?" asked Miriam.

"Roy, ma'am. He'd been night-watch for a long time below, and one day he took a notion to see the world above, and there was an end; he's never been up since."

"It killed him, of course?" said St. Denys.

"No, sir, not that; but it broke more bones than I'd 'a' thought he had. We patched him up and kept him like a lady till he was healed; and he seldom comes near the shaft now, nor will he come up to the daylight. He says, being put down so strong, it's but fair he should stay. Will you go down further, Masters? There's little below but water and deads. Yonder's the lode we work."

Pausing on the platform, they glanced into the profound again. One or two torches, small and bright as fireflies, flickered about the face of the blackness. There was a murmur, broken now and then by a dash and gurgle, that told of running waters; and the clang of the workmen's hammers came to them with only a deadened reverberation.

"It is as great a mystery down there as it was when we started," said Miriam. "Can't we go where they are at work, papa?"

The man who accompanied them was one of authority, being an underground captain; and making her will his law, he stepped from the landing, and conducted them along a tortuous way,— now on single planks that bridged pits suddenly sunk to murk, dizzy, and never-sounded depths; and now crawling through passages precipitous on one hand, and the three remaining sides all within reach of the other, while to the flare of their candles displaying in a glittering profusion bright sheets of vivid green and rusty red, and singularly white, pellucid oozes,— till the narrow sides spread into the wide halls of the explored vein. The roof that they could have touched before, supported, as it was, by great pillars of ore left unwrought, stretched suddenly upward, without brace or buttress of any kind, higher than they could see, and shrouded in completest gloom. A natural cavern, a vast hall flanked by vaster galleries with a thousand avenues, all like as many mouths gaping for darkness, was rendered only obscurer and more awful by dim, scattered lights fixed in the wall, the walls themselves giving back countless reflections, and glistening in rolls of gorgeous colors, as the mundic sprinkled its lustrous facets over the unhewn metal. Great barrows, piled with rocks whose rough resplendent angles told of the treasure in their bosoms, passed them; and heaps of the earthy matrix lay waiting to be conveyed in their turn, with giant crystals of quartz and shining slabs already split away from them, through whose transparency the metal branched off and wandered along with all the delicate arborescent intricacy of a fern or a sea-moss. The clash and clatter as of Thor with a thousand hammers, resounded and beat about their ears in a deafening clangor, and all the air was hot and oppressive. At one moment the black distance of some far-extending galleries would be powdered with showers of tiny sparks, followed by quick explosions that echoed like the multitudinous rattle of musketry, as small fragments fell, loosened by force of some detonating blast; and already so suggestive of terror had the gloom become, with its wild hints of greater depths and darker precipices where the miners were already kindling the Saturday fires, that Miriam clung to Sir Rohan's arm in a strange kind of fascinated dread, while the Captain explained to St. Denys all the difficulties and attractions of the works. "It was pleasant," said St. Denys, afterward, "to observe the affection which this man entertained for the mine, always using the feminine appellative, and glorying in her wealth as if it were a personal attribute."

Advancing down the cavernous mazes, they stood upon a brink, deep in the heart of whose chasms firemen were piling fagots and logs under a hundred arches and beside every hanging wall, feeding the hungry flames that licked the vaults with long tongues, and as they passed to and fro across the ruddy glare, waving their torches at unlighted piles, seeming more like the gnomes who turn the crystal sluices of hidden streams and cook the gems and metals of the earth's bowels, than like men who ever breathed in the atmosphere above.

"Perhaps," said Miriam, "those things, those

imps down there, hold the strings of the earth's motion and keep her even in her orbit. If I should hit one of them with a stone, I wonder would she fly off like a comet or not. We are in a sort of fairy-land."

"Stranger things have happened," said Sir Rohan. "Throw your stone and see." And they both delayed, looking at the masses of metal which ran molten in the blaze,— prismatic copper, and here and there delicate drops of silver.

"How that heavier metal plashes down! Compared to it those silver sprays and plumes," said Miriam, "seem rather to rise than fall, like feathers in the air."

A frequent movement of Sir Rohan's, a sharp, alert survey, had annoyed Miriam ever since their entrance.

"Sir Rohan, how nervous you make me! you positively frighten me!" she exclaimed. "What is it you see with your rapid glance at either hand? Is there any danger?"

It half seemed to him when she spoke, as if his secret were discovered, and he realized what he had always doubted, the relief that could be afforded by a disburdened conscience.

"No danger, Miss Miriam," he replied; "there are no fire-damps here, I believe, though we should not linger too long in so vile an atmosphere. The firemen will have spread their labors through the mine soon, and then all leave it till Monday morning, unless poor Dick stays down."

"There it is again!" cried Miriam. "What did you see?"

"I saw, Miriam, a figure such as the witch saw when Samuel came to Saul," he replied, after an instant's pause.

"Gods ascending out of the earth?" quoted Miriam.

"I did not mean that exactly. A figure such as when Anne came to Richard, very pale and faint and wild, that glides between those distant columns, out of one concave into another, and always over the shoulder throws a dreadful glance at me."

"In other words, a ghost?"

"In other words, a Ghost."

But when Sir Rohan had said so much, a great fear seized him lest he had revealed himself. He knew, when he spoke, that she would not believe him, and he felt himself to have trifled with something too sacred for approach. Could he smile at the Fates? And would not the curse fall with greater burden that he had raised it a moment by a jest? Yet here it was fitting for the Ghost to reassume her function, if every place which she had once filled with the dazzle of her youthful beauty might be haunted by its phantom now, for here she had once been, on as fair a day as this, not twenty years ago. But as if some spell bound a portion of her influence, she, who not long since would have confronted him in her direst mood, could now exert no more authority, nor spread a wider van of horror than the wan glimmer fading away from arch to arch in a perpetual pursuit, and he could laugh at his Ghost.

Turning hastily, as he spoke, they wound through other alleys after St. Denys and the guide, till they again reached the great hall, where, having seen quite enough of the mine, Miriam, in answer to St. Denys, expressed a wish to re-ascend, and they slowly crossed, listening to the remarks of the garrulous Captain. Several of the miners were haling an immense boulder down one gallery; above them, known by its faint breaths of air, flared a forsaken shaft, looking up to which,

Miriam, half expecting to find the blue, found only a sphere of crystal darkness; and down an opposite aisle a torch advanced, rapidly swinging from side to side, while its bearer sung a rough-voiced recitative of some only half-remembered ballad. Either they had become accustomed to the din, or a large portion of it had ceased; for they heard his words distinctly enough, and his rude salutation to the Captain. He was a tall man, properly, but so gaunt and haggard as to add an unnatural length to his stature; clothed in leathern nether garments, a red shirt falling open from his tawny bosom, and a small skull-cap above the matted rusty locks that mingled with his long and scanty beard unkempt and unshorn. So sallow and hollow were the cheeks with their parched skin clinging to the bone, so toothless the jaws, so sunken and deep and glittering were the eyes, so racked and ruined the whole distorted frame, that it was evident he had long breathed the fumes of arsenic which the burning mundic evolved, and had been drained of health by the profuse sweat of the furnaces above.

"O Heavens!" whispered Miriam, "it is an automaton that will drop in pieces before it has passed."

"It is Dick Roy," said the Captain. "He is tough, ma'am, or he 'd died long ago."

"I thought your arsenic burners lived but a short time," said St. Denys.

"Well — we don't look for them to trouble us long; they are in the houses above. But Dick is only exposed to the poison once a week, — when we kindle the fires over Sunday, — and then he 's out under the old open shafts; so he lasts, and he likes it; but we may find him dead some Monday morning."

Touching his cap with a mechanical deference, the man was shuffling by, when he paused, looked round with a wild hesitation, lost all his stupefaction on the instant, and suddenly turning, tossed and flared his flambeau repeatedly in the face of Sir Rohan, and then of Miriam. Passing his hand quickly across his supernatural eyes, again he peered into their faces.

"Ha' I dreamt?" he cried sharply. "Ha' I been dreaming? Is it no score o' year sin I came into the heart of earth? Is it no score o' year sin I saw the blessed daylight, or a star, save it glinted as yon now in the bal above ye? sin I snuffed a wind creeping in fro' the sea, or heard aught but its roaring, — for ye 're under the sea now, d' ye ken? and there 's no white godoleans on high, with their steel eyne snappin on the gale, an shrilling an shriking as yon o'er the moor! God! han ye never gone yeself, ye and the bonnibel beside ye? Then I 've no broided bones, nor did I fall. I ha' been in a swound. Sure, it 's the glaze on my eye that makes your face so old and deadlike, — but the lass is young as I kent her. No, no, ye must han a drug up above to keep beauty and life, but ye 've not drunk it yourself."

Sir Rohan made a movement to pass, and the Captain motioned Dick away. He obeyed, but in an instant shouted across the distance, "Wait a bit, I 've something for ye!" and was soon lost in the obscurity. Before long, his light was again to be seen, and shortly he waylaid them.

"Look at this!" he cried, extending something that glittered in his hand. "Ye don't mind it, Miss, when ye wor down before? How the master gave ye the siller, and ye turned and gave it me, sin it wor so like the ring ye wore on your third finger? Ye 've no ring there now."

"I don't know what he means," said Miriam. "I was never here before."

"Hoot! so fair and lie? O lissom lass, mind ye!" and he laid what he held, in her hand.

It was a piece of silver, as it is sometimes found in mines, crystallized in a slender stem and some singular inflorescence that in shape resembled a violet or the plant called heart's-ease. As she looked at it, he snatched her hand, twisted the supple stem round her finger: "God give ye good-den," said he, and vanished.

A deadly pallor had overspread Sir Rohan's face; he had dropped Miriam's hand, and standing apart, was surveying her with fierce, fixed eyes. The dreadful thought crossed him, if it were indeed his Ghost; the words faltered on his lips, but he strode away quickly without speaking, and led them to the. foot of the ladders. Soon the white glare of the opening blinded them, and in a few moments the fresh breath of the upper world illustrated the horrors of the atmosphere below, and with the cool winds blowing in and out the open windows of the coach, they were rapidly proceeding homeward.

VI.

Fanchon.

THE next day being Sunday, St. Denys inquired if there were any practicable church in the neighborhood; and soon, under Redruth's guidance, departed with Miriam to find it, leaving Sir Rohan to his primitive desolation.

Instantly, a loneliness utterly new overcame him. These people, who had not been with him half a week, and one of whom he had known but three days, became suddenly as indispensable to him as the air he breathed. The unusual stir about the house, proceeding from the kitchen and its occupants, only reminded him of the silence around himself; and unused to control any emotion, except in its exhibition, he allowed the little annoyance to vex him unbearably, while he paced the long drawing-room and execrated the murmuring air that his rapid step set in motion about him like another presence. A scarf of Miriam's, a tiny silken thing, lay across a chair; he took it up tenderly, as if it were a part of herself, for so full of life did she seem to him that he fancied her imparting her vitality to all around her. 'But I am myself half dead," he murmured. A glove of hers had been dropped at the door, and scattered violets from the bunch he had plucked for her at sunrise marked her path across the lawn. "It is a generous prodigality that distinguishes her," he thought. "Her heart is so large as to receive every creature with kindness, and she looks at all men with equal eyes." Sir Rohan was on dangerous ground; so he rolled the scarf and glove together without lingering over their delicate perfume, placed them by themselves, and went up to grind colors. The clock struck the quarter before two as he lifted the curtain of his painting, and simultaneously feet and voices echoed through the hall, and Miriam, searching drawing and dining-room, called aloud, "Sir Rohan! Sir Rohan! Do you know what day it is? Do you work on Sundays?"

Sir Rohan dropped the curtain, despite the faint and revengeful look that gathered over the face beneath, and joined his guests like one ashamed.

"What a queer little church!" said Miriam, as they sat at lunch. "It stands so lonely on that long slope, and buttressed by those great cliffs, with only three little lonely graves and the sea before it, that I believed Uther Pendragon to have said his prayers there; but nobody since. I said so to papa, going in, and a quick voice from no-one-knew-where replied, 'I apprehend the gentleman you refer to did not accustom himself to that amusement.' One might have known who spoke, but I could n't see him, till half through the service, in the great pew opposite, there were his evil eyes staring us out of countenance, at least if Marc Arundel's eyes could do so much."

"Miriam, you don't mean to say —" cried St. Denys, dropping his fork.

"Precisely that, papa. He bowed with the condescension of a Prince Cardinal."

"You did n't return it in service, Miriam?"

"O no! we were past the creed. So I was oblivious of all the Arundels since the flood, till leaving; when I put as much graciousness and as many smiles as could be crowded into a nod, and gave it him."

"You are a coquette! But I did n't see him."

"O dear, no, papa! Your eyes were blinded by your prayer-book."

"And where were yours?"

"O, mine are like those bugs, that see all ways at once. What a superb altar-cloth that was!—amaranth velvet, powdered with silver fleurs de lis; we must have one like it, at the Castle. Did any ladies of your family make it, Sir Rohan?"

"No, indeed! There have been no ladies in my family, you know, for many years; that little church flourishes under the Arundelian dynasty."

"I should n't wonder if Marc worked it himself," said Miriam. "It would be very fit employment; he has such a finikin faculty of mending, picking up, patching,—surely he knows the scandal of every family in the kingdom, papa! I think he 'd like to make flourishes in gold thread."

"You are growing vituperative, young lady," said St. Denys. "But there is one fortunate thing about this rencontre. He does not know where we are."

"O, papa, that 's too soothing a medicament; he saw Redruth with us!" she replied, pulling off her bonnet and suffering it to fall from her fingers.

"You should have been less devout, and by staying at home have avoided your friend," said Sir Rohan.

"That's a remedy too late. But there's yet another; let us use expedition, and depart."

"Miss Miriam, you will not leave me yet?"

"Why, Sir Rohan, if we stay we shall see Marc Arundel."

"And if you go, I shall see worse."

"Do you really mean that you want us here?"

"Most assuredly."

"Then, if content to have your retirement broken in upon, all your household upset, and your immutable decrees turned topsy-turvy by a romping lass and an angelic gentleman, what did you seek it for?"

"Miriam, child," said St. Denys, "what affair is that of yours?"

"Do you be quiet, papa, if you can't return your partner's lead."

"One may weary even of chosen pursuits, Miss Miriam."

"Then you'll soon weary of us, and we had better go before that catastrophe."

" Give me, at least, the opportunity of trial."

" Now, papa, am I not a good diplomatist ? You said, this very morning, we might be trespassing after all, coming as we did into a student's quiet without an invitation, like an irruption of Saxons; and now I have procured you one, although not starting with that intention," she added, merrily.

"I don't know, little chatterbox, where that tongue will lead you," said St. Denys. But Miriam was already half dancing away, moved by some fresh caprice.

It was toward the conservatory — Sir Rohan's mongrel between hot and green-houses being thus styled — that Miriam now bent her steps; and always choosing the most unusual way, she preferred crossing the sill of the oriol at the back of the drawing-room, to seeking it by either of the hall-doors. It was built apart from the house, and was kept by Sir Rohan with exquisite care, in which labor an experienced gardener, one of his nearest tenants, shared; and here the owner's useless wealth had been lavished. Scarcely a rod from the window, it looked thence, when the noonday sun illumined its gorgeous nurslings, like some sunset cloud blown into a nook of the great buildings, and screened there from all harsh dissolving winds. Since it had been the place where Sir Rohan grouped his colors and studied forms, where, also, he had been least dejected, it was less a formal hot-house than a wilderness of delights. Once within it, and you fancied yourself in the heart of the zone that girdles the earth with all the beauty of that magical one of Venus.

Miriam had not seen this place before, and indeed had no business there now, for it was as private and peculiar to Sir Rohan as his painting-room; but she was one of those who take possession of whatever they see, and entering an open door, a long green leaf and white-impearled plume of the rice kissed her cheek in welcome. She had not passed the threshold, before, rapt into a new world, every sense concentrated itself into that of scent; every known perfume was wafting toward her; every blossom on the face of the earth, she thought, was steaming with delicious fragrance. There were no forms or tiers, but the plants grew in broad beds, terraces, and mossy mounds, where practicable, while the walks were mosaicked in thick-strewn autumn leaves; serpents, parded, barred, and mooned, like agates; wings of the Purple Emperor of the Woods, and gay fallen feathers. At one point, long alleys lined with splendid shrubs formed, in the sun, arcades of diamond brightness, while half up their height hung narrow galleries whose vines trailed over balustrades of gilded network. Where the crystal wall arched out in crescents, great cones of the dark, shining leaves of orange, myrtle, and camellia were massed against the fresh brilliancy of tamarinds and enormous ferns whose intricate meshes glittered like cobwebs in morning dew; while again, the rich green of the maranta was thrown into deep shade by the startling light of a mimosa tossing from its rude trunk a spray of airy, tremulous foliage and long wreaths of golden blossoms. Opposite these, an Indian coral-tree loftily reared itself, clad in profuse scarlet flowers; and by its side the regal poinciana, still breathing of Madagascar and southern wealth, poised its clusters, crimson and magnificent, on large twin leaves all winged and nervous for flight; while counteracting discord, over them and across, with snake-like coils, the tropical bauhinia clambered and hung its white festoons, elegant, unequal, countless. From this excess of color and contrast, the eye passed to a passion-flower trellised in broad lace-work against the glass, looking backward from the increasing height, with its doubtfully blue and odorous blooms, upon a bed of late, shade-loving violets at its feet; on low brackets at one side here stood vases of the rich, violet-colored gloxinia, and paler daphne; and higher, on the other, a wide urn full of the purple Brazilian cleome, each blossom like the claw of Jove's eagle grasping his arrows, and round the urn the torenia twined in wanton luxuriance with its dark-purple, velvety bells. Easily the prevailing hue changed to the soft shades of the poncra's buff fascicles, the cream-dyed asystasia clinging breathlessly to the wall, and the globy abutilon; till turning suddenly round a dwarf-palm whose great fronds waved with dreamy rhythm, she came again upon a blaze of pomegranate-flowers, orange-colored sesban, crimson clianthus, pecking like a bunch of parrot's bills at the sunshine, an acacia,— the Persian Gul-ebruschim,— rosily tufted with great silken-threaded tassels, and the blue thunbergia twisting the light columns near by with involutions of classical acanthus-leaves. For all these flowers Sir Rohan forced to abandon their own proper times and seasons, and bud, bloom, delay, die, at their master's despotic pleasure. So, by some secret of superb skill, ordaining for them such unwithering perpetuity that the buds of May became the bantlings of December.

Here, glowing carnations took the noon to their hearts, and among. them nestled the ivy-leaved cyclamen, white, eager, listening; and there, the perpetual shiver of the hedysarum filled her with a vague response, and the snowy tube-rose satiated with a cloud of sweetest spice. Thrown, as things were, into masses of intense hue, they attained such individuality only by gradations as minute in one place as daring in another; while on this exaggerated scale the combination of color might be very different from that allowed by the fine finish of a lady's toilet. Swinging from tiny cups on high, grew the acrides, delicate and sweet; and above, hung in every way, the most fantastic, most delicious orchids. White doves and swans seemed floating in a world of greenery up the dome, falcons with light on their pinions shooting from spray to spray, vermilion-colored spiders sitting on some broad leaf, and rainbow-tinted fish swimming the thinner medium of upper air, while, grassy or pulpy as their stems might be, they all wore a degree of grace, beauty, and novelty, not to be rivalled. One epiphyte dropped its spiral slowly down as she advanced, till a great moth, with broad-balanced wings stained in crimson and gold, danced gaudily before her eyes; and round her head, as she walked, waved the long, wide ribbons of Sumatra grasses.

Miriam wandered along in a maze. She had brought her little bible with her, but sooth to say, it was yet unopened, and at last she threw herself into a chair of rough Madeira-wood, to recover a moment from the intoxication. Beside her here were all strange, mystic plants, with immense leaves; all tropical vines, sighing for their sultry, gloomy forests; lush, dark things, still stained with the steam of hot, humid regions; rank trailers, whose blue lips dripped with poisonous honey; and rich, feculent, aromatic scents, whose every draught held death. It was Sir Rohan's idiosyncrasy. Over the whole place the pandang shed his powerful breath, the rarest in the world, and sacred to the gods themselves.

Near the other extremity, Miriam now saw a group of figures, risen in a cluster, and through the shimmer of water that surrounded them, still rising, one might say. Some were above the others, and one was uppermost of all; with her right hand upon the shoulder of the next, she seemed to have sprung for a wreath which she held in the uplifted one. It was a wreath of lilies, and from the heart of each slowly issued a single drop, diffusing and gathering again at the apex of the petal, and falling forever, while tenuous threads of water shot forth in pistil and stamen, and with the perpetual drops wrapped this upper figure in torrents, and powdered, as they fell, to a drizzling rain that bathed the others in a veil of mist, till they all seemed like dimmest, farthest shadows risen from watery depths at some mortal call. In the silent basin at their feet were tender aquatics, the gems of Indian archipelagos and remoter seas; and the canals into which it ran lost themselves, without borders, in a soft green moss. Beyond this, baskets of roses, comprising all shades from black over sanguine and damask to purest white, transfigured themselves through the vapor into a splendid fleece; and flaming cacti made a rich

background for the noiseless fountain, and asserted their own identity more vigorously because
robbing a hill of heliotropes behind of theirs.

While Miriam sat surveying this pandemonium
of scent and tint, the heat and fragrance had become oppressive, her sense reeled under so strong
a cordial; the sun, calling forth the heavy incense
of every leaf, threw his own life into theirs, and
when the gardener came and went, having drawn
the canvas awning over the roof, it seemed to shut
in the whole soul of the ascending atmosphere
and press it upon her.

She leaned back in her chair, inhaling the perfumes like a voluptuary, yet half doubting if the
enjoyment were healthy. Her eyes were partially
closed; but in an instant they sprung wide open.
Something in the softened light, through the ful-
vid noon, was moving here, was taking shape, rising from the gray heliotropes and bringing their
passionate fragrance with her. Something so
pale, so fair, so thin, so sad, requiring no room,
yet making all room, where she once was felt, a
desert. Something floating toward her, never
tinged by any of the gorgeous shades under which
she passed; white, through all the lurid changes

of purple and gold and scarlet. Something that seemed to imply strength for so much direr a form, should she choose. Something still advancing, till the heat became as if an iceberg had melted in it; pausing; gazing at her with such infinite tenderness and pity and mournful beauty; passing on, and fading like a moonbeam into the sun.

Miriam sunk back again, dazzled and dizzy; a distant shout met her ear,—she thought they laughed at her dream, and wondered had she really slept.

The only thing to contradict such supposition was a purple heart's-case,—which she was sure she had never plucked, she said,—lying in her lap, pricked and threaded with the finest, finest, long, dark, human hair. But as if seized by a wind, when she would have touched it, it whirled from her finger and disappeared.

She was frightened and trembling, faint with awe; all her muscles were relaxed,—either the close air or the vision had rendered her power-less; she felt abstractly that the position was becoming perilous, when suddenly some one dropped the sashes of the roof with a clang, and a free current of cool wind swept gloriously in, tossing all the blooms, ruffling the smooth masses, bringing forth new splendor and freshness and life at every sigh. The reviving gale fanned Miriam's temples a moment; then, without seeking the cause, she clasped her bible and ran.

The cause was Sir Rohan; he had unconsciously drawn near the conservatory, had beheld Miriam as the vision took shape, had watched her through it, had withdrawn the sashes to relieve her, and now himself stood pale, cold, and cursing fate. For no magnetism was delicate enough to impress upon her sight this burden of his thoughts, and Miriam for the first and last time had seen the Ghost.

In an hour or two Miriam re-entered the dining-room, and finding no one, stepped into the garden, where the two gentlemen were walking and leaving fragrant wreaths of blue smoke behind them as they walked.

"I wonder why people will make perambulating chimneys of themselves," she exclaimed, as they abandoned that occupation. "You, for one, sir, promised to show me those south rooms at the top of the house, where the sea is so plainly to be seen. Come now!"

"With pleasure. St. Denys, will you join us? I fear you disappoint yourself, Miss Miriam."

"O no, that is not possible," she cried. "I never have passed any time before under the same roof that sheltered crumbling walls, forsaken rooms, and deserts of dust. There will be unexplored closets, and old escritoires bursting with lost records, and when we have broken out the blackened panes,—the prospect."

"Probably the storms have saved us that trouble. We may capture a swallow skimming round there, or waylay a little owl."

"Then we will believe some damsel of the Ladies Belvidere has been cruelly enchanted into that form, and we are the powers come to loosen the spell. Upon which the lady will leave the owl, and live happily all her days, as the story-books used to say."

"God forbid!" said Sir Rohan, more heartily than appeared reason, before she concluded. But Miriam only laughed, and tripped on before them up the stairway with the keys, which Mrs. Redruth had given her, in her hand. At last, however, she resigned them to their owner, who threw open door after door into rooms destitute of furniture, where the paper hung peeling from the wall; but Miriam found them all too small, and flitted restlessly forward.

"Here is one," she said, as Sir Rohan would have passed a door; and so pertinaciously and like a spoiled child did she return to the attack, that, after hesitating till he was embarrassed, he turned the key, and they entered one in full as ruinous a condition as the others. The curiously netted rafters overhead had been eaten by worms into the similitude of quaint and delicate carving. The floor was warped and depressed at the sides, and heavy articles slanted against the wainscot or had pitched forward and fallen into fragments. One large window lighted it, glass and sash quite gone, and moss bedded upon the stone lintel within. Adjoining this window was a diagonal closet built in one of the octagons of the wall, with two oaken doors, looking through the collected deposits and rusty hinges as if unopened since the erection of the house.

"This promises more than any other," said Miriam; "were you ever in it before, Sir Rohan?"

"Once or twice I may have been," he answered, involuntarily glancing at one of the closet doors.

"I should think it was a place of pharmacy," she added. "See that furnace and its little stone crucible, and those phials and retorts upon the table."

"Doubtless it was."

"Ah!" said she, pulling a ribbon that lay on the floor at the foot of the closet door, half escaped therefrom. "And was any woman the victim of their cabalistic arts? We are approaching the mystery, Sir Rohan." And she examined the ribbon, once some bright-colored thing, that yielded to her grasp and hung in threads across her fingers. "What did it belong to?" she asked. "I wonder who wore it."

There is always something touching in decay, and this little faded ribbon seemed to impart to Miriam, for a moment, an air of sad sobriety. But with his first glance Sir Rohan had endeavored to withdraw her attention, and approaching the window, said: "But the prospect! In your sentimental lute-string you will lose it," and he tore aside the sheltering ivy. Miriam bent forward, rapt an instant in the glory of the great unrest before her.

"Come, papa. See it!" she exclaimed, drawing St. Denys toward her. "It is scarcely better than when out of sight of land one feels in dark nights a world of water slipping under the keel; but what else equals it? What color! What expanse! What light!"

Indeed there were few scenes to compare with this; for isolated from all surrounding scenery, the bowery tree-tops of Sir Rohan's grounds tossing below, and the whole set in the ivied framework of the great window, you saw only the vast loneliness, and heard only the tireless song of illimitable sea. A narrow strip of yellow sand bound the shore, washed by broad creamy waves, breaking, without sparkles, in low humming tones, and sobbing back into the gulfs again with a stifled sough. Long blue lines of depth and richness, as one sees the channels of rivers, trailed across the ever shoreward advance; and beyond these, purple fields of stillness inflected its surface, and further yet, where some island cliff towered to the winds and turbulence of weather, great sheets of foam aslant took the stray sunbeams into their bosom and produced a miracle of radiance. Overhead the sky soared faint yet clear, with the dim haze upon its skirt that ever haunts a sea-horizon.

"And it is always so, Sir Rohan," said Miriam, glancing at him a moment; "all summer long, all day, till the moon comes with her white sereneness, and swings it to and fro upon her queenly will. And in clear nights of sweet darkness how it must brood to itself, and what calm and hush come instead, and overshadow it with unwavering wings!"

Now and then a little shallop furrowed some cove, and again, from a misty distance a broad white sail broke into life, and tacking through the sunshine, buried itself from view in other firmaments.

"The sky is as worthy of study," said Sir Rohan. "Observe how the sea near the shore borrows its hues and changes, but further out and near the horizon, the sky borrows those of the sea. The beauty here, one could swear, is eternal. It is because we see it in the vast, the mass; the details are not so pleasant."

"O, do you think so? Don't you find any beauty in those sea-anemones, and madrepores, and nettles with their fine scarlet and cool purple? I believe there are no such shades on your easel. Surely you 've seen the sun-fish shining white and lucid, like a ghost under water, and the dying colors of the mackerel along these shores."

"I did not think of those in speaking, and they are hardly what I mean. Perhaps it is a peculiar prejudice. In the midst of a thing, one can hardly form a correct idea of it. One needs almost the supremacy where may be seen the earth rocking her great tides now on the long coast-line of the Americas, now on all the broken gulfs and reaches from Africa to Thule. We must come up here some dark night, Miss Miriam, and see the briony," he added. "Redruth and his boys shall go out in their skiffs and whip the water till it is all aflame, and over the sea of fire you will look to have the heavens roll together like a scroll, and the last day dawn upon us."

"Don't send them, then. I will enjoy here a little longer. I don't care, yet, for that Last Day."

"Miriam," said St. Denys, "why do you persist in speaking so lightly?"

"I never thought, papa, — please forgive me," she answered, turning quickly toward him. "You won't be angry with me, frowning Puritan?"

But the indulgent smile was reply enough, and

her sole care dismissed, she returned to the enjoyment of her view, while St. Denys moved away to
examine the garniture of the room.

"There was always a charm to me," said Sir
Rohan, "in the myths of those old existences of
ocean.   Not Neptune, nor yet Nereids, and hardly
Mermen, but Spirits of the Sea."

"Yes," answered Miriam, "and I have frequently thought, if I were not a woman,—which
is a state so much sweeter, you know,—that I
would choose my metempsychosis to be into a
water-mist, or any part of its great source."

"The sea is, nevertheless, foreign to me.   It
seems when sparkling, too much like a living
thing rejoicing in the hurry and bustle of the
great world."

"To me it is a Beneficence."

"What! with its caprice and treachery, its hol-
lows of green darkness beneath the shining shield
that sleeps in the sun, its rage and its laughter; —
remorseless, and yet, I can fancy, kind."

"All that is because you must float on it some
calm noon, in the shallows, where the sunbeams
bend into it and stain it a *mort d'ore,* as if yellow
waves were rising and falling below the skin of

brown ripples, and every instant you might see some glorious creature come sliding up their under swell, all radiant with these Murillo tints, these browns and gold."

"Like yourself, Miss Miriam."

Thus speaking, the dialogue paused, and they continued for a time silent, together watching dim purple vapors that rose as Thetis rose to Achilles, — yet uncertainly, like smoke, — and then crept in silently over the land. For Miriam it was the incense of the ocean, but for Sir Rohan the palest and mournfulest of shadows fashioned herself from the ascending cloud to gaze at him, vanishing as it spread, and gathering form again in each succeeding one.

"We must wait till sunset," said Miriam; "how kind to bring me here!"

"You have an artist's eye," he rejoined; but looking at her to avoid the phantom, the relics of the old ribbon caught his own again. Miriam observed the glance, and immediately returned to the topic from which he had so successfully diverted her. "I wonder who wore it," she repeated. "May I open this closet, Sir Rohan?"

Without waiting for his response, she turned

the rusty key quickly, and looked within. A gray cloak lay on the floor, and a cap, linen and once white, of some rustic pattern. Sir Rohan could neither move nor speak; too well he remembered the day in which he had thrown those garments here, too homely grown for their wearer's use; and now was this strange girl, — inquisitively raising them, throwing the cloak round her, setting the tattered cap gravely on her hair and holding it by its single string, — was she their angel of resurrection? — to drag them into what judgment! What right had she to come and search his wounds with her curious fingers? — perhaps, he thought on the moment, to heal them with " sweet inspersion of fit balms."

Miriam had laughingly displayed herself to St. Denys, while Sir Rohan repeated another question which again and again had recurred; but quickly dropping them off, she exclaimed:

" And now I wonder what is in the other closet. There is no key to it; was it never opened? "

" Never, to my knowledge."

" But can't you open it, Sir Rohan? "

There was nothing more which he dreaded to have her see; indeed, he did not suppose there was anything else to be found there, and with his knee against the panel, he shook it lightly and brought away, as it unclosed, the lock and a part of the rotten case. Immediately a great cloud of offensive dust blew wildly out, seeking freedom in the room; flew into his eyes and nostrils, suffocating and blinding him. He half turned for breath, and at the motion some shelf gave way with a little crash, and countless yellow bones tumbled rattling upon the floor, into his bosom, striking his face and his extended arm; and a human skull rolled away, splintering to fragments at Miriam's feet.

"Fanchon! Fanchon!" he exclaimed, shaking them off with a fierce gesture.

"What does it mean, Sir Rohan? What does it mean?" cried Miriam, springing back.

"You must ask Redruth!" he retorted, scarcely knowing what he said, and striding from the room. "Let him look to it!"

They followed noiselessly, St. Denys first pausing to lock the door; but Sir Rohan had preceded them with such rapidity that he was out of sight when they resumed, and at the grand staircase they met Redruth ascending with a box, and a

pale, shivering housemaid with dust-pan and brush,
the teeth of the girl chattering in her head.

At dinner Miriam was surprised to see their host
cool as usual, and hurried that she might ask
Redruth to explain it; moreover, the silence she
kept concerning the hour in the conservatory
excited her.

"I am afraid Miss Miriam is frightened," said
Sir Rohan, when she had gone. "She was so different, so still."

"She may be a little curious," replied the
other, cracking his nuts, — "not much more."

"It was very singular. You remember I once
told you the little legend, — but never put faith
in it."

"This confirms it, then?"

"Yes. See that; the maid found it among
those bones;" and he put into St. Denys's hand a
gold girdle-clasp once set with jewels, and wearing in old English text the word **Fanchon.**

Miriam found Redruth in the housekeeper's
room, looking over an old gazette that St. Denys
had brought with him.

"You are pale, Miss Miriam, — paler than
usual," he said, putting it aside.

"Truly I may be," she replied. "I think the whole house is paler; I can't stay in it,—I shall have to run away."

She sat down on a stool near him, and resting her head in her hands, said:—

"When I asked Sir Rohan what it meant, he said, ' You must ask Redruth! let him look to it!' So you may tell me why he cried, ' Fanchon! Fanchon!'—Pah!" she declared, shaking her head and making a wry face, "I can smell it now,—that dust!"

"You might ask me? Sir Rohan said you might ask me?" he replied. "Why, Miss, it's not much to tell. You must know, in the first place, that Sir Rohan and I, though I am far the elder, are a sort of foster-brothers; for his mother died before he was a weanling, and mine had just lost her own child. Well do I remember this little dark baby crying pitifully in so strange a world, as my mother held it. I was a tall younker then, and something taller when his father sent him away to school, and me with him; and there I picked up a little learning myself, as you may guess. And when Sir Rohan went to the university, another servant was sent him, and I returned to manage the lands. And his own father, in dying then, bade me never forget we were foster-brothers, and serve him with the love which one blood begets. Well — I believe I have obeyed; and who could help it, — could help loving my master, Miss Miriam! He went, when he finished his studies, to a place in the North that his mother's brother left him, for his father had been a strange old man, and lived much as Sir Rohan lives now; and the place was damp and full of underbrush and mould, and when he came here, that time I told you of, he did n't like it. But by and by he fitted it up fine enough for a bride, then returned and lived alone and let everything run to seed. My dear young master!" continued Redruth, in an altered tone, "you see him now so sad and worn, Miss, and admire him of course. I wonder what you 'd have thought when, so tall and dark and slender as he is, he had a color in his cheek and light in his eye, and though never, may be, a handsome man, yet with a power about him, a stern singular way of constraining you, so that I fancy he might have won any woman's love —— "

"But what has all this to do with the bones?"

"True enough. I ramble, don't I? Only that I am his foster-brother, and long ago, a great many generations ago, there was another foster-brother. But the heir then was a maiden,—Dame Fanchon. My master is not in the direct descent with her, for she was the last of her line, and the title went to cousins,—the second house, I think. But as I began to say, Dame Fanchon was accounted beautiful, and there were many who asked her in marriage, and her father greatly desired to see her choose a husband. Yet she seemed in no hurry, and time passing on, the foster-brother got the old man somehow in his power, and demanded Fanchon for his wife. She refused disdainfully, to be sure, but her father implored her, and then undertook compulsion. She was a proud lass, but they bowed even her spirit, and at last she yielded. So, on a time, her women dressed her for a bride, and pinned in her hair the wreaths and veils and gauds, and led her down to her father and the bridegroom. And as near as I can recollect, she said to him in French, 'My father, one foster-brother has ruined your line, and another will bring it to dust.'

"Then she said she would yet go up to her

room and pray, before starting for the church; and she never came down again. When they went to seek her, my lady, she was not to be found, and never has been found till this day.

"They searched the country through, away beyond the Dart, and looked somewhat in the house; but who dreamed of her hiding herself there? Perhaps she meant to come out o' nights for food, knowing her white raiment would startle whoso saw her; though I can't think what she meant to do with herself. They did n't do their work thoroughly, Miss Miriam; one should not half break a spirit, — it 's labor lost.

"But young Dame Fanchon never came out again, for up there just now I found, slipped down the crack of the closet threshold, beyond reach of her little fingers, this key. She had locked herself in at the sudden freak, and dropping the key, it must have fallen there, leaving her with nothing but despair; since, if she made any efforts, the door resisted them, and there was no one to hear her cries in that far corner, had she raised her voice, — if, after all, she did not choose that starvation to the other fate, and by losing the key put succor beyond her reach.

"I remember now hearing that servants, sleeping in that room, died of strange fevers or wasted away; but how it came to be guessed where she was, I never knew, though no one could tell exactly in which room she had secreted herself. But you know, Miss Miriam, murder will out. That is why Sir Rohan called Fanchon!"

"And why must you look to it?"

"Why! O, I suppose because I am a foster-brother,— though God knows there is no service too great for me to render him! Bring his house to dust? I would die before I would do him an injury, — before I would let a sorrow reach him!"

"You are a very good man, Mr. Redruth," she said. "I don't believe you ever would harm Sir Rohan. I don't know how you can. Poor Fanchon! Do you suppose it was her ghost I saw in the greenhouse to-day?"

"A ghost in the daytime! Come, Miss Miriam, that's silly."

"Then sunshine and blue sky are silly. I don't believe, now, that they ever come in the night."

"You saw a ghost?" he asked, with a singularly perturbed air.

" Why, Mr. Redruth, you must n't laugh at me.
I don't know, — yes.   Was it hers ? "

" Hers ? — No, not her ghost, — not hers."

" Whose was it, then ? " she said, rising.   " How
absurd I am !   What would papa say ?   Well, I
can't help it.   Poor Fanchon ! "

VII.

TESTIMONY.

A FEW more days vanished like the others, when one morning Miriam said,

"Do you know, Sir Rohan, this is our anniversary? We have been here just a week, we have known each other just a week. At least it would be, if seven days made a year."

"I presume you would think me very uncourteous to say that it seems to me a year."

"Indeed I should."

"I have just begun to live; and to the little child days, you remember, are ages. I am perplexed to know why it should seem so long a time," he returned. "Possibly, because so full of happiness that it will take me a year to recall it."

"I don't know, sir. I should think you might always have your life as pleasant."

"You have found this time pleasant, then?"

"O yes indeed. All-time is, to me. No one could help being happy where papa is."

"Do you suppose happiness independent of him would be possible?"

"O, I hope not. I wonder, almost, how you lived before he came."

"It is not all papa, Miss Miriam," he said, quickly; but a glance at those innocent brown eyes silenced anything like compliment, and presently St. Denys entered.

"It is odd that we see nothing of Arundel," said he, after the morning salutations.

"I should n't be surprised," Miriam answered, "if he came to-day, it is so fine. We were talking yesterday of visiting one more celebrity, while here, Sir Rohan. Can't we go at once? Which shall it be, — Trevethy stone or Tyntagel?"

"You can have both, Miss Miriam. Why not?"

"It will take so long —"

"And when I go to Kent you shall show me every hop-field in the county. I shall be in no hurry."

"But when we are there, will you ever come to Kent?"

"It is my turn to ask now, — 'Do you really want me?'"

"And mine to put on the air of a Monseigneur, and answer, 'Most assuredly.'"

"Then it will depend upon whether you stay here a suitable period without grumbling."

"O Mr. Fox! nobody knows better how to ask a crow for a song! But we can't go to both in one day. I'll toss up and see," she exclaimed, laughing. "But I've no pennies!"

"Never mind," said St. Denys; "two roses will do as well."

Miriam seized one, and a broad grape-leaf. "If the rose fall first, it shall be Tyntagel," said she, "and if the leaf, — why, Trevethy!" And throwing them into the air, the rose dropped instantly, and the leaf fluttered downward in doubt to fall or not. "Tyntagel it is!" she cried.

"Scarcely so fair as the flinger, though," said Sir Rohan.

"Now, now! The rose is a little the heaviest, and I had a little rather go to Tyntagel," she returned, pushing back the drooping hair. "Besides, Trevethy means a place of the dead, — old British dead too, you said. But one can see a grave everywhere, and it is doing the business too cheaply to have one stone for a whole congregation."

" But what present congregation, at the end of a thousand years, will be known by so much as the fragment of a stone ? " asked St. Denys.

" And what is Tyntagel," pursued Sir Rohan, " but the monument of a whole race ? "

" Well, gentlemen, I am going to Tyntagel, and therefore to breakfast. If you prefer stones to bread, you can stay and discuss the question," she merrily concluded.

Thus it came to pass that the afternoon found them at the inner base of the great cliffs of Tyntagel, and singly winding up the narrow footpath. As Sir Rohan followed the others, and the peril of the precipitous way became more obvious to him, his heart beat with a loud fear lest some false step of the adventurous girl's might hurl her down the dizzy height ; and he could have found such a wish, that his strong hand might save her. But nothing of the kind occurred, and they stepped safely across the breach of the old fortress, into the open area of the outer portion.

Behind them now lay the great gap in which some earthquake had rent the rock, and far down whose griesly chasm sea-birds built their nests and black tides washed in and out, once spanned by a drawbridge connecting the twin cliffs and forming a part of the most impregnable strong-hold Britain boasted. The low ruins of the walls reared a parapet around the edge, and leaning on this lightly, at first, that it should not crumble at their weight, they looked down and out upon the Atlantic which dashed at a vast and perpendicular depth of hundreds of feet. Above them, the heaven hung burning with yellow light and clearness, like a giant chrysolite; and the sea below, full of stormy vigor and tumultous activity, leaped joyously to catch the breath of the soft cool wind that came singing in from western continents, and tossed a thousand white caps in air with sonorous glee. Under them, hidden caves rumbled to the pent up element and the sucking flow of water; and now and then a mightier wave showered its powdery foam half up the unyielding barrier, and thrilled it to its centre.

It was too grand a thing to behold and speak,— this broad and boundless phase of the whole ocean's immensity; these warm swells rolling in from reefs of the Corrientes and Florida, from Africa and the Western Islands; this wind that, it was pleasant to believe, had touched no land since

it bent the unexplored forests on the mountains of
the Americas; and they received it in silence.
At last, as if the white gulls had thrown the melody of their motions into a sound, Miriam's voice
rose on the monotone of the symphony, in the
words of the song.

Thy giant rocks, O Tyntagel!
    Toss back the javelins of the sprays,
Nor ever can their shouldering swell
    Remove thee from thy flinty base.

Idly the winds blow o'er thee now
    That once have swept a continent; —
Who putting ashes on thy brow
    Long since to ancient ruin went.

The spell that Merlin's magic keeps,
    Though not omnipotent to save,
Still hovers round thee, while he sleeps,
    Sleeps bound and sealed within his cave.

What perfect forms of old romance
    Crown thee in visions soft or stern !
How fair across the bright expanse
    Still looks and sighs the sweet Yguerne !

Still waits his shield upon the wall,
    His knights in chivalrous content; —
Still from his airy palace hall
    Great Arthur climbs thy battlement.

Thy foes their laurels pluck from thee,
  Saxon forgets that he is such,
And Time's resistless enmity
  Turns to a lingering, loving touch.

Dance yet the Fays within thy ring,
  The Fays who knew and served him well,
Whose royal gifts hung on the King, —
  Thy valiant King, O Tyntagel?

O listen with them, when the dawn
  Stirs in the night, to that wild bell,
Whose selfsame peals rung in the morn
  When Arthur fell, O Tyntagel!

As the last word died from her lips, Miriam turned, with a broad smile, and flinging off all sentiment, said,

"That's what the song says, Sir Rohan, and what do you say? Do you believe in the Round Table, in Galahad, and Lancelot, and Guinever?"

"Devoutly."

"Let us shake hands upon it! So do I. Papa laughs at me; but why not believe in them? They were much better people than ordinary then, and surely it's refreshing."

"My dear, I deny your major."

"Then, papa, you'll have nothing at all to say

to the kernels of truth dropped in debate, and we had best carry the argument to more general grounds."

"There used to be another song about your hero," said St. Denys, " though not in so grandiose a style, concerning some foray or marauding affair, —it would be called petty theft now, if there were any law for these epic monsters. It related his address in stealing three pecks of barley-meal, and the Queen's skill in putting into it lumps of suet as big as my two thumbs."

" Fie, papa ! "

" Those were the fabulous exploits," responded Sir Rohan. " Miss Miriam and I believe only the canon, and reject the apocrypha."

" Chronicle or Romance, Sir Rohan ? "

" Chronicle, Romance, and Tradition ; a pretty braid enough,—let the Romance be the golden strand, though," he replied.

" We must discard you for an infidel, papa, while we settle the points for ourselves. Here, Sir Rohan ! Look at your feet. Who drew that old circle in the stones ? "

" Merlin, undoubtedly," he said.

" A part of some horoscope. Very well, let us

stand in it, and summon the shadows of our antiquity. They are very far off; imagine that we have burned incense and these shapes grow from the curling smoke. How dim they come! You begin to see them? Stately Sir Caradoc and his faithful Dame, the bold butler, Gawain, Tristram; now a throng glides up, now separate and singly. Who is this, King of men, this mightier one, his brow lofty in the shadow of a plume waving from his starlike helm, clad in the shine of armor, and bearing a spear of light? And who this bright, willowy shape, all wrapped in gleaming lawns, an April face of smiles and tears, glancing askance at Lancelot already here?"

"Or perhaps Guinever is in a sadder mood,—chilled in the atmosphere of the King,—pale, white, sorrowful," interposed Sir Rohan.

"Hush! It wouldn't be Guinever. Don't you see her personality? Tristram's lady may know sorrow; Marc's, repentance; but Lancelot's, only love. The others might question of right or wrong; but it was a part of Guinever's self to love Lancelot and not the King, and conscience never stings her. Very wicked, indeed, Sir Rohan! But then what a pretty picture Guinever always is! A lawless, soulless, wanton, witching, lovely thing, without a moral perception, changing and beautiful as a shower with broken bits of rainbow in the clouds. And her queendom and all its gorgeous accessories shrine her fitly, and heighten her charms. Who blames Lancelot? She must be queen, not because Arthur is king and mates among his peers, but because she is Guinever. Everything she touches gains in splendor. Lancelot might be a clown — who knows? — if Guinever did not love him. Does not a fresher green burgeon on the forest shawes as they ride beneath? Are n't her falcons, snarling at their bells and jesses, transformed Genii? Does she toss a flower to her knight in tourney, — it is a rain of unknown petals. I wonder how he conquered, for the sun must always have been in his face! And it is the same Guinever who tries on the magic belt. See, it was a narrow golden band when one by one the faithless ladies tried to clasp it. Guinever takes it; the King is angry-eyed, perhaps, — there is a flush on Lancelot's cheek, — none on hers. Laughing, bright-eyed, dimpled, she reaches it, brings it round the slender waist, essays with taper fingers to shut the buckle. Of course, it is in vain; of course the gap yawns finger-wide; but where is the narrow golden band? Beneath her touch what miracles of chasing, wrought-work, fluting, have blossomed! It hangs unclasped and heavy with jewelry, dripping with chain, filigrane, and aiglet. What loops and fringes of sparkling costliness, strings threaded with precious ransom-holding beads, festoons and tassels of gems, brilliant with every tint, a sun inside them all, and defying the wondrous work of the King's hilt! Nine years it took for that,— for this, an instant. And when she looks up with that radiant laugh, I suspect the King had rather see it than the shut buckle. As a piece of art, she is faultless; her beauty is her virtue,—a perfect, splendid creature, in her way. Let her go."

"Ah, before they pass, ask her of these intervening centuries,— in what region they dwell; these immortal lovers,—what life they lead. Will they speak?"

"I wonder, Sir Rohan," replied Miriam, abruptly, "if people who never used or cultured their souls did n't lose them, like beasts of the field, as we assume;—living in a world of sense, if, sense dying, they died too. If they dwell at all, these immortal lovers, it is in some happy region, they are so blithe and fair to-day. No, Guinever will not speak. She does not know our language, and is of a different race; and Làncelot does not see us. They are shadows of dreams, I think."

"What then keeps them? Whose power holds them now at your call?"

"Did n't you ever notice how the old masters claim property in their pictures, sir? Down in the hem of some garment, on the under side of a spire of grass, just half beneath a stone, a tiny scrawl, the 'Ghirlandaio,' or 'Beatus hoc fecit'? So invoke what scene you may, whose background is the stones of Tyntagel or Carlisle, there is always the signature of that son of the royal nun and the Genius; Merlin, Sir Rohan, hoc tenet."

"You are learned in the lore. Tell me, Enchantress, will Arthur come again?"

"A many times," Miriam answered lightly.

"And his Queen?"

"No. He comes because he went. Guinever and Lancelot, it may be, never died."

"What said they, meeting at the tomb, that autumn day?" Sir Rohan asked again.

"Peccavimus. O bah! it must have lost all

piquancy when the great hero was gone. I don't like the book after Guinever grows good ; I don't believe it. It 's getting tiresome now. There they go! Passing on and up in what a glorious cloud, with flashing faces breaking from it in radiant smiles. Let them pass!"

Sir Rohan smiled, and St. Denys said : "What new freak now, little one?"

"Freak? — Why, papa, such a wind fans one's life into notice."

"And how much youth goes to the fuel of this precious flame?"

"He throws my years in my teeth!" she returned, pouting and laughing. "But I 'm not a sexagenarian yet."

"Don't exhaust your spirits before you are, nor forget the true San Graal in your admiration of the Emerald," he said, strolling away.

"He would n't scold if he enjoyed La Morte d'Arthur."

"You enjoy it, Miss Miriam?"

"Certainly. It 's a toysome book, — better than playing at dolls always."

"But your lore is far more Rabbinical than orthodox. La Morte d'Arthur is not responsible for it all, I hope. And you don't like books, you say; what attracted you there?"

"Who knows? Papa says I live in feeling, not thought; in the sensational, emotional, nothing of the intellectual. But what odds, so one is happy?"

For a little while Miriam, leaning over the parapet, crumbled the bits of stone and moss into the sea, and Sir Rohan still remained within the circle, looking inland.

"Do you see Sir Kaye come riding up the path, that you are so earnest?" she asked, glancing back at him. "Or is the nation marching to Camelford by moonlight, and Mordred looming beyond the town? Remember, sir, that the Queen beseeches Arthur not to risk the kingdom, but wait till Lancelot and the flower of the chivalry return from France."

Sir Rohan felt as if he were possessed, her words and tone carried such a life with them.

"Is n't it grand to think, Sir Rohan," she continued, walking to and fro with very long steps, her arms folded, and her eyes on the ground, "that Arthur walked here, as I am walking now, his spurs clanging on the pavement, and Excalibur rattling in his sheath for longing of the strife?" And she looked up, her eyes sparkling, and cheeks burning. "Or here, long before," she resumed, approaching and standing beside him, with her hand upon the stone, her eyes dewy, her smile vanishing, "was the bower of his mother, that sad Ygnerne of the song, who sat waiting in vain for her lord when the banners of Uther Pendragon were spread. There, perhaps," she added, changing her expression to one of exultant sagacity, "the old magician learned his incantations of the stars, when all the castle but sentinel and watch-dog slept; or rose and passed them unseen to meet Fay Vivien in the woods, or bury himself in the Welsh hills. To think that actually here, in this very spot, they lived, loved, moved!"

"You are intensely dramatic, Miss Miriam! Such talent of fusing your individuality is not to be wasted," Sir Rohan exclaimed, as he watched the vivacious changes of her countenance.

"I am brought from my world with your gallantry!" she replied, shrugging her shoulders. "I should think the ghosts of these heroes would come and haunt you, since you believe in them, for such levity. Do you remember the sword the

Lady of the Wood gave the infant St. George, teaching him to fight with shadows? One I cannot give, but for the other,—you too may fight such shadows."

With the words, his old chains fell back on Sir Rohan; he recalled what nothing but her presence had made him forget, and the angry gleam shot again from his eyes, but unnoticed by Miriam, for St. Denys was drawing near with a flat piece of stone in his hand.

"Is it not singular, Rohan?" said he, displaying its surface, where lay the impression of a small and delicate hand with a ring on the third finger. .The inside of the left hand, but not a wedding-ring, if one might judge from the fact that being twisted round it had stamped its jewelled sigil there. A hot color suffused Sir Rohan's face; he struck one hand into the other with a vehemence that caused his companions to start, and see his eager glance fixedly bent upon the stone.

"It is a piece of steatite, such as is abundant in the vicinity, and forms a large portion of the Lizard," said another voice, proceeding from none of them. They all looked up, and Sir

Rohan surveyed a gentleman, not short, but rather stout, florid, and with a most singular cast of features, the prominence of nose and chin sinking the mouth into an abyss where it was obliged to have recourse to an unvarying smile to avoid total collapse, while the eyes, large and light, shone shrewdly beneath shaggy brows. This person was not well dressed, since somewhat too showily, but had a pleasing, persuasive voice, and a graceful manner.

"The steatite, you are aware," he continued, "when first broken into is soft, and will receive any impression; and this being probably done at such a time, brought here and forgotten by other sight-seers, is after all not so curious. How do you do, St. Denys? A handsome hand, though. Place your own upon it," added this easy personage to Miriam. "It will fit it to a T."

Miriam scornfully turned her back upon him, while St. Denys gravely inquired concerning his health, and half hesitatingly touched his proffered hand. "You need n't be afraid, St. Denys," muttered he. "I won't eat her."

But almost immediately Miriam returned, and presented him to Sir Rohan as Marc Arundel.

"Happy to make your acquaintance, sir," said the latter. "A little odd, though, that one must come from Kent to introduce neighbors."

"This stone is like the ring the miner gave me," said Miriam.

"What! you were those down there, then?"

"Yes. The earth opened and swallowed us up, the other day, Mr. Arundel," she replied.

"I was passing the shaft, to-day, when I saw a maniac-looking fellow lying on the grass in the midst of a group. He had ascended from the mine, they said, not long before; but the world spun the other way for him; he was dying, — raving feebly. about a ring, and people, who, I see now, must have been you. You remember him, Sir Rohan, — Dick Roy?"

Sir Rohan replied with such graciousness as he could command, and as St. Denys relinquished the curiosity, took it for closer examination, and then dashed it into the sea where it was swallowed by a hungry wave. It seemed to burn his hand. He found himself more miserable than when alone; for then he had often been strung to the required tension of stoical endurance; but here, every hour gave him desire and hope of freedom, only to be blasted in the next by encounters with the Ghost of his youth.

"I never learned till now," said Arundel, bluntly, as he watched him, "that you and my cousin were friends."

"We have been friends a long while," replied the other, absently.

"They can hardly show you a kickshaw like this, at home. Were you ever in Kent, Sir Rohan?"

"Some years ago. A short time."

"Good soil that. Healthy farmers, worth a lease; but they put all their liveliness into their hops. Do you think they could dance a reel, now, St. Denys?"

"A reel or a saraband, if they chose," was the curt reply. Sir Rohan's frigidity was contagious, and Arundel crossed to Miriam.

"You have not wished me good evening," said he.

"Good evening," she returned, abruptly.

"It sounds much more like good by."

"You can take it as you please."

"You are cruel," he said in a lower tone.

"From your kindness in the church, I was led to expect a different demeanor."

"Dear me, Mr. Arundel! One must have a little meter to mark the finer grades of feeling, and accommodate one's manners to your moods!"

"Rem acu tetigisti. Precisely, Miriam. And that meter, you cannot fail to know, is —"

Miriam yawned with her hand at her lips.

"Is n't it time to go, papa?" she said to St. Denys. "It will be dark before we reach home."

"Home." Sir Rohan liked the word from her mouth; he smiled unconsciously while his glance met Arundel's. On the instant, they comprehended each other.

"See Redruth sitting down there," she added, bending over the path, "as still as —"

"Is he asleep beside those remains of lunch?" asked Arundel.

"The cliff. One might drop a tortoise on his head and crack it," she continued.

"Crack which?" Arundel interpolated.

"But where would Redruth be then, I wonder?"

"Still squeezing his wine-bottle!" said the

quick-eyed interrupter. "He takes less scruples to a dram than an apothecary does." But having finished her sentence regardless of the rejoinders, Miriam seized her bonnet and almost bounded along the path, followed by Sir Rohan who, together with the others, expected momently to see her dashed down the declivity.

They descended more leisurely, and as his unwelcome company was not to be avoided, Arundel soon seated himself beside them in the coach. Sir Rohan, however, was now alive, and quietly ordering Redruth to take a different route from that by which they came, had the satisfaction of dropping Mr. Arundel at his own residence, and rolling homeward at liberty once more.

"Well done, Sir Rohan!" cried Miriam. "Now you 've seen the man, tell me, do you affect him?"

"We are not likely to be friends," said he, dryly.

"And need not therefore be enemies," said St. Denys. "The sight of him warns me, Rohan. I must hasten."

VIII.

THE FOREHEAD OF THE STORM.

TIME passed now more swiftly by them all: by St. Denys, examining the great estate with Redruth, offering suggestions, and relating incredible feats of some machinery he had used on summer fallows; by Miriam and Sir Rohan in rides through the bridle-paths of the forest, where tangled vines impeded progress and occasioned sweet delays, and in rambles over the long swelling moors seemingly grand and boundless as the sea, purple with crackling knee-deep heath in whose fragrance the winds were smothered, and broken only by some white thorn-bush bearing here and there a cluster of last year's scarlet haws, and with eagles screaming far above them. Nor is it to be doubted by whom he passed most pleasantly.

In Miriam's thoughts Sir Rohan had become associated with all the beautiful scenes in whose enjoyment they had been companions. He had lost, to her view, the air which at first character ized him, or familiarity had made it more agree able. There were a thousand points, with which St. Denys did not sympathize, that united them; and there was moreover a kind of magnetic attrac tion about Sir Rohan, that with his courtesy and natural powers effected more for him than any youth or beauty.

And as for him? He found Miriam only more lovely than the loveliest margin with which he could surround her. Delightedly he listened to the bird-like voice; her slightest touch thrilled him; — bitterly his old pain and despair threatened to fall should she ever leave him. Most men, when numbering his years, are best pleased by that which recalls old reminiscences; but he, waving those constantly away, was like one who has just found his youth.

One sunset, as the two gentlemen were stand ing near the shrubbery, Miriam came running up the fields from the shore, a color blown into her cheeks, and her arms full of sea-weed, reeds, and all manner of marine growth.

"Do but look at them, Sir Rohan!" she cried. "These blubbers, nettles, what-nots! They are crimson and purple and dusty with gold. And these corals, fine as fringes, like ragged rainbows. And oh! these bloody sea-docks. But what is this?"

"Why, Miriam, you are loaded with that wet stuff," exclaimed St. Denys.

"A fucus, Miss Miriam," said Sir Rohan, taking it. "The sensitive plant of the sea. It sways to the heat of my hand as if blown across by a breeze."

"See these sponges, papa. They are the very royalest purple, and fern-shaped," and she plunged among her booty to bring one up. To her chagrin, it had forsaken its rich hues with its element, and was only a yellowish brown. "O my heart!" she ejaculated, "when I almost drowned myself to get them! And what's the matter with my hands? They are covered with white blisters!"

"It is the vengeance of the nettles."

"Where they stung me? The ungrateful things! I'll carry them back directly. Into the water you go, every one," and she sped down again to fulfil her menace.

"How oddly the sea looks, Sir Rohan!" she said, as he accompanied her. "It is so covered with a kind of mist. And far out, do you see, a great white line shining like a low cloud, only it keeps changing,—now high, now broken, gone, collected again."

"It is the white forehead of a storm coming over the horizon," said he. "Or to speak less poetically, you see the blore. It is many miles away; listen, and you will hear the rote. We shall have a Cornish storm soon, and to-night can see the briony without any help from Redruth."

"These little birds, with their wings stretched on the waves, look like its prophets. How I like such a fresh salt wind!"

"It whistles the megrims off one's nerves."

"And I suppose when we looked at the sea that divine day at Tyntagel this storm was ploughing along the distance and hurrying to meet us. I must wade out again, clearly. Don't you think I shall catch my death of cold, get pains for my pains, go to school to the rheumatism and learn to compare ache, acher, achest, with the chance of a lot in God's acre?" she asked, laughing. "All water is damp, you know, but that with a storm in it must be the dampest kind of water!"

"It is too costly an experiment," he returned. "Give your bundle to me, Miss Miriam; here are some stones upon which I can step, and deposit it for you."

"And that will sting two pair of hands."

"Unnecessarily. Let me manage them, and it will soon be done;" and in a minute more the treasures were afloat, and Miriam had challenged Sir Rohan to a race up the slope. Suddenly she stopped, with her gay laugh broken in ringing, and pointed at a horse waiting near the firs.

"Don't you know it?" she asked, with a look of mock dismay. "Who is that with papa? My hands need some liniment, Sir Rohan, and my eyes too, after seeing him. I shall go to Mrs. Redruth for it, and then I shall go to my room and be altogether too ill to come down again. Good night, Sir Rohan!"

He watched her till she disappeared within the casement, and then by another path joined St. Denys and Mr. Arundel.

The latter, who had, of course, seen Miriam, did not inquire for her, and did not regard Sir Rohan with more favorable eyes at her absence. By turns affable and sarcastic, he mingled in the conversation till obtaining its command, when he conducted it to elicit Sir Rohan's peculiarities, causing him to shrink nervously from the scalpel so suddenly busy about him. He remained with them upon the lawn till the great bell of the hall clock tolled ten, when mounting with a parting prophecy of rain, the galloping hoofs of his horse were soon lost in distance. The wind, momently increasing, bent the tall trees heavily when the sound became undistinguishable, — and it already blew a gale as they went in.

IX.

SUNSHINE.

IN the morning, Miriam found Sir Rohan's promise fulfilled. Torrents lashed the panes, the bowing branches swept the lawn, the wind whistled round and through the house, the gray sky seemed to open and close with gluts of rain, and the great roar of the sea filled the diapason of the tempest. But to Miriam there was a world of sunshine within, and when she met Sir Rohan, himself like one fired with purpose and strength that day, and St. Denys with his unvarying equipoise, she could not have been gayer had sunshine reigned without as well. Nevertheless, indoor amusements were not many in that house, and on the third day of the storm Sir Rohan had recourse to a last expedient; and as Miriam rather shyly proposed it, instantly invited them into the room which she dignified by the name of studio.

16

Here, strewn in every position, was a day's delight for her : portfolios of bold drawing ; rustling water-colors, as many and strong, she thought, as the brown leaves of an oak in autumn ; and wonderful things, where the artist in experimenting with his tints could not avoid expressing beautiful conceits. Leaning against the wall, one upon another, were strange, half-finished pictures without frames, pitifully dented by their mutual weight ; and here, scattering them around her, Miriam sat upon the floor for their better enjoyment, while St. Denys betook himself to a black-letter chronicle, and Sir Rohan stretched a canvas.

A few, such as an aspen shaking through a south-wind into the likeness of a silvery ghost ; the centre of a forest rich in every shade of green, gorgeous with every flower and fruit and plumage multiplied in stagnant pools below, but from whose virid mosses noisome vapors rose, and in whose countless reeds the fiends of plague and malaria lurked, — a spot fecund with every venomous reptile and stinging insect, — a spot damned with luxuriance ; or the awful brows of an eclipse brooding over space and stifling the shrinking earth ; or a little chrisom baby stretched stiff and stark on a yew bough, and watched by a school of wizard eyes; or yet again, a dread assemblage of the artist's imaginative terrors, flocculent faces, that had stared in his eye, hissed in his ear, flapped in his path, and from whom he could gain no release except by imprisoning them here; — these and other kindred Miriam flung aside, as she would have flung the study of a foot or anything not promising immediate satisfaction.

Indeed, in every one there was an anomaly, a trait of the artist's individuality, that could only be described by supposing a soul to the picture, expressing, after all, that wherein his pencil failed; and this expression was always the Ghost, as much as if thrown herself in broad dashes of glimmering color upon the canvas. But in the others, where it was less explicit, Miriam soon found sufficient enjoyment.

Here was a pearly, crepusculine sky, through which the spirit of the tenderest young crescent held up her lucid vase to catch the earth's light that foamed high as the rim of the old moon between its golden horns; here a white midnight moon rose behind a line of broken columns surrounded by tideless lagunas and crowned by an albatross taking her glow on the tips of his white drooping wings; and here a long stretch of green waves washed themselves to froth, and clamored for a falling moon that sunk hastily into their bosom.

"She has drunk her pearl, this sea," said Miriam, "and now for the asp, Sir Rohan."

"The darkness will bring that soon enough," he responded, quickly.

"I think you must have experienced a kind of lunacy in painting these three," she said, laughingly.

"Or found," he murmured half inaudibly, "relief from it."

"You are moon-mad!" she exclaimed, taking up another sea-scene, where, in an atmosphere of delicious darkness a yellow waning moon peered half risen over a gloomy tide, and in the light of whose trailing splendor myriad sea-sprites rose in shoals, with twining arms and tossing hair, springing from the spray.

Soon she turned to others. One, where a mountain brook falling from a ledge, half-way down tore itself to diamond dust out of whose depth looked a face like sunlight, below a wind-blown scarf of rainbows; another, a delicate shell, from whose inmost spire protruded a minute and perfect foot lying rosily along the whorl; a third, where stepping from a colossal lotus, clothed in a white shimmer of raiment, her brow rubescent with lambent lanceolate flames, stood the goddess of the Ganges; and one whence casting out rays like a shooting star, a rebellious angel plunged headlong over a black vault, known by his shining wake and the fixedness of sad still stars behind. Again,—one of the immense yellow-haired Cimbri, nude and brawny, slid gleefully on his shield down the icy glare of an Alp, the hollow of a starlit sky above, and around him frozen boulders fulgent and sparkling in prisms, while beyond the horns of some towering crag a fleshless hand rose, like an apparition, and gathered the night down closer over his young savageness. In another, he had caught all the changes of an endless moor, the shadows of sailing clouds, the warm hues of sky and earth; and over the rosy edge of one only heath-flower in the luxuriant growth appeared the face of a tiny curious being, who, full of droll amazement, stared at another sleeping in its heart. But all these Miriam piled together, when catch-

16 *

ing a glimpse of the next, in which were the beginnings of a certain grandeur soon melting into pathos.

"O Sir Rohan," she cried, "what is this? Where did you see it? Is it your genius, your dæmon, — or is it Demogorgon?"

"Your ideas are larger than mine, Miss Miriam," he replied, glancing indifferently towards it. "No. It is Spring, or Autumn, or something of the kind."

"But has n't it any precise title?"

"You can call it the Nemesis of Spring, if you like."

Miriam bent over it spell-bound, all her fancy charmed in the long champaign, the golden-green quivering of a near willow, the dull red hollow, the rich violet haze that bathed the level distance, and far, far away, a titanean head and shoulder heaved to sight, a dim brow receding in the light, slanting showers falling from half-closed eyelids, and a watery smile breaking over the sad, grand mouth.

"Do you like it, Miss Miriam?" he asked, at length.

"O sir, so much!"

"Will you accept it?"

"Sir Rohan! Truly? Will you give this price-less thing to me?" she exclaimed. "Listen papa,—look!" and she sprung to his side to display it.

"Yes, my dear," he said, absently. "But you don't thank Sir Rohan."

"Thank him?" she repeated. "I don't know how. To think I can see this always! Upon my word, I believe I never said 'thank you' in my life,—it is so awkward now! It must be very tedious to have thanks."

"Small fee will answer here," said Sir Rohan. "But now, Miss Miriam, essay the art yourself;" and he placed palette and brushes in her hand, and commenced his instructions which, amidst peals of laughter, she did her best to obey, producing gro-tesque caricatures in design and color, and soon showing him that her customary drawing-lessons had not been wasted, although cultivating no pecu-liar talent.

"The way to catch God's idea in a landscape, or an architect's in a building, I have heard," said she, "is to look at it with inverted eyes. Now it's not so easy to turn the world upside down, but for my picture,—presto! it's done in a minute!"

and she twirled the work round in her fingers till whether it were saint or scaramouch one could not tell.

"What are you two doing?" asked St. Denys, looking up.

"Canvassing matters of art," she answered, gayly.

"I should think you were canvassing votes, by the noise," he rejoined.

"Do you catch any idea?" she asked, inclining her head critically on one side and the other. "I don't. I am afraid I 've left it out."

"How is it, Sir Rohan," she continued, after a pause, "that all your female faces, when you put anything of the weird into their construction, resemble me? — though one could not be more matter-of-fact flesh and blood than I. They were painted, too, before you saw me. It must have been a prescience of my coming."

Sir Rohan started; — did they? But he could not convince himself that such was the case, and guided her pencil along a difficult curve before replying,

"It would n't be singular if when Heaven is to come into my house, I receive some premonition."

Miriam bowed with the *coupée* of a minuet, palette and maulstick waving in either hand, and glancing over her brows at him, with eyes full of merriment.

It was not long, however, before she deserted her new employment, to look at the blossoms snowing the grass; and after lunch some needle-work was found, in which she busied herself, while St. Denys read aloud from his book, with an oral commentary.

Listening as long as she could, she exclaimed at last, "O papa! The man who wrote that chronicle was afflicted with chronical dulness."

"For shame, Miriam!"

"And what a dirty book!" she resumed. "As yellow as a war-whoop, and the great wry letters making eyes at each other! I wonder it don't use its cleansing power inwardly, it's such a soporific. Where's the use now, for a book of old sinners with new names, as full of scandal as a teacup? It must have been written by a *confrère* in wickedness, who scampered through his life while he could, and when he was prevented, made his book racy by imagining all the course he should like to run. See how indifferently he huddled kings and queens and crimes together, like flies in a swarm. If he had any sconce, he might have emblazoned other things than royal peccadillocs and saintly impostures."

"Apollo pastured the flocks of Admetus," said Sir Rohan.

"Long ago. Pasturage past your comprehension. Really, Sir Rohan, do you care a rush for what papa reads? I don't believe a word of it; it is just inef-fable, and not to be re-lied upon; like a bee in a blossom, all a humbug."

"You 'll burn your fingers, you Will with the Wisp! Language and powder are dangerous playthings."

"Both can blow one up? Well, papa, proceed with your augury, though some of us, Sir Rohan and I, may be unwilling to endure such a somnolent procedure. There, don't fear any more interference; that was a cobbler's armorial shield, — my last and my all."

"Miriam, I am ashamed of you."

"Nonsense! As if you would n't have said it yourself, if you had thought!" she retorted.

Indeed, far from interesting to the child who lived in the present was this archæological gossip;

and after the preceding *feu de joie* and one or two vain efforts at wakefulness, the voice lulled her into a dream, nor did she wake till dinner was announced, when Sir Rohan had sketched her sleeping face for that of a Semele.

As the night fell, they all gathered round the fire in the drawing-room, (which was now quite repaired,) and Miriam, sitting on a low cushion between the others, bent forward, her face illuminated by the blaze, and recited the savage tales she had heard from the Pifferari at Rome, till the blood forsook her cheek.

"You have succeeded in thoroughly frightening one, at least, Miriam," said St. Denys.

"And another too, papa, I dare say, only you must be desperate and conceal it. I should n't like to have felt so, the first night we came, though."

"And what makes the difference?"

"Why, I feel almost as much at home here as at the Castle, now."

"That speaks well for your hospitality, Rohan."

"Thank you, Miss Miriam."

"I should be better satisfied if you, sir, looked slightly perturbed or pallid. But I solace myself by thinking no brigand of the Apennines would succeed where I fail, since you are so bold to live here alone. Marc Arundel tells a good story, though; he 'll im-pale you on its point!" and quickly making her adieux, her feet were heard scampering along the hall, as if expecting each flag to sink under them before gaining another.

But Sir Rohan might well afford to laugh at such machinery for terror, when, in the lack of any other excitement, he could always fall back on his Ghost.

X.

MR. ARUNDEL.

THUS the week of storm passed, stranding them again on sunny weather. And with the first clear day came Marc Arundel, a brace of birds, shot on the way, hanging across his saddle-bow.

"You are a summer friend, Mr. Arundel," said Miriam, in greeting. "Rain don't agree with you, — melts you. Are you sugar, or salt?"

"Both, as one bites. To the friend sugar, and you have not yet tasted the salt."

"Vastly polite. Now go and threaten papa with it, and let us begin sparring comfortably all round."

"You began it yourself, Miriam."

"And you follow your flugelman admirably."

"I've heard of thunder's souring cream. Crisp as a curd, this morning. Though how could one keep good-humored in such gloomy quarters, and with a man so possessed as Belvidere?"

"These are not gloomy quarters, and Sir Rohan is not possessed," said Miriam, judicially.

"Ah! Is it so? What a sweet air! You don't inquire for my health, — but I never felt so well as on this fine day. I 've been longing to see a relative, these twenty-four hours, to learn if the pulse of the whole race is as even as mine. Where is my cousin? Speaking of a meter, the other day, this of blood is about the best."

"Your cousin in the third remove is there," replied Miriam, slightly vexed, " coming with our friend."

"My friend in the thirtieth remove, counting each day since I knew him as a further distance," Arundel said, with a sneer.

"Sir Rohan has n't much patience, I suspect; and you had best conduct yourself reasonably," she added.

"Or he 'll pitch me, neck and heels, out doors?"

A look of contempt curled Miriam's lip. "Your phraseology is choice," she said.

" That 's as I please."

" How can you hope even peace should remain between us, when you treat me with such disrespect!"

"I would treat you like a princess, if you allowed. A man should have the patience of Job, to see such a prize carried off under his nose. Let me tell you, my dear—"

"You are too familiar," she interposed, moving off with a flashing eye.

"Fiddle-de-dee! By the sun, moon, and seven stars, Miriam, if he show his airs to me—"

"Don Braggadocio!" she ejaculated over her shoulder.

"But honestly, Miriam—"

"I, certainly, am no relative of yours," she uttered, turning upon him; "and let me say, in language most intelligible to you, Mr. Arundel, that I always use a handle with your name."

"Ten thousand pardons! Miss —— Miss What?" he asked derisively.

Miriam had half the mind to strike him; but she had drawn it upon herself, and walked away without another word.

"Silenced you!" said Arundel, as he gazed after her. "And a woman's easily conciliated. It's your turn and your heyday,—mine will come!" with which he advanced to pay his compliments to St. Denys and his host.

"Now we have you in Cornwall, St. Denys," said he, "hope you'll not leave us till I can take you to our assizes and other lions."

"I thank you, Marc," St. Denys said, "but Sir Rohan and Mr. Redruth have already shown us everything of interest."

"I regret not knowing your arrival sooner. Have n't thought to ask how you came."

"By a packet from Brittany, in at Falmouth."

"Bringing your coach, I suppose."

"Of course."

"Yes, you travel at your ease. I 've not been long in the country myself, though. Positively, I feel hurt that you should have come without advising me."

"We thought you behind us, on the continent."

"And took that opportunity to see Cornwall? Kind of you!"

"No. We designed taking ship for Torquay, but this offered first. We did not come as sightseers. What do you find to amuse you here?"

"O, I don't live on my expectations, St. Denys," he said lightly. "There's my place to be looked after, and being bred to the law, — why, I now and then find a case."

" You like the bar ? " Sir Rohan asked.

" Why, no, not particularly. Though there 's something like a zest to ferreting facts, especially when I have one such as yourself in the witness-box."

Sir Rohan was silent, but St. Denys said, " Ah ? how 's that ? I scarcely understand — "

" I mean a reticent fellow, who has plenty to say, but don't mean to speak, and behind whom there lies a most excellent case."

" And what case has Belvidere ? "

" Sir Rohan ? O, I referred to his reticence, not to anything else, I assure you. There are few of so blameless a past as his, to endure such a test," he replied, bowing to the one of whom he spoke ; and Sir Rohan bowed in return, though well knowing that Marc Arundel never would have said it had he thought it true, — impudent in either event.

" I have heard, through my steward," he answered, " that Mr. Arundel meets with great success."

" Yes," said Marc, tapping his boot with his riding-whip, " I flatter myself there are few men in the circuit with a longer docket. I can refer to the antecedents of every family in the county."

"You are industrious, Mr. Arundel," said Sir Rohan, half scornfully.

"And fortunate. I never met with a failure in my life."

"Never ?"

"Not completely ; none irrecoverable. I fancy a thorough-bred lawyer enjoys himself like a good setter, — once on the scent, and heaven and earth can't stop him. How long do you stay, St. Denys ?"

"We go to-day."

"Then I am in time to see you off. Another good fortune, Sir Rohan. You will find a great vacuum in your house, sir, after the presence of so lively a child as my pretty cousin."

"I expect to," was the brief response.

"But, probably, to a person of your habits, one easily filled," he said, watching him as he spoke.

"Then you would find it so in my place ? "

"How can I tell ?" replied Arundel. "Miss Miriam never conferred so much honor on me !" And with this thrust his manner told the wish to ascertain how much honor she had conferred upon the other ; but he obtained no satisfaction from the face over which Sir Rohan was, for once, master.

In a short time Miriam returned, equipped for her departure, and Sir Rohan left the two for her side.

" You do not ask me to the Castle, St. Denys," said Arundel, as they stood alone.

" No, Marc.   It is plainly impossible."

" Well, well, I 'll overlook it, since I know you 're too fond of me to be so rude intentionally."

" When you cease your persecutions — "

" I could n't go now, indeed, should you press it ; I have some work that must be done before I see Miss Miriam again.   Till then, I do cease these persecutions.   A fine suit, St. Denys, — it might interest you.   A large amount of property may change hands by its means, and I 'm not certain but it promises more."

" I hope you will meet with success, Marc, in all points where success is right."

" That implies a doubt of me," he returned, looking toward Miriam, who stood by Sir Rohan with the painting which he had given her, and which he was now wrapping.

"Is it possible that any year comes to you so sadly as that?" she was asking him. "When you visit Kent we will show you happier seasons."

"All seasons will be prodigal of happiness," he said, in a lower key, "where you are, child!" Yet by a singular self-contradiction, as she met his glance with one so unconsciously pleased and happy, though it gave him a quick joy, he turned away with a sigh.

"The carriage waits, Sir Rohan," said Redruth, at the door.

Sir Rohan did not stir till he had finished wrapping the bundle, when he gave it to Miriam, and gave her also a glance into which he concentrated all that other men could say; then, taking her hand, led her down and placed her in the coach, without trusting himself to speak farewell. The luggage was already on, the servants, who had at first been left at the inn but were subsequently domesticated here, disposed of, and St. Denys only pausing on the step, to repeat urgently his desire of seeing him very soon again; while they both gave Redruth a hearty invitation to visit Kent with his master. Arundel wished him good morning, and mounted. Again the handsome face flashed on him from the chariot, but this time with how sweet a smile, — and they were gone.

He went back into the house alone, and taking a book, attempted to lose himself; the words swam on the page, conveying nothing; he threw it down, and ranged from room to room, seeking what was not to be found. In the heat of advancing day, all household bustle had ceased. Silence reigned throughout. No more light steps, or jocund laughter, — no friend for speaking, no child for loving. Child? He knew he did not regard her in that light; he knew that, fresh and buoyant as she was, no presence more womanly had ever crossed his path, that the thing she had touched could not be graced by others, the sunlight that fell round her was sacred. But for loving? Yes, he answered himself; with his whole heart and soul. — And how much was that?

When they had entered his house — not slightly unwelcome — it had been St. Denys for whom he cared, to whom he turned; but long before they left, Miriam had held his thoughts day and night. What solace had they brought him, — what peace, brief and blissful, — how much had been crowded into these five weeks! He remembered Miriam at one time, dancing and singing in his path, the impersonation of a spicy summer; and at another, half aware of some under-current of feeling, adorned by that same gentle dignity in whose guise he had first seen her. Who would sing to him now, — who, when the dreadful night fell, would charm its terrors away, — who, in any stress of stormy weather, would fill the room with light? Who was there to teach him that he lived? Who for him to make happy? Alas! they were gone, and had torn delight with them.

The house was more lonely than a desert; though swarming with memories, only a desolation It was unendurable, — he would leave it, he would go to Kent as they wished. Why did all wretchedness choose him for its victim? The question answered itself, stinging him to elder remembrances. Had he not deserved it? and so was it not inevitable? This was only the old stain of his existence spreading over new spaces. Should he cover Miriam with it? She was young and cheerful now, he thought; how long would she remain so with him? Could he carve her wrinkles and inspire her sighs? Youth had many salves for sorrow; even if she loved him now, absence would attenuate and break the connecting thread; the pain would pass into forgetfulness. Truer love was in keeping away from her. No matter what he suffered in his loneliness, he would not go to Kent.

A good resolution, but will he keep it? We shall see. Until this time, I think, Sir Rohan has never performed a thoroughly noble action.

All nature had sprung up from the tempest into warmer life. Home was insupportable; Sir Rohan took his hat to go out and see what fresh store of coloring, what new gleanings of beauty, might be in the woods. Had he gone with that avowed design, I doubt would he have brought home anything; for the gold, unhesitatingly put at a comrade's disposal, who displays to the professed pickpocket? Nor are these secrets to be had for the asking. It is the bosom friend who wanders with us into our retirement, abounding in quiet sympathy and love, — whose vicinity disturbs no vibration, whose slightest touch is harmonious, — that gathers them. But since Sir Rohan always returned richer than he went, the intention of his walk was like a draft at sight.

Driven rapidly at first by his mental vehemence,

he had heedlessly traversed a league of the foot-path, when he found himself all at once within a rod of the highway, which, according to the perverse tendencies of its class, preferred winding round the base of the hill some eight or ten miles, to taking the direct cut by which Sir Rohan got there before it. It immediately occurred to him, that proceeding slowly over the bad-conditioned road, and pausing to take leave of Arundel where his more lonely way diverged, St. Denys had not yet passed this spot, and he concluded to await him. So still was Sir Rohan, so gentle all his motions when in the woods, that the wild things regarded him as one of themselves, and his approach was inaudible to a man who stood half concealed by the crusted trunk of a tree. This man wore a spur, — which accounted for the horse Sir Rohan had passed beyond, — some game lay at his feet, and he was reloading ; an occupation left, as the sound of distant wheels caught his ear.

He turned sharply and peered through the interspaces, as if satisfying himself of the identity of some object. A horrid suggestion answered by a horrid resolve, like lightning made in the south and reflected again at the uttermost parts of the heavens, writhed across his lips and brow. For a moment a visible agitation chained him with a shiver; then glancing round as if a fiend had whispered, he deliberately finished charging the gun, which, as the sound grew more distinct, he cocked and raised to his·shoulder, displaying, with every vein knotted, the flushed face of Marc Arundel.

Intuitively, knowledge of the other's intentions seized Sir Rohan, but interference was as impossible as if he were changed to marble. The coach drew nearer, the rolling wheels spun through the open trees, and puffs of dust blew across the hedge. They had passed him, they were passing Arundel. Not so. There was at this point in the road a gully worn by the brook that babbled by them, and over which a rustic bridge was built; a plank of this had been displaced, and the coach stopped while some one alighted to readjust it.

The gun trembled at Arundel's shoulder; the aim was not satisfactory; he lowered it, and bending on one knee, again settled it, again unaccountably suffered the muzzle to fall. Some strange hesitation seemed to restrain him at the very moment he had awaited, or there may yet have been too much tremor to trust death upon. Was it Miriam or St. Denys whose fate lay in that ball, that hesitation? Not Miriam, certainly.

Slowly the arm rose again, slowly fell. They might escape in his vacillation. How much he must desire what such effort was unable to accomplish! Lusting after murder, too dastardly to snatch it. Faugh! It was in cold blood. What impetuosity, what passion, of one kind or another, was there in this? Arundel was evidently a man whose whole moral sense and life were hardly higher than the level of this moment, if, indeed, this were not higher than they. Of the two, ghost-ridden and soiled as he was, Sir Rohan felt himself the better stature.

The plank was replaced, the coachman had again climbed to his seat, and St. Denys was entering while the footman held the door. What suspense bound the moment! Once more Arundel drew the bead in sight. The gun was steady now, the hand sure, but the face white with fear and horror of the deed; perhaps his heart would yet fail him. He wavered an instant longer, then — whether for retreat or advance, who can tell? — planted his foot more firmly among the running vines. Torn by the spur, one snapped and sent the foot slipping over a round pebble. Something, he never knew what, struck up the barrel, he lost his balance and fell forward ; there was a flash, a report, and without his agency it had gone off. In the cloud of smoke, Sir Rohan withdrew again to his former position, content with having broken his spell, baffled the design, and seeing the ball pass over St. Denys's head, — for all this had taken place in an instant.

Arundel's decision was made as quickly. He wiped away the flowing perspiration, seized his birds, ran down, leaping lightly over the hedge, and accosted the startled travellers.

"There 's nothing like being a good marksman," he cried, tossing the game into the boot. "Dress them at the first inn. You 'll have little else, I can tell you ! Good morning again," and he sprung back. While Sir Rohan, as if he himself had been the guilty person, retired noiselessly, and crept away without a word. In offering Arundel a week's shooting on his preserves, he had never dreamed of placing such quarry at his disposal. He saw the coach rolling on, they were safe, and he dismissed the matter.

Absorbed at last in the pleasure of the noonday woods, he advanced, searching the eyes of a tiny fluttering partridge caught and loosed again, watching the tawny gilding of some newt who walked the water with the dignity of a doge, or ruffling wild swans in their sedgy nests by his invading steps. The half-ripe bunches of the roan-trees hung like oranges amid their shivering leaves; the wild grapes were beginning to redden; the indolent birds sat silent on the boughs, hardly distinguishable; the trumpet bignonias leaped from tree to tree, scarlet in exuberant beauty. Sir Rohan with determination banished everything but the present enjoyment, sensuous though it might be, from his mind; and examining the inflorescent galls of the blueberry, downy as if sprinkled with fresh-fallen snow, and brilliant with stains of carmine and cream, scraping the lichen from stones, the moss from trees, following the sparhawks wheeling above in open spots, or the little serpents twisting like tendrils or green sunbeams among the eggs of a deserted nest, he still extended his walk, meeting no one but some solitary peat-digger splashing through regions of shaking heath; nor did he return till the sun had passed the meridian, and he had gathered marvellous hints for his painting.

The servants had not known of his absence, and as he entered the shrubbery a familiar horse, tied there, met his eye again; and passing the great cellar-doors, he observed that they were open. Somewhat surprised, he paused a moment to glance in, without impeding the broad stream of sunshine that flooded it with mellow warmth.

A cask had been drawn into this light, on its head were two or three flasks, of choice seals; and by it, at opposite sides, sat Redruth and the ubiquitous Marc Arundel. The former, with flushed face and fiery features, holding up his long glass to catch a sparkle in its crimson depth, and speaking with animation. The latter, looking like the man's familiar, with a cool perseverance about him, and his glass untouched. It was evident that the garrulous Redruth had drank too freely, and that Arundel was profiting by his frailty.

"The blood of summer, Mr. Arundel," he said, but half intelligibly. "Are rubies so red?"

"Ah! Rare wine indeed, rarely kept. But as

you were saying, sir, your young master — " Sir Rohan heard replied.

" Had been gone not a day from the — I mean not a year from the day he and the young lady came," resumed Redruth, " when one dripping wet night, looking as he had been dragged through a city, he came back without any warning."

" And alone, as you said.   But did n't stay long ? "

" Did n't stay long, you asked ? " he replied feebly. " No, he left just as suddenly, in a week's time or less, and seemed wild and stunned, and then restless and uneasy, as if expecting something ; and all in a hurry flew to the wars, and did n't come home again for ten years or so."

Sir Rohan's first purpose had been to pass without interruption, the next to confound such insolence by his entrance ; but he could not endure to meet what he felt must be the man's consternation, and would have proceeded on his way had not their words attracted him as he lingered in doubt.   How much Redruth, under the influence of his potations, had told, how much of his past life Redruth was able to tell, he did not know. It could be no great amount, he thought.

" And after he went, you received this singular message. Repeat it, Mr. Redruth."

" Singular message ?— why, sir, you 've no memory at all! "

" True. But you 've a most extraordinary one. Enough for two. A wonderful memory."

" Ha! ha! Thankee, sir. Fill your glass, Mr. Arundel ? Clear juice! "

" And this message ? "

" O! A tramper brought it to me from an old woman in one of the east counties, he said ; to tell my master that she would n't disgrace the memory of her grandchild by hanging him, but there were them as lived by Ronald's Tower that could."

" Ronald's Tower ? That 's his place in the north, I think. And why did n't you give him this message ? "

" Why did n't I give him this message, — why did n't I give him this message ? " reiterated Redruth thickly, endeavoring to gather the import of the words through a vague sense of danger. " Try another bottle, sir — message — O ! I may have thought it was only some spiteful person's impudence," he said, speaking as though his mouth were full, and makin ' much effort to articulate ; "or maybe I was afraid. I don't clearly remember, sir, just now. It 's a dreadful warm day ! "

" And before that ? " queried Arundel.

" Before that ? Who told you anything about before that ? " exclaimed his *vis-à-vis*, with the sudden pugnacity of another glass. " I should like to know what for are you round prying into your neighbor's affairs. My master 's a good master, sir, and minds his own business, which is more than all masters do ! And as for his Miss, —— what 's that to you ? you —— "

But here the impetus failed him ; he looked round fearfully, then vacantly, and dropping his head upon the cask, burst into maudlin tears.

Arundel rose to go, and as he turned saw Sir Rohan standing gravely in the doorway.

" I am concerned, Mr. Arundel," said the latter, stepping down, " that in my absence you should be obliged to seek refreshment in my cellars, and waste your conversation on servants. Let me beg you to finish your repast in the dining-room."

" Thank you, sir. No occasion for concern. Not this morning," said the other, buttoning his coat coolly, as he recovered from a temporary abashment.

"You did n't proceed so far as you intended," Sir Rohan remarked, viewing him quietly.

"O, quite! And remembering that Mr. Redruth was witness in one of my suits, returned, and found him here."

. "You lie, sir!" exclaimed Sir Rohan, pale with rage, and kindling at the spark.

"Where did I find him, then ?"

"You lie, you coward! Must I repeat it? That's not what you came for! But there's powder and ball above, and you don't go home without them!"

"Not I, sir," answered Arundel, who had too precious a booty to be shot down for it. "I 've no dispute with you, sir. We 're quits, certainly, if your eaves-dropping — "

Sir Rohan seized an empty flask to break upon him; his own lips were blue, his cheeks bloodless, nostrils quivering, eye flashing,—he had undergone a complete metamorphosis. But the other, cowering beneath and avoiding the blow, sprung past him from the cellar, when, quickly reaching his horse, he vaulted into the saddle and dashed away.

Sir Rohan walked toward Redruth. Some bold

vengeance swept through his mind; but he was not so young as once, and now, after a delay, he clinched the old man's shoulder, and caused him to raise his head and turn his stupefied gaze on him.

"Redruth!" he said, between his set teeth, "if you wish to live an hour from that time, never let my name be in your thoughts or on your lips again when speaking to a third person!" And dropping the nerveless shoulder, he left the place as he had entered, sought the hall-door, and mounted to his painting-room.

XI.

WORK.

SIR ROHAN, recalling the occurrences concerning which Redruth had been cajoled into imparting all he knew, could not discover that that had been much, or that Arundel could in any way use it to his disadvantage. He had himself learned one new fact, — that of the message ; but the old woman referred to could have spoken only on surmise, he reflected, if there were any such person at all, which he doubted ; and considering the affair of no further importance he dropped it, and once more recommenced work.

There had grown to be something painful about this picture now, as though it were a thing long held in suspense and reproaching him. He had neglected it lately, and had only with difficulty prevented Miriam from raising its veil, for by some instinct he could not suffer her to look upon it; and he had found that the spirit that fed his pencil wavered, as if invariably subject to some antagonistic attraction. Now again constantly as ever he employed himself, the lark not earlier, the glowworm scarcely later. The last brief weeks had infused a healthier sense, and he hoped to realize it in his performance.

Other weeks sped by, and a few more would complete it. What should he do then, he one day thought; but resolved to let that time decide for itself. - The memory of Miriam he tried to banish; but as well hold the wind from blowing. She asserted herself as firmly in his mind as the Ghost of yore; yet he clung to his purpose resolutely, nevertheless.

Working, as before, when the light grew dim, again he saw fine points of white lustre pass from his brush and diffuse themselves beneath it. In the mornings, frequently, something like a mist seemed to cover the surface, which clearing away at his approach, left a darker atmosphere beneath, emitting faint coruscations till sucked up by the canvas. And as he drew nearer conclusion, every night, he thought, tenuious balls of fire shot from the spot on the lawn where he had seen Miriam crowned with azalias, into his painting. Far from ascribing these things to his Ghost, as once he would have done, he believed them to be owing to the electric and miasmatic agencies of the place, and planned a new home for the future, in his fancy, should she leave him longer in this apparent freedom.

Now he ventured to add some last tint to the eyes; what wonder if Miriam's had escaped from his heart to the work, brighter and larger than the truth, and gathering life, as it were, at every trace of his pencil? The air rustled about him there before his easel with low sibilations, oven the darkness, as he lay in the room with it, put out an arm toward it, and his idle pencil glowed like the finger that wrote *mene*, *mene*, on the wall. A slow infiltration of some unknown chemistry seemed in process,— a dangerous alchemy transmuting all he did with its own gloss, and holding his latest stroke in flux, till at turn of tide a hand — how dim and weak, like the ghost of a ghost — took shape, and flitted with mysterious falterings round pencil, palette, and picture. It was his Ghost, he knew, essaying to come back and add her few dreadful touches; but what power she had met superior to diminish and dissipate her influence, he could not imagine, nor why that which had so often mastered him should now, at his recognition, retreat round the easel and vanish into a hostile gloom.

But at length there came a morning at the close of summer, when he believed nothing was left to do, and some such rejoicing exclamation may have passed his lips. For simultaneously, all the air of the room seemed seized by a strong throe, swelling, through sharp and tremulous palpitations, as if bursting with unseen fulness, till it shivered in a quick rebound, and a long-drawn sigh of exquisite relief died away into silence.   It was finished.

Sir Rohan swept aside his implements, and determined not to see it again immediately, that coming the next time with an eye grown somewhat unfamiliar, any remaining defect might strike him more obviously; and although a feeble affinity still drew him back, he resisted, and left the work alone.

In the drawing-room Sir Rohan found everything nearly as it had been left, for all the servants had not yet been dismissed, and Nell and

Nan, Mrs. Redruth's maids, contented themselves
by keeping the rooms in order, without interfering
with their arrangements. Here was the book as
St. Denys had laid it down, there the little lace-
wrought handkerchief that Miriam's careless wont
had left in a crumpled heap on the clavichord,
and still withering in their vase from which all
the water had long evaporated, were the stems of
those flowers she had gathered on the morning of
her departure. But the charm that had animated
the whole place was gone, — all things were
crammed with life only because of Miriam. The
first respite he had enjoyed from the misery of
nearly twenty years she, he fancied, had produced ; and questioning how those few weeks
should be capable of such effects, he saw them as
the point throwing all his past life into perspec-
tive. The cloud no longer overshadowed him ; —
he had passed out from it, he believed, and Miriam, in her youth and beauty, was the first to
meet him. Should he therefore sacrifice her ?
But if he suffered pain then, was it happiness that
this loneliness gave him ? Once, he knew, he
could have imagined no greater height of bliss
than to be free of the Ghost. Less agonizing than

the Ghost, but hardly less bitter, he felt this renunciation of love to be; and he longed to see her again, as the watcher longs for morning. He never asked if he were pampering a fond vanity, for it seemed as natural that Miriam should love him, once known, as that she should command the love of all others. But he repressed the aching at his heart, and dangerously resolved again to cherish the thought of her in distance, to let her memory sweeten long wakeful nights and lighten dim days, — to worship her, in short, without a word, in a real self-abnegation, free from all hope of reward. Was it not more blessedness to love than to be loved? Surely love, so used, crowned and glorified itself. But it was in his fancy, — not in himself. Perchance, had he kept his vow, the Ghost had kept her truce. Ebn Thaher reasoned, says the old Arabian tale, but Aboulhassan loved.

He had received a letter from St. Denys announcing their safe arrival, which he always carried about him, for a postscript had been added over Miriam's scrawling signature. Which document we give below, having taken the liberty to spice it with punctuation and capitals, the thing being none the less hearty because she had omitted that ceremony.

"I was so glad to be at home again,"—it ran, —"that I never thought how sorry I should be, directly, to have left you. But we miss you so very much, Sir Rohan, that you must come immediately, and not misuse us."

This he had not answered, yet something of her later presence seemed haunting it, and as he paced the room he laid it for an instant by the handkerchief.

A little urchin—whom Miriam, with kisses and sugar-plums, had frequently seduced from one of the cottages, with whom he had seen her frolicking in the grass, and whom, bending towards him with the gentlest caress and merriest smile, he had seen her leading over the lawn—now came with abundant daisies clutched in both hands, as doubtless he had come before, and flattening his small face against the window, looked in with wistful eyes for Miriam. Sir Rohan knew what he wanted; he wanted it too; and his impulse was to beckon him; but he could not remember the time when he had spoken to a child, and while he hesitated, the visitor, frightened at his stern, pale look, retreated. It was odd that such a trifle should strengthen Sir Rohan's resolution.

But now that the old occupation was gone, the dreary man felt the necessity of fastening his attention elsewhere, and for once, being in the mood, sought for some good to be done to others. There was sufficient awaiting, without leaving his own land. He would regulate and repair his house and its surroundings; he would improve the condition of his tenantry, of whom, questionless, many were suffering; he would place education within the reach of those who desired it; he would inspire the desire. It was not too late to expiate his youth. He would commence at once; and with a new energy he stepped into the hall, scenting the powerful fragrance drafting through the open doors, from the greenhouse. Well, they were pretty dreams!

But at the foot of the staircase a change overcame him, the color fell from his face again. An instant ago so elastic, now, with drooping head and pensive air, he could scarcely move. Some powerful attraction seemed drawing him above; but if he yielded to this, would not the more powerful attraction of Miriam conquer again?

Nevertheless, whatever force it was, battling it at every step, or wearily acquiescing, he submitted, and slowly ascended to the door of his painting-room. Once there, the door seemed to burst open for his entrance, and the alluring power to bring him yet more swiftly till he stood before his picture. Let us also look at the thing.

It is not a small canvas, being about four feet in height, although rather longer than broad, and is set in a quaint frame of black, carved wood, with an inner reglet gilt to relieve the want of that color in the painting. It is full of purple, misty shades, with one or two flashes of light, yet at first sight devoid of interest, for the only object seems to be a tiny balance held by invisible fingers. One scale descends, the other ascends; in either lies a violet. These violets are exquisitely finished, the hue soft and rich, while the tissue of the petals is of ethereal delicacy. They are relieved by a doubtful reflex of crimson drapery. In the heart of the upper one rests a dew-drop, a large liquid diamond that has caught the very spirit of concentrated lustre. It is singular to observe that the only light in the picture radiates from this dew-drop as from a sun. But its jewel has not enhanced the beauty of the flower; on the contrary, it is wilted, and the fierce rays have creased the frail film, and exhaled the sweet juices. No dew-drop seals the heavier violet. It lies alone, as if just plucked from the woods, nursed by sunshine, fashioned by south winds, yet fed, cherished, and utterly impregnated with the life and beauty of morning dew. Its soft blue bloom is unimpaired, its fresh grace seems imperishable, one fancies that it fills the room and picture with a subtile fragrance; a long-stemmed leaf of tenderest green, pulled from the parent root, lies beside it. Your eye lingers on the ungemmed violet, for the confused tinge of the remainder of the canvas does not entice, and you wonder why it was not framed in six inches.

But gazing so long, something seems to unfold, some mist to lighten; you are aware of the suggestion of a finger on which the balance rests, and tracing it up, a round arm, that grows whiter as you pierce the smoky wrapping, till it melts into a shoulder of the perfect mellow mould of a ripened pear, a curve of the neck, a face, while long hair like a cloud of refined shadow shrouds the rest, and is hardly distinct from the dark purple background.

Delighted at having discovered a face, and almost imagining yourself the first who has done so, you stay like one entranced till the beauty you are sure must be there resolves before you.

Behind the mist, the gauzy vapor, the oval brightens with a faint color in the cheek, you even see the dimple in the chin. Each feature gains clearness, and the eyes illumined by the dew-drop open on your sight.

You feel sure that the room must be swarming with other intelligences waiting upon those eyes. Words fail to express their charm. They are full of a dreamy languor, they are large, serene, and obscure, they are like a flame or sunshine or gold seen through wine or any brown transparency, they are a little darker than topaz, they imbibe rather than emit a sparkle, they seem to have filled themselves with the whole glory of a Roman summer.

You are still satisfied, but in a measure trained, and glancing down an instant, it appears that the upper scale with its violet and dew-drop forms only a superb ring for some one yet undetected; searching for whom, you detain in the lower corner a face turned upward, fainter far than the other, white, earnest, the eyes almost quivering with eagerness, the brow beaded, the darkness receding from it in folds as if brushed aside by keen motion, the whole suffused with a wild radiance. It might be Lucifer. The light is so managed that this is the only object casting a distinct shadow. His extended hand is a flash.

There should be something counter to this; and erelong, higher up than, but not far distant from the first face, another issues into life. It is not remarkable except for its placidity. It looks down from its cloud as if full of heavenly content; you perceive the shades are lighter around it, and at once notice its air of vigilance and certainty. All the calm influence of the painting spreads from that. It might be some seraph whose crown is won.

The composition of the three is good, having the effect of a broad sunbeam falling slantwise; and the coloring comprises a rich succession and mingling of tones and semitones, although on a scale of strict selection.

It is curious that while the first form is so vague and dim, she seems nevertheless the only real one, and these two remaining faces but the people of her reverie : one, perhaps the image of life, temptation overcome ; the other, the ardent dream of passion. You do not doubt into which arms she will fall.

You are apprised also of something foreign in this form, something, so to say, supernatural. That absorbed smile seems to part and float across the face, these colors to change with a quick pulsation ; you fancy, if released from the frame and scales, it would soar up and away ; you feel uncomfortably, as if the eyes saw you. You believe the artist to have worked beyond his will, and to have wrought that of which he was not conscious, a power above his control inspiring his pencil. It is a wonderful picture, and opulent in tints that would cool an August noon. But having glanced away, as you return it is once more enveloped in its smoky drapery, and only by a similar process would you again discover the same objects.

This is what you and I see, — little enough for a man to waste so much life on ; but what did Sir Rohan see ? A mistier shade, a whiter film, something not of his creation. Vengeful arrows shot from the proud pathos of those eyes ; through the haze he had wrought over them, the lips quivered at his gaze with flecks of blue flickering flame; though fixed, it hovered; though inanimate, it lived.

"Had he been mad, so to deceive himself? Could he ever escape it? Here too! Here too!"

But Sir Rohan had no time to utter such words, or frame so distinctly their thought. The sense alone smote him; he was wrapped again in the black and poisonous cloud. So shortly since so buoyant, so hopeful,—what had ruined him now?

He stood tensely, half turned away, but his eyes by irresistible attraction drawn toward and returning that gaze, livid and agonized.

Great God! the Ghost was in the picture.

XII.

MORTMAIN.

NOT long Sir Rohan remained inactive. Without pausing to consider consequences, without hesitating at destroying such labor, he seized the little palette-knife lying near and dashed it madly through the canvas.

A sudden shock, like a stroke of lightning, smote him; then, for a space, the very silence seemed to sing in his ears. A vacant space, into which ebbed a tide of air, a rush, a tumult, and with all her pristine strength and hate the Ghost flared forth and enveloped him.

Voluntarily she had entered this prison, to torment him truly, but yet once there he could flee from her; he could escape from her and he had returned, she was bound and he had freed her.

Again the Ghost threw her net over him, again dragged him captive in her toils. There are no

20

means to depict, were it desirable, the horror and darkness that overwhelmed him anew; his fetters galled the more that he had been free. But in coping with material objects she had manifested an incapacity; her usual cunning seemed to have failed her, her dreadful art served her only for those of the soul. Wrapping his forehead with her clammy breath, she stifled him; her cold, long fingers were upon him, her hideous embrace around him, that shadow of her hair brushed his cheek, those fierce eyes searched him through and through. Did she breathe, he wondered; did those glances gloom and flash with the current in her veins; was that heart palpitant above him? Then, laughing despairingly at his absurdity, he saw that by her sympathy with the whole free universe its forces were kept in ebb and flow through her existence, and that thus drawing after her in infrangible connection a strength that was almost omnipotent, she acquired a personal determination, a deceitful limitation and power infinitely beyond that to be dreamed of from any mere effort of breath or blood. Now the air sobbed away from him, now poured back echoing her horrid laugh. All voluntary motion left him; the Ghost moved him hither and thither at her will. Each moment became a cycle filled with what unutterable pain! Like a pricked bubble all his dreams fell dead to the bottom of his heart, and numberless hopes escaped and swam in her lurid light, a whole heaven of possibilities and sorrows as they broke. The morning crawled away, and left him yet in her vindictive hands. Noon passed; day; evening drew near. He hoped some human being might enter and perhaps dissolve the charm; but no one came, till dusk brought the housekeeper. He wanted nothing, she heard him say; he was not ill, she could do nothing for him. He longed to ask her to remain; the words were on his lips, he thought them uttered; but the Ghost snatched them off as they rose, and tore them to shreds of inarticulate sound, for Mrs. Redruth closed the door behind her, and again he was alone with the Ghost. Now once more she stretched vividly before his aching eyes the scenes of his youth, and contrasted them with some dim sketch of Miriam pallid, haggard, miry; and once more shook the web of fire between them. Now she laid her icy cheek on his, peered askance with her chatoyant eyes close beside his own, stained his lips in her filthy kisses, and then retreating with grimace and flounce, leered at him from behind a screen of gathering darkness, or flowed forth brandishing keener spears than hitherto, before which he cowered and hid his face only to be drawn up again and forced to encounter the terrible dualism. She heaped upon him all the cumulative force of her hibernation. Sleep forsook him; night crowded herself with other Essences ready, it seemed, to assume shape at the Ghost's command. Thought refused to yield him comfort; he was capable only of torturing sensation. Morning came at last, and the unwearied Ghost sung its reveille, but never left him. If he traversed the house from room to room, still she sailed by his side, opening the doors before them by the power of her will; or if in some long passage he fancied himself alone an instant, she burst in countless reduplications from every panel, and swept on with her myriads to environ him. Burying himself in the forest, all the air murmured of her; the leaves of the birch shivered with electric, luminous points, the needles of the pines whispered her messages. Nature, who brings the sick wild beasts to medicinal browse, who heals the gashes of her trees with slow sweat of crystal tear and fragrant gum, had no remedy for this man who had wounded her. Misery had beset him; not dead, he suffered hell.

Now and then, Sir Rohan indulged himself in a trifle of extraordinary logic.

It is impossible to imagine a new color; beyond the three primary ones and their modifications, the imagination cannot go; the conception of another, original and creative, exceeds mortal capability. But one day the Ghost appeared to him invested in robes of a new color. She floated finely before him, and trailed their lengthening splendor after her. For a moment he stood amazed; then entering his forsaken painting-room, opened chests and drawers, and proceeded to investigate the sources of this mystery. The Ghost followed him, displaying the full field of color with a mocking apery of vanity, holding it here for a light, dropping it there for a shade. But he searched vainly for any tint owning an affinity with it, following it into shade, or ruling it; nor could he produce it by any artful mingling of prime or tertiary. Cinnabar, nor realgar, nor any brilliant madder, overpowered it; mort d'ore was in no wise akin to it; no pigment could catch its life, alien to them all, a monarch of other chromatics than we possess. He put the things aside, and still stood gazing on the strange hue which the Ghost so accommodatingly paraded. It occurred to him that if he could only prove the color to be an optical delusion, he might also infer that the Ghost herself was no more, on this occasion; and if on this, why not on others? But while meditating, he could not bring himself to believe in a power of imagining anything which might not exist. If the elements of an object's construction are in the mind, he said, they must also be in the world; and thus even had he imagined this color, it might exist, and his Ghost then as well. But on the other hand, was he able to imagine it? Could his will reach up into the heavens, and pluck this secret from God? As well create another sense. No; he must needs confess his weakness there. The color was before him,—no illusion;—he saw it, he had proved it new, he could not doubt it, and the Ghost must be as real. As this conclusion forced itself upon him, the novel drapery forsook the Ghost, and with her old laugh she soared aloft, swept round the easel, and descending beside him, lay recumbent on the air, with one visionary hand upon his shoulder. But thin and immaterial as was the airy hand, its weight was that of a mountain.

He had not dared use his pencils before this day ; he did not dare again ; the Ghost had usurped his province ; but he felt now that if he might, his brain in this great heat would strike off glowing thoughts, to circle, like fresh planets, in an immortality of their own.

Anon the Ghost took a quieter mood, and hung beside him only a sorrowful shadow. Then the memory of Miriam came and poured soft balsams on his wounds; — he caught it, held it firmly, turned it in his mind, and clung to it tenaciously. But at the moment, the Ghost sprang up again, redoubling all her energies, summoning all her alien forces, and every day increasing her threatenings as he refused to resign it, — yet holding her estates by mortmain.

It became a question with him if there might be no scheme to evade her, if flight would free him, or if other chains might be forged for her; — a question, howbeit, that soon answered itself. Issuing one morning from a closet that had been partitioned from his painting-room, he shut the door hastily, and thought, with the exultation of Macedon on conquering new worlds, that he had shut the Ghost within. He said with a chuckle that he had been too quick for her ; perhaps she humored the supposition, for all that day he enjoyed a quiet that was rare. A quiet so far as she was concerned ; but after a little, he began to worry himself with conjectures, where could she be, and what could she be doing ? At last, a curiosity not to be curbed possessed him. There was a nail in the partition at some height, and if it were removed he thought likely he could discover. The Ghost could not be omniscient. Accordingly, having darkened his room that no light might enter the closet through the aperture,— a thing easily avoidable, especially as the other owned a window, — he noiselessly drew the nail, and bringing some steps, cautiously mounted them and applied his eye to the hole. At first he saw nothing; then raising his eye he rubbed it vigorously, and again looked. What did he see ? Only another eye at the opposite side, scanning him as he scanned it, scintillating with malicious sparks, and laughing at him in keen mockery and devilish cunning.

There was no deceit for the Ghost, no more pris-
ons of his making; for him she was, he found,
omniscient and omnipotent. When she had seen
him escaping her by devotion to his easel, she had
entered his work and poisoned his art; but she
was not one on whom he could revenge himself.

Soon, not alone she came, but swept before his
vision day and night with a train of other ghosts,
all separate, all glaring, all silent. They spoke no
word, but used only that dreadful language of the
ghosts, — the eye, the wild gesture, the tempestuous rush, the sigh. From the mantling pools of
the heath at noon they gleamed like the faces of
corpses; wading out in the surf at night, they
broke to view in every crest; he never, never was
alone again.

Sir Rohan had at first congratulated himself
that he would no longer be with his single Ghost,
but a short time taught him the difference was
truly that between one sword and twenty. Their
silence, too, exasperated him; he longed for some
thundering denunciation, some taunt, some doom.
Anything but these tacit threats, these multiplied
stings. The eternal wordlessness, solely, was fren-
zying. He wandered about without aim or knowl-

edge, frequently seeing nothing, but hearing the perpetual rustle of unseen movements, as one hears the murmur of a conch. But was he not indeed laying his ear upon a vaster hollow, and striving to see, painted on the gulfs beyond his own identity, a face, the reflex perhaps of his imaginings? He had walked for hours, at one time, beholding no individual of these milliards, and hearing only their mysterious susurrus; he had endured it in a corresponding silence.

"Speak!" he cried at last, and turning, found himself sitting on a tombstone in the lee of the little church Miriam had described,—the three graves, the long slope, and the sea, behind; and before,—between the gap of the cliffs reddening with morning,—the cross-roads, and a sunrise boiling wildly athwart low inland plains. One region of the heavens was wrapped in the pomp of crimson brightening vapor that, curling and sailing higher, put up a golden lip to take the morning star; through it broad rays blanched the zenith; in it the thin moon, waning her last quarter, slowly and more slowly dissolved away. At his demand, deadlier stillness seemed to hold the air; but as if they had always been there, he was aware, on looking again, of a phalanx of motionless faces clear with metallic brightness, turned, not at him, but toward the disc of the sun. Before Sir Rohan might have suffered his glance to follow theirs, something shot across and led it on till resting there. It was the tiny blade of a penknife held in long slender fingers, but increasing and swelling as it withdrew,— and when it lay on the shining disc, large and flexible as a Damascus blade. A moment it remained quiescent, then waving like a zostera gently from side to side with rippling undulations, it was grasped more nervously, and, as if it were a shuttle, tossed to and fro, bending, slashing, twisting, rising, falling, all at once, like not one, but a hundred swords, and with a rapidity that bathed the controlling fingers in a cloud. Now, like the swift wings of birds flashing in the prime, it darted darkly across the light, singing as it went; and now, like a myriad fish in a sea of aerial brilliance, it swam with curves and whirls, swaying at graceful pleasure. But that which always gave distinctness to the object, and brought it back to its original purport, was a stain of brown rust upon the edge,— a stain that had been blood,— the coagulation of a life. It was the one returning point, that arrested its swiftest motion, that caught it from the most fantastic transformation, and shook it terribly before him. By a peculiar process, Sir Rohan could not resist the belief that the stain was not so much on the knife as on his own soul; that it was that in truth drawn and played with by those ghostly fingers, black against the radiance of dawn. In a kind of trance, he stared at the swift glancing of the blade, till suddenly it leaped toward him from the sun, like an arrow, but fell short of its mark and stuck upright and quivering in the ground; while that old touch, like compressed wind or a breath from a rarer atmosphere, circled his wrist again, — spiritual, chill, and melting like snow.

When he looked up again, the morning was advanced, the faces faded, and the only object before him was an upright stake driven through the heart of the suicide who had been buried at the junction of the four cross roads. It was the speech he had demanded of the Ghost and her Legion.

When Sir Rohan trusted himself to look upon his life, he saw it as one who has ascended an apparently extinct volcano. The old lava-streams are gay with wild-flowers that have bedded their roots among them; the blackened channels over-grown with vines; and bending down the savage rifts whose deserted margins are green with moss, nothing but everlasting quiet and sombre shadow meet the eye. Suddenly, the earth trembles, thick vapors, rising, assume wild shapes and darken the lift; sulphureous flames follow in broad columns; the old craters yawn and rock the hills, and new mouths belch forth fiery rivers; while all the demons and spirits of fire, who have slept so long in their caverns, start into activity, and forward the work with diabolic glee. And yet as often Sir Rohan wondered if he were not as responsible for these fierce imps that haunted him, as the Ghost; and such gleams of recognition broke upon him, that he half fancied them the creations of evil thought, or the informing life of all his vicious deeds, now first surrounded with shape.

He climbed among the gables of the old house, ivy above, within, beneath his nook; owls staring at him with great horny moons; bats wheeling around him; but there too they came. Unimagined revolting phantasms roaming the dark firmament, travelling the winds, dropping on long threads and swinging before him; silent all, but restless, capricious, malevolent. Abolishing distance till they showed him a false Miriam in Arundel's arms, or haled her by the hair across his sight, dead and freshly bleeding; or while the white bush at the foot of the lawn glowed into the shape of the Ghost, surrounding it with wreaths and arabesques of head and limb and mop and mow, horns, wings, tusks, till rising in a cloud, the Ghost at their head, they charged valiantly and drove him from the lair that seemed instinct with life and stinging in every spray, still pursuing, as he fled, with fresh dismays.

Strange to say, the most frequent of all these extramundane faces was one resembling Arundel's, pale and shuddering as when taking aim at St. Denys.

He walked mile after mile on the endless moors by night, and with the empty shell of the sky above, cheated himself into a whim of freedom, till the momentary transport checked his pace, and the rising moon confronted him. It cast long shadows from the margin of the moor toward him, it cast also his own shadow behind him; what then cast that same shadow, pale and varying, in the path before him? Turning with frightened eyes, again his Ghost in her dim red aspect of triumph was at his shoulder, and each time the shock was no less intense.

In the excruciating pains given by the noxious vapors creeping treacherously into his bones during these nightly wanderings he hoped that he might merge his mental distress; but as if his soul were fed by corresponding pulses, every physical pang merely aggravated the wild throbs of anguish there.

By day again, let him go where he would, a blinding heat and light crowned and dazed him, refulgent atoms of lightning flitted through his vision in clouds, and every actual object wavered as when seen through a veil of fervid air. He felt it impossible to give any material its relative value.

He never looked in a glass now, for there the Ghost was most clearly to be found, as if it needed the substanceless depth of the mirror to paint this essence and evolve her from her shadowy sphere. Yet at horrid times she burned away the awful nimbus that surrounded her like a personal at-. mosphere and separated them as the glass seems to separate you from your reflection, — but which was, indeed, the impassable barrier of worlds, that interposed between her and corporeal things infinitely more effectually than rushing leagues of tempestuous sea-foam or ranges of heaven-kissing hills, — burned this veil away with a subtile inter-penetration of light, and stepped from her sphere to the shore of his, or rapt him into the bosom of that, till his flesh lay chiller than snow upon his bones, heavier and more lifeless than lead.

Not infrequently a great horror and darkness fell upon him, wrapping him completely from all outer objects; and when, after a while, it withdrew and he became conscious of his Ghost, he demanded if she were not the image of that thrown out bodily, more especially as his mind was of the class prone to individualize and assign every ideal thing its equivalent of personality.

Hardest of all to bear was the hopelessness of release, the fact of her perpetuity, the knowledge that it was she, and that she was always there. If by any chance tired habit snatched him into sleep awhile, it was only to wake pricked through the eyeballs, and meet the baleful face hanging within an inch of his own. The breath of life itself had now become fear to Sir Rohan; apathy kindled to anger, and one trepidation built itself upon another. A mouth passed, and still the Ghost was his second self, and still as he turned to the thought of Miriam she called her awful legions to destroy it.

A perpetual distress of this period was the total loss of all privacy. His mind, like some fair cathedral nave with pillared aisles withdrawing to lofty twilight, rich in antiquity, experience, the beauty of genius and aspiration, instead of being swept and garnished by pious and orderly hands, and with closed portals repeating the quiet footfall of silent worshippers, was set open to the gaping view of all passers, thronged at the vestibules with hosts of curious intruders, clanging to the fierce tread of haughty scoffers. Rude iconoclasts shivered the shrines, tore up the mosaics, splintered the tracery that crusted mullion and arch like the moss of centuries; while the air that had wafted only blue-rolling incense, harmony, and prayer, was now scattered by explosive laughter, and silence fled shuddering to far monastic cloisters, still to be caught and destroyed by the ribald profanity that chased it.

There are few of us, even the most candid, that

do not keep some inner niche, where we retire alone with our chosen oracle, our single memory, or our hidden hope, — but this was denied to Sir Rohan; and since so few hold their thoughts to the gaze of a friend, who would choose an enemy for their revelator, and that one whose enmity was to be measured, if at all, by the strength of a former love! Yet at such mercy he lay. Again, though we commonly shrink from investigation of our least wish, and do not desire intrusion on our sorrow, the delicate and fastidious hold their joys in a far greater degree sacred to themselves, and scarcely in their confessions to God pray all that is in their hearts. How, then, could they bear the prying search of an indifferent eye, and what desecration would their holy of holies meet at such insolent touch as this man experienced!

One of the most fearful circumstances with which the popular idea has chosen to invest the Day of Judgment is that on that day all secrets shall be revealed; but this Sir Rohan suffered instantly, already. His thoughts were known in their conception; there was no ward in his heart of which the Ghost had not the freedom, every nerve of pain or pleasure quivered at her presence, she exposed the flimsy texture of every dream, every fancy she scanned, every desire she held up and shook derisively. And if such scrutiny be painful from those who, by the kindred of a race, share our frailties and aims, how must it exceed itself from beings who have not one attribute in common with us, who do not even breathe our air, and own not a single human sympathy? Whether the allies of the Ghost followed her insulting march, or she communicated with them without by some more than electric celerity, Sir Rohan could hardly discriminate, or if their intelligent torture would be keener than that effected by unwitting malice. It was enough to feel all hidden things brought to light, each recess rifled, all sanctity violated, and his soul alive and resonant with foreign and malign manœuvres.

Contemplation of any object is apt to impart to ourselves a tinge of that object's archeus. Thus I should not care to have, too often, the inspection of an elephantiasis, amaurosis, or leprosy, lest the drop serene should be grafted on the mind's eye, or a more dangerous mental leprosy be induced; and thus Sir Rohan, who at first may have seen his Ghost simply because he knew she was to be seen, at last felt himself in jeopardy of partaking her nature. But hideous as this nature was, had he not made it so?

Previously he had dreaded death, and driven all his thoughts from it; he had feared, indeed, worse than he was suffering; feared too, that he should become of like substance, part and parcel of his Ghost, able to endure finer inflictions. But if he too had laid aside the flesh, would not some ghostly poniard be his? No, no, he interpreted her look, anew; he had had his turn. At least some foil for defence, he persisted, then it would be impossible for her to bring him such pain as now; and truly he desired this release. But whom should he ask? He dared not take it, and to those who demand him Death never comes. Once, in the evening, as he crossed the dark drawing-room, the light from the hall streamed in at the open door and lay upon the carpet; the long mirror, nearly opposite, caught this light and shed a brighter air round itself, and a parallelogram of fainter clearness on the floor beside the other. As Sir Rohan entered, his own shadow fell in the first, and he had seen the image of that shadow dimly in the glass, together with the white misti-

ness that, swaying at every breath of air, still un-
falteringly served him ; and now returning, before
he reached the mirror, he saw again his own approaching shadow, with the Ghost's, not in the
glass, but thrown from its bosom upon the floor.
Uncertain enough, surely, was the double reflex of
his material form ; but how utterly impalpable,
ethereal, and evanescent, this accompanying film !
It was as if the freak of light had stripped her of
the medium in which she clothed herself for visi-
bility, so that naked to the core, her true substance lay in that representation hovering over the
carpet ; so that he saw, not her mere refinement,
but the reflection of the reflection of the shadow of
a shadow. He no longer desired Death to endue
him with a similar ghastliness, and abandoned all
thoughts of conquering the Ghost by becoming of
like stuff. The intangibility and nothingness were
awful. He felt that she would embrace him more
completely were he free from the flesh ; that in the
body, with all its infirmities and susceptibilities,
lay his peace or his salvation. He was like those
who, having bargained with the fiend for the next
world, fix themselves resolutely on the swinging
blossom of this, and pierce it for its lingering drop

of bitter honey. He half fancied that since Nature had made one such exception for him, in the case of his Ghost, she might also make another, and decree that he should never die.

But time fleeting, the fitful darts of pain became the heavy pressure of aching. Again his fancy flew to Miriam.

He forgot that the Ghost had been growing feebler before she came. Faint enough, he said, had been that influence in her presence; had she not finally banished it all? And he suddenly believed it possible that having encountered the vigorous nature of this joyous girl, the grave-soiled weapons of the other had been found of no avail. He had resolved for Miriam's sake, not to involve her in his own sphere of pain. But had she been miserable while here? In saving him had she lost herself? Doubtless she was happy now: would she be less so when vanquishing, by her calm virtue and that voice like a sance-bell, these ghouls and vampires that preyed upon him?

There are many who have the magnanimity to resign that which costs others too precious a price; few who have the courage to think, as Sir Rohan did, of the greater price of their accepted resignation, to weigh with careful poise their benefit and the other's loss.

Not immediately did Sir Rohan collect his argument; he had chance in the ceaseless operations of his foe for thought but in jets; yet finally the one conclusion held him,—he would seek Miriam, he would never return without her.

Great need was there now for the Ghost to thrust on her blows with violence, to exert all her sovereignty, and sway her sceptre over the farthest of her winged auxiliaries, investing them with a new power; and when she resorted to the boldest of her expedients, the danger must have been imminent. She had ruled a passive victim, now it was an enemy resisting her. Out of his sudden hope night shut down upon Sir Rohan. These wings blackened the sky. That was a fierce time of joy to the Ghost, of agony to him. He yielded to it like one in the centre of a hostile battalion, crushed, torn, and bleeding. You, with your healthy organization, laugh at it. To him, diseased, sensitive, and replete with consciousness, swords could not have been sharper; and not the least piercing thorn was that his own hand had loosened the horror, as the fisherman opened the jar for the Genius.

I have asked myself if this man were mad. But when, if he were, the madness became infectious, when these phantoms became apparent to others, I am forced to deny him that relief.

For now the servants knew of his approach before they heard a footfall. If they met him at dusk, they averred his eyes were burning coals; if at noon, they unconsciously made way for two. Enormous shadows, they said, danced as though one tossed flambeaux in his path. The maids fled like frightened doves among themselves, and told with sharp whispers of the cloud in which their fancies girt him, as if it held some half-guessed monster to crouch above as he came down the stairs, some form to sweep on either side, some dimmest semblance of a weeping woman always to be seen floating before his eyes: eyes like a sleep-walker, they said, though he so often raising his hand to brush it away; eyes wide with confusion, oppression, and fright. He looked, they said, as if he walked towards hell, and its shooting flames already threw their expectant shadows across his lurid visage. His old and gentle condescension, his suffering, and kindly patience, availed no jot in the regard of these people, who beheld in him the victim of unknown, and thence the more terrific agencies. Redruth also, they declared, saw such images, though he said nothing, and one, indeed, was always whispering by his ear.

But Redruth soon was not alone. These fantastic creations filled the house, darted from every closet, lurked in every corner, chased them till their haunted work lay unperformed and they dared not leave one another. Could I ascribe all this to that power in Sir Rohan of stamping his own sensations on the nerves of others?

Fearful legends now were rife in the place; the story of Fanchon was bandied about with additions, and it was even circulated that some ancient Knight of the Belvideres had agreed upon a day with the Powers of darkness wherein the whole house should fall with a crash, and the dust of its ruin choke the welkin; this day they believed to be near, and with the superstition of their class they rose to meet it.

In people of no high grade of intellect, we often find a material perception, so to speak, a species of instinct, that serves them in these emergencies; and thus they may have felt rather than seen what they described, and receiving impressions so more strongly through the senses, these emotions may have acted upon them in that direction, and taught them to appreciate their master's condition more quickly than by other means.

Of all this Sir Rohan was aware. He was worn, thin, exhausted, and racked with perpetual pain. But the hour his determination was fully made, he descended heedless, a moment, of the crew that followed. His head throbbed, his cheeks flushed, his eyes burned with the fire in his veins ; a fever boiled his blood ; he ordered his horse in a rage, and mounting, dashed down the lawn with the Ghost, and turned into the path through the park that led to the highway traversing the county on his road to Kent.

At hurried instants when this whirlwind of flame broke and flashed away from him, his thoughts vaulted buoyantly, and travelled along the track of memory, drawn by unseen but invincible chains, over the waste of years, to the pleasurable scenes of youth ; so that he remembered the beauty and joy of that phase, the hot passion, the indifference, the regret, till out of them leaped a wild hasty deed like a crease from its sheath, and then Remorse chased him ; Remorse that begat a feverish longing for the restoration of what he had destroyed; a longing which assumed the semblance of love, and led grief by the hand; while the first foe still followed, never flagging with his whips, and chasing him into madness. There his thoughts wallowed through a miry flood, till the longing became loathing, the love hatred; and struggling to free himself he slipped in viler sloughs, where successive horrors encompassed him, receding and advancing like the waves of a sea, till on their long rolls they tossed up the Ghost. And these same thoughts dimly perceived himself now, with the great darkness falling again upon him, that, as he peeled it in broad flakes from one place, fell upon another.

His frenzied violence at departure was not unnoticed by Redruth, who followed at a distance through the wilderness of neglected growth. Toward nightfall, while he still wandered hardly knowing why, crackling boughs and an intermittent trampling drew him from the path, and in the thickest of the woods he found his master thrown senseless at the trunk of a tree, the snorting horse not far off. There was a wood-cutter within hail, the sound of whose cutting fell with clear echoes, a ringing musical chopping; and having secured his aid, they exerted all their strength, raised the senseless man to the saddle, and led him home.

Physicians were soon summoned, but Redruth bethought himself of a nurse tenderer than the others, though so far away, and wrote that night to St. Denys, directing his letter by the one he had found on the clavichord. Scarcely had the mail time to reach the Castle and return, when Miriam and St. Denys stood by the sick man's bedside.

XIII.

SIR ROHAN lay prostrate under a fierce fever; only a constitution of iron strength, wiry and elastic, could have arisen from it. For many days the unrelenting heats stung him along narrow ways. Goaded, parched, and panting, at last sleep overtook him; the delirium consumed itself; and waking, purposeless and dejected, life fluttering at his pulse for release, as he hung in the balance of Fate, he found the Ghost gone. It were an idle speculation to question if she found sorrow in the work imposed upon her or self-assumed, — she was flown with her battalia to assist his other enemy.

As his languid eyes opened, and he slowly received perception. of what he saw, Miriam, sitting at a low table with her needle, seemed as much an apparition as all things else; and again he suffered the weary lids to fall. But she had seen the

22 *

glance, and rising with her sweet smile, came toward him, moistened his lips with the cordial, rearranged the pillows while the physician raised him, welcomed him back to life with low happy tones; and as he raised his eyes again, met them with so kind a gaze, so pitying, so tender, that his faint heart trembled in his throat.

Some change he felt in her nevertheless; what, he could not trouble himself to find, but a happy one; and at all events, she was here, she was real, the Ghost would never display her in this guise. It was St. Denys, too, entering now, frank, warmhearted, rejoicing, reassuring him, and bringing smiles to his pale lips. He was right, he said to himself; he knew Miriam would free him. Too weak to be glad, he only felt the vacancy left around him, as one dwelling on the coast misses, when travelling inland, the measured beat upon the rocks, the distant whisper of the surf along the sand. But with these brief hints of the Ghost, his heart beat so hotly that, life now again invaluable, he was forced to cease all thought and abandon himself to the luxury of repose, of receiving care, of seeing Miriam.

Day by day now brought returning strength,

health flowed back in its old channels, he sat up several hours. During this halcyon period, Miriam read to him what was to be found,—a task that perhaps she would not have chosen to please herself alone, reading just light enough to beguile his mind, while the musical accent soothed his ear; or recited, in the twilight, pastorals slipping along a stream of smooth vowels, that she had picked up somewhere in her wanderings, or ballads whose breath was a lengthened sigh,—recited them, till from their dim and tearful atmosphere she seemed only to have taken shape for the nonce. She surrounded him with sweet-smelling flowers, served his dainty diet with a fastidious grace peculiar to herself, ransacked her brain for devices against monotony. Always she had a treasury of sparkling gossip on which to draw, till judging he had heard enough. She imparted health as a heated iron imparts caloric.

Before long she ceased to be with him so much, and very soon Sir Rohan found means to descend to the drawing-room for a part of every day. Then with St. Denys they drove out in the open evergreen glades of the park, imbibing health, though scarcely equal strength, from the sweet resinous perfume that loaded the air, where the sun had lain all day on the pines, more richly than that of orange-groves. Or in the clear mornings Miriam drove him into the neighboring town, where the gay colors and voices, the bustle and merriment, consequent on the autumn fairs, pleased him like a child, and full of jokes and glee he assisted in the shopping, and manifested the airy sportfulness of a boy, relapsing into completest fatigue after the first draught of exhilaration. It was soon decided that, when able to travel, he should return with his guests to Kent, spending the winter there ; and meanwhile, for a man thus palpitating from recent misery, this was bliss enough.

Autumn now was at its height. The woods of beech and elm had burned themselves away like the funeral pyre of Summer, the oaks were yet brown, and the sky a perfect blue full of softer shades round the horizon. With Miriam by his side, Sir Rohan, believing himself almost restored, enjoyed the air, the quiet, when one afternoon Arundel was announced. Before he greeted the others, by more than a familiar nod, he walked toward Sir Rohan.

"It was a great liberty I took, sir," he said, in

a low tone. "I most truly beg your pardon. I hope you will believe that if I had been myself such conduct would n't have transpired. And if you still desire it, am ready to afford you the satisfaction demanded, although I can't but trust you think better of it, and will number me among your friends."

"Point device!" said Miriam.

Sir Rohan shook his extended hand warmly, forgetting everything in his present moods.

"I have satisfaction enough," he replied, "in returning health, and my friends are not so many that such an addition is unacceptable."

But hardly were the words spoken, when the scene in the woods rushed upon his recollection. He colored and bit his lip. After all,— who knew? —Arundel might not have fired; Sir Rohan would give him the benefit of the doubt. Meantime, the wily lawyer was proceeding with volubility.

"I have been waiting more impatiently than you will believe, for this opportunity of offering apologies," he returned, "ever since my trip to the North; and I am pleased to find you so much better than I expected;" saying which, he turned to salute his relative and Miriam.

"Since I couldn't go, you came, St. Denys," he said, "the very person I was wishing to see. You must allow me to congratulate you on your excellent management of invalids. You should take out letters overt for the art."

"That palm, Marc, must be laid at Miss Miriam's feet."

"O, she is a perfect Hygieia, begging her pardon for the heathenism," he rejoined. — "But strength is needed, Sir Rohan," he added, returning to the charge. "You remind me of the prayer of an old Methodist friend of mine, for his dissolute son: 'O Lord, take my son John and shake him over—' a place I 'd mention if your polite ears were not here, Miss Miriam, — 'but, O Lord, hold on thy grip!' And I should say the Lord had taken the wrong person."

"An old story, Mr. Arundel," said Miriam, laughing. "I was boasting once to Sir Rohan of your historical powers, but this seems rather of the lyric order."

"So! Are we never to sing truce?"

"O that 's no matter! But when will you tell us something to make our hair stand on end, as Nell and Nan say? Something really tingling

with terror ?   You 've been up at the North ?
Then certainly you have picked up a new story."

"And you want to hear one, Miss Miriam ?"

" Yes."

" Well, as a price of peace, when the evenings
are longer, and I have untied the last knot in my
last case, I will tell you the story of 'that.   It will
be well worth your while."

" I am very glad to be at peace, Mr. Arundel,"
Miriam said, smiling.

" And how do your farms do without you, St.
Denys ? " said he, approaching him.

" Very well, I fancy; they are used to the experiment.   It will not be long, though; we hope
to take Sir Rohan with us for a season."

Arundel was slightly surprised.   " Indeed ! " he
exclaimed.   " Is Kent more salubrious than —"

" O no.   But it is a change; and then it is time
Miriam went more into society, — her kingdom has
waited long enough for its Queen.   And while she
is dancing round I 've no notion of sitting alone.
Perhaps you will come too, Marc," he added, with
an effort.

"You credit me with fine remembrance.   No,
it 's impossible.   I can't leave home again till
spring."

Miriam had said to herself, when he was speaking with Sir Rohan, "So Judas kissed his Master;" but now, on the contrary, she was actually pleased with him. "He was quite bearable," she declared afterward; "apologized for an affront, promised a story, and refused to go to Kent!" And perhaps if she had thought on the subject a moment longer, she would have joined, from mere good-nature, in St. Denys's invitation.

"You are indefatigable, Mr. Arundel," said Sir Rohan.

"Success requires it. But while you are here, St. Denys, I am at your service."

This was more than St. Denys had asked, but he thought there were certain reasons for feeling more kindly than usual toward Arundel, and therefore would have replied urbanely, had not Sir Rohan himself thanked him for his offer, — judging that the attempt upon St. Denys would not be repeated, even if that whole morning were not a madness. It is a peculiarity of those who deal with unreal things, that they soon are incapable of distinguishing the true. Moreover, Sir Rohan indistinctly felt St. Denys to be safer in the open society of Arundel, where there could be fewer opportunities of ambush; and now that Miriam's fortune was probably secured, there could be less motive.

"With only a convalescent as companion, and in so gloomy a house," said he, "my friends will have to call too largely on their inner sunshine."

"That is one of the inexhaustible things," replied Miriam. "The more you use it, the more there is of it."

"Nevertheless, Miss Miriam," said Arundel, "you do not illustrate your assertion. Where is all your gayety gone, — 'Quips and cranks and wanton wiles'? Your spirits are as still now as they were exuberant a year ago."

"Not spirits, but manners; one is not so happy when boisterous," she returned.

But at Arundel's remark, Sir Rohan threw his searching glance at Miriam, to question if it were a fact. True, he had himself observed, that her ways were more quiet than before, that only now and then the blithe roysterer broke from a cloud of mild proprieties, that the once sudden angles of her motions had rounded themselves into curves of a slow grace; she scarcely spoke so much, nor was her laugh so loud, nor was it always to be known which way she went, as formerly, by her scattered properties. But her brow was clear, her smile sweet; no, it was not change, but development. Do we not always accumulate — so slowly, so gradually, that the process seems imperceptible — emotions and experiences for a new phase of life, and wait for some sudden event to give them crystallization or destiny? So it had been with Miriam, he thought; and so, while away from him, she had passed in a beautiful efflorescence from child to woman. She seemed to him too rich in some real happiness, to bubble up with an effervescence of joyousness. She had reached the first period of self-consciousness, a period as full of bliss as of pain. The heir apparent to so regal bounty, as this perfect creature must be, need not hasten to assume her crown and display the dazzle of its gems, he thought.

"Moreover," resumed Miriam, a little aside, to Marc, while he thus meditated, "I may be triflingly stunned by your agreeability."

"Ah? I did not think of claiming any share in so delightful a transformation."

"Now you are going to be rude, Mr. Arundel!" she said, half pouting.

Arundel looked at her a moment with a peculiar expression, then, without replying, startled Sir Rohan by exclaiming, "Half-past four! Do you ever dine here, or do you live on the ambrosia of—. I must bid you good morning, Sir Rohan. I shall see you soon again, St. Denys."

"Once in a while we dine," said Sir Rohan. "Will you stay and try potluck? It would give us much pleasure."

"Why, no, sir; but let me hope that at some other time I may, Arab fashion, eat your salt." And he turned to go, first exchanging a few low words with St. Denys.

XIV.

MIRIAM'S KINGDOM.

MIRIAM had slipped from the room, but as Arundel stepped into the hall he heard her light footfall, and in a moment more was beside her again.

"I brought you this bouquet, Miss Miriam," he said, notwithstanding he could see the overflowing greenhouse as he stood, "and was so ungallant as to forget about it. It is faded now, yet perhaps you will take it;" and he offered it with a glance and gesture that broadly told of a heart offered anew with it.

Miriam hesitated a moment, then receiving them, said, "Thank you for your flowers."

"And the heart goes for nothing?" he exclaimed.

"No, no, Marc, do not speak so; you know we are to be friends."

"Friends! I don't want your friendship, — I ask for your love!"

"Love would not be worth taking, without the other."

"Miriam, how long must I serve? Could you ask for more constancy? Love will come, once sealed by marriage."

"Marriage is too divine a sacramental bread to be broken between us," she said.

"Marriage is n't a sacrament in our church," he retorted.

"Not a sacrament, but too frequently on one side a sacrifice."

"Then you won't be my wife? I need n't ask, I see; you 've your old answers pat. But they 're all false; only this one true — you love him — him! But he never shall have you," he added in a lower yet fiercer tone. "Your words can be his ruin; it hangs on you. See! I never will ask again. Refuse me now, and it is forever!"

A quick, angry answer leaped to Miriam's lip and flashed in her eye; but something taught her that if the man loved he suffered, and repressing it, she only said pleadingly, —

"Don't make me angry, Marc."

He turned upon his heel as if to go, but retracing his steps, came and bent toward her face. Miriam sprang back indignantly, then heard his short laugh, as he exclaimed, —

"Ha! ha! we should do capitally on the boards. No two better actors in the kingdom. If St. Denys should die and leave you unprovided for, I'd advise you to try it!" and before the wrath that overwhelmed her could find expression, he was gone. His last coarse words, she saw, had betrayed him. It was St. Denys's money, not his ward, he wooed. He should have it all.

Yet a year afterward, — when she heard that Arundel, still doubtless on his way weaving snares for others, was himself caught in one that forced him to seek safety in emigration, where, with an ocean between them, she was never again to be troubled by his sight or influence, — Miriam did not regret that words had failed her on this occasion.

Meanwhile, within the drawing-room, St. Denys, as Arundel went out, looked up and surveyed his companion from head to foot.

"For Heaven's sake, Rohan," he said, "why

are you not like ordinary men, and twenty years younger?"

"Things without remedy should be without regard," sadly quoted the other.

"I wonder if I am doomed to mistrust that man continually? He seemed to you very affable this afternoon?"

"Yes, very."

"And I have always observed him so, when most pleased at any piece of mischief he has in hand. Before this spider spins his toils round her, my friend," continued St. Denys, somewhat cautiously, "why not win and marry my little girl?" This proposal he made with the air of one ashamed of himself, as an Englishman would barter a Circassian.

"Impossible!" ejaculated Sir Rohan, looking at him with wonder, and now that his own wish was urged by another, summoning every reason to oppose it. "I am wedded to an inexorable past."

St. Denys seemed confounded an instant. "You are speaking figuratively?" said he then.

"I mean that I will not poison your 'little girl's' existence by the shadow of my own."

"I hardly comprehend you. But if Death has ever brought you a sorrow such as it brought me, I cannot imagine where a dearer consolation is to be found than mine, than Miriam. You love her now. And as for the poison,—pshaw! She was never so gay as in your house."

"Do you know that I think I must have been mad awhile ago, if not a great portion of my life?"

"More mad now, if you persist."

"I beg you not to mention the thing to her. If unconscious, let her remain without making me abhorrent by such an idea."

"Don't slander my friend, if you please. And remember that, since you cannot be improved, nothing would give me more happiness. Try."

"I am ill and old."

"How old are you, Rohan?"

"Forty."

"A vast age! and I a lustre more. What gray-beards!"

"I wonder why," said Sir Rohan after a pause, "you cherish this romantic friendship for me. I do nothing to deserve it, all to forfeit it; and after sleeping twenty years, it is all at once bright as ever."

" It has not slept twenty years. What use is it to recall our boyhood, I should like to know ? We were friends then. I could not have been living but for you, Rohan ; and after that, had we any games, studies, or thoughts but in common, till you left me ? Who had ever more morbid weaknesses corrected by another than I by you ? I owe infinite sums to your courage, your friendship. You don't forget it, though you have buried yourself alive. How can I ? "

" And can you look at me with clear eyes, and fail to see that I should make her miserable ? "

" Certainly I fail to see it."

" Then why do you wish me changed ? "

" Checkmated ! Why, sir, that you may fill a young lady's ideal."

" And you think that possible ? "

" Perhaps I ought to ask if she fills yours."

" You should remember that I have no ideal."

" My child, indeed, has had no mother," said St. Denys, apologetically, — " has wanted for all feminine instruction, and lacks a little that unbroken dignity of the thorough lady ; but — "

" She is the freer from artificiality therefore ; the rarer, richer," interrupted Sir Rohan.

"You think it? Then why not follow my advice, — win her?"

"By God's help, I will!" Sir Rohan was about to say. But what right had he who had broken law to require help? It was an obstacle not to be destroyed, so he turned his back upon it. "As I live, I will," he said.

St. Denys took his hat and stepped upon the terrace, in search of Redruth, the glamour of friendship still sealing his eyes; and Sir Rohan, with beating heart, waited an instant before opening the door and unexpectedly confronting Miriam.

She stood where Arundel had left her at the foot of the staircase, one hand upon the balustrade, the other hanging by her side, with drooping head and sidelong glance, absorbed in reverie. At his advance, she started, and caught her foot in the heavy mat. He bent to disentangle it, and as he rose with the flush of stooping on his face, said simply, " St. Denys says we must leave soon. When I return, shall it be alone? Will you come with me, Miriam?"

She hardly knew what he said ; her mind was not yet clear from the storm Arundel had aroused.

Ire, to be thus addressed again and so soon, renewed the confusion, and with a curling lip she sprung past him up the stairs and into her own apartment.

Yet once there, her face sunk into her hands. What had she said? What had she done? Had he asked her to return with him? How? As his wife? Yes, yes. But was it true, what that wretch had said? Did she love him — Did she not love him? "O my heart!" she cried, as it rushed over her, "is it too late?" And impetuously as she had entered the room, she left it.

But at the first step a sentiment, totally new, routed her; — a timidity, a shame, a doubt; — and more and more slowly she descended, till standing in the selfsame attitude at the foot again.

Sir Rohan remained, according to his custom when suddenly excited, as the blow struck him, upright, motionless, and frozen one might say, but for a scarlet dye upon his cheek. The hush about him was like that preceding some explosion, when every breath seems drawn into stillness. He appeared not to notice her as she stood there, till at last, as unreasonably, he turned slowly toward the beautiful face bathed in tears, the great eyes raised a moment to his, full of love. He stooped forward, his breath swept her cheek, his lips touched hers, grew to them, in a passionate daring. Then, as wildly, he tore them off, and commenced walking the hall.

How long she waited, paled and flushed alternately in uncertainty, hope, and fear, Miriam did not know. She abode like a culprit, while her sentencer measured the tiles with his stride. The great tongue of the clock struck six, and only with its resonant clangor did his step cease.

" Miriam, Miriam," he murmured like one in a dream, " do you love me ? "

" You know I do, Sir Rohan," she answered pathetically.

She felt him draw near, though she dared not see, — felt his ardent smile, his outstretched arms, the embrace with which they held her ; and silently, Miriam had found her costly kingdom.

And for Sir Rohan, — all things were swallowed in the fruition of the moment. Life was sweet, he said ; rest and joy. Life was Miriam.

XV.

THE TWO.

THE next week to Sir Rohan passed in a delirious rapture; every hour with its blessings
repaid him for a year's pain; and Miriam, crown-
ing his ecstasy to-day with her sweet gravity, to-
morrow with a triumph of wild and overflowing
gayety, filled him at first with keen delight, and
then with an alarm as exquisite, lest some sudden
sorrow should fall and quench the flame. In her
felicity he believed as fully as in his own.

St. Denys, glad as and more hilarious than
they, left the lovers by themselves, and made
arrangements for their departure, whose day he
finally fixed.

When Sir Rohan considered his happiness, it
appeared too great a thing to be true; and if Miriam left his side for a time, he feared lest it should
prove some illusion that would shortly refuse to

deceive him. He felt himself again in the vernal flood of youth, and cast not a thought on the dark tide between, for

> " True love hath no powre
> To looken backe; his eies be fixt before."

As for Miriam, she was more glowing, more radiant, than a Mænad. Her eyes flashed vivid lightnings all day; existence was to her like a sculptured frieze, a perpetual scene of never-varying enjoyment. The contrast which they presented was that between a picture blazing with gorgeous Venetian tints and another abounding only in quiet cinereous colors and stern outlines; but his tranquillity was as grateful to her as cool draughts from a rocky well to one in midsummer. Her life was full of salient points, each one beaked in sunshine. He was still and grave: she needed toning down. Their difference in age exceeded twenty years; nevertheless, he was still young, and that was all she was. At least, so Miriam felt.

As St. Denys saw them thus together, he remembered that in the midst of the fierce August heats that brood over a languishing land and sting out the red bells and pricking growth of later summer, there sometimes comes a day that scents the fresh stir of advancing autumn, the clear air washing a cool retiring blue with frosty sparkles of vigor and hope, and all the earth turning, as it seems, to a new phase of fine and sweet maturity.

One asks what is this love that never palls, that, shift the kaleidoscope as you will, presents a new configuration. It must be the universal sympathy alone, you answer, which will not suffer it to tire. About ambition, jealousy, and crimes, the world varies; that age demands a good hater, this repudiates him. But Love is the flower of every age, and foreign to no clime. Is it any fable, the flower-juice dropped on sleeping lids? Is it not, rather, the fanciful expression of a broad truth? In what subtle atmosphere do lovers move, that, once breathed, intoxicates with all imaginative freaks of infatuation? What delicate ether is it that creeps from heart to heart to bathe both in one medium? Whence come the threads that knit each to the caprices of the other's slavery? What lodestone, what cynosure, with all magnetic secrets and latent force, equals the fearful and delicious attraction that draws either soul into eternal subjection and revolution. We know the secrets of the earth's magnetism, her currents, her poles, her meridians ; we know nothing of this airy evanescence that flees at a glance, and baffles all our ponderous pursuit, yet swings a planet at its will, and is the Viceroy of creation. What wise magician shall ever come to read the ancient and mystical book of its lore, text and commentary, to translate to us the strangest of familiar things, the simplest of enchantments, the most terrible of blisses — to tell us what is Love. It is the crown of all experience, say its prophets. It is a fulness, an imperial largess from overflowing spirits, a wealth of joy like generous sunlight, a strength, a glory, an aureole, say its devotees. It is a void, a need, a pain, say its victims. And those who stand without, who see the dance and do not hear the music, — what more weird fantastic folly, the madness of the saturnalia, the sacred fury of eleusinian or evantian choir, ever dawns upon their dazzled darkness !

What drew these two (of whom the story tells) together, what made of them a single creature, with one wish, one thought, one life, nothing clearly defines ; but no rod of divination is needed to detect the kindred quality of each. A stream that runs its melancholy race in dark, subterranean caverns, is no less the same when it bursts to light above in joyous flashes filled with the sun so long denied,—no less it falls from its brilliant frolic and flows on quietly to the great sea beyond.

In any unseen vase of flowers we discriminate the odors, and there is honeysuckle, we think, that mignonette, this sweetbrier. But that of two oriental coronations — no more nor less than twin garden pinks — with its ineffable spice of clove and cassia, who thinks of separating? The two do not emit different rays of perfume, but slipping into each other, form one. They are the same thing. What else were Sir Rohan and Miriam? And what more frail and perishable than their unsupported happiness?

I linger a moment over these few brief days, days marred by nothing, days coming but once. They have for me that fragrance of a book where I have pressed a rose, and a shade of soft sadness always tinges such in the remembrance,—it may be, like an attraction of opposite poles. And thus the image of Miriam, resplendent in loveliness, bathed in wafts of light and grace, a flowery thing

24 *

of smiles and joy, standing in the dark halls of the gray old house, beneath the stone heraldic cope,—if seen through this magic lens that mellows all the landscape and imparts a golden air, borrows from it also that pathos which distance and excessive beauty give.

XVI.

IN THE LANES.

ONE morning shortly after this event, the gentlemen were walking to and fro in the shrubbery. There had been no frost yet, but the dew lay in tiny globes on the broad leaves as if shivering and clustering for company. To them came Miriam, in a daintiness of morning costume but recently indulged.

"Papa," said she, "I wish I could talk slang."

"My dear, I don't find you deficient there."

"I expected that! But I mean jockey slang, so that I could challenge Sir Rohan to a race over the downs, in real sporting phrase. It's so clear and breezy, and would do him such worlds of good!"

"I take up the glove without the accomplishment," said Sir Rohan, "and back Pharo against the Benshee at any odds."

"Will you make a book, papa?"

"Not I!" St. Denys returned. "It would be difficult to decide where the most money were to be lost."

"O, I don't know. The Benshee has n't been out this season. You rode Pharo to the hunt last week, I did n't hear that you checked the hounds though. It will be rather stupid for so old a hunter as Sir Rohan to ride without anything ahead, to kill, that is; but then my hat is killing, and he will always have that before him."

"Like certain Easterns then, I ride for a bride. Don't flatter yourself with hopes of escape!" said Sir Rohan.

"So at the best of it," she laughed, "when you catch me, you catch a Tartar."

"Well, little one," said St. Denys, "you seem to have attained your object without too much slang, though I have my doubts if your opponent can do more than swing in his saddle just now. What put that particular branch of education into your head?"

"Oh! Don't you know? There are some gypsies somewhere across the moor, real north country people, and they talk slang, of course. And one of them, papa," she added, lowering her voice, "the housekeeper says, was hung in London, a little while ago, for something he did on the way here; and they are very angry about it. How they wander round! Do you suppose they came down to see the land's end?"

"An old woman, belonging to them, was here last night," said Sir Rohan. "Did n't she speak with you?"

"Yes. She was talking with the maids, and I went out and crossed her palm. But she was very odd. She only muttered some gibberish — slang, maybe — and threw my hand up to my face, looked at me a minute, and whispered, 'So you think you 'll marry him, the pale villain yon. Toss it away, you won't. You are one of us.'"

"Miriam, — she did n't say that?" asked Sir Rohan.

"Truly! Who cares? I should like to see her forbid the banns!" said she.

"Saucy Miriam! where are your blushes?" exclaimed St. Denys. Whereupon, the breakfast-bell ringing, she ran away.

In an hour or two, at Sir Rohan's direction, Pharo and the Benshee appeared in the avenue, and very shortly, side by side, with their riders, they were finding their way up the long field. Before them a fence reared itself, with a lofty gate which Sir Rohan rode forward to open.

"Not that way, Sir Rohan!" cried Miriam, and making a short turn, the Benshee took it like a bird, and flew along the other side with the speed of a racer. In a moment Pharo followed, thundering close behind. Miriam turned in her saddle to see, then shook loose her reins and flew on. The Benshee was thorough-bred, and exhilarated with her new freedom and kindled by the pursuer, covered the ground well; and though Miriam was a light weight and a light hand, and though she spanned an ugly gap kicking the dirt into Pharo's eyes, she could not rid herself of him, or put more than that distance between them. A naughty glee was in Miriam's heart, she wondered how one could be happier than swinging through the air with such a lordly swiftness, drank in great draughts of the fresh air, and inwardly staked every hope she had in life on keeping foremost.

A lane with rough fences here intersected the course; if they turned down the fields, Pharo would certainly lead ; Miriam determined to take the fence, badly as it looked,—and ignorant of what might be beyond, giving the Benshee head, she rode straight upon it. Sir Rohan called to her in vain ; she pointed forward with her whip, and dashed on. The top of many Cornish fences is flat and broad, so that one usually walks upon them,—and suddenly a peasant, with a bundle of fagots on his head, started into view as he slowly rose to pursue his way. The Benshee saw this apparition, swerved aside, reared and plunged, and then, before Miriam knew what had happened, bounded across with such a leap that she thought she would never light, and shot like a whirlwind through the miry lane, round a sharp curve into a by-way, over a gate and field that opposed her, till she found herself in another lane, where, putting down her head, heedless of curb and snaffle, first showing a wicked eye, she flung out her flanks with a quiver, and used a pace that only fright and her previous excitement could have aroused.

Daunted in the first heat, and then resolved on conquering, Miriam kept her seat, knowing the speed could not last ; but at length having taken a stony ascent at a gallop and raced down like an arrow, the Benshee closed as unexpectedly as she had opened her career, and stood trembling, flecked in foam, with hanging head and starting eye. Miriam alighted, loosened the girth, caressed and stroked the animal, using all her limited means to aid it, and dreadfully afraid, even in her pity, that she would lie down and leave her solitary among the moors. Sir Rohan had followed, to be sure, but then he had not been able to put Pharo to a speed anything like that of the Benshee's, and in the bewildering turns and ways followed since, he had lost all track of her, while if she did not succeed in finding the homeward path, she had the prospect of spending the night in the lanes.

Finally she dared to remount and advance very slowly, hesitating long as to which of the two ways that now diverged before her she should choose. She trusted the Benshee, who took the sinister one. It led into deeper and deeper dells, and deceitful sloughs. Hoping it would open on some fairer way she continued to proceed, while the day drew near close, darkness falling round her; and to add to her discomfiture, a drizzling rain set in that brought the night with it. Still she jogged on, till at last completely at a loss, in a thick gloom, with a wet wind blowing in her face, the Benshee stopped.

Miriam was not easily discouraged; but now, after a moment, she bent down to shut out her thoughts, her heart sinking within her. All at once, the wind seemed to be rolled away, and some of the darkness. The Benshee shook and started in terror; something led her, and they went lightly forward. Miriam could see nothing, she was more alarmed than ever, drooping masses of hair like threaded air seemed to sweep her forehead, she fancied an icy breath licked her cheek, and only cowered closer to the living creature beneath. They emerged into a broader, smoother way, where the wind puffed back, the airy hair, the breath, were gone, and the Benshee sped along as in the day. Far ahead, Miriam now saw a light that burned steadily, while lesser ones danced round it. Anon she lost it, or saw it fainter, and when the Benshee slackened her pace again, she was not many feet distant. Pausing now under the lee of an untrimmed hedge, she found herself in a small hollow quite thickly wooded. One or two carts were tilted around in odd positions, and a rude tent occupied the foreground. There might be others among the trees, but in the faint light cast from the red embers whose flames had been extinguished by the rain, she was not able to discern them. From the tent, voices harsh and low proceeded, but the words were some incomprehensible jargon. Now and then, Miriam thought she heard a more familiar tone, and was at no loss to conclude that she had blundered upon the gypsy encampment. Home, then, lay across the moor, but at which point of the compass? And how could she reach it, with not even a stone to go by? The voices rose within the tent.

"Not a penny," said the familiar one. "Mind you! I don't pay a farthing. *He* 'll hand over the hush-money, — enough to buy you a farm apiece in Mesopotamia."

Angry unknown words were here interposed, followed by a lusty English oath from the former speaker. "To be sure he will!" said he. "You 've nothing to do but threaten disclosure of what you saw, and what the old woman told you. What good will that do you? Stupid

oufes! What did I bring you down from beyond the Lord-knows-where for, but that? And
now you 're here you 'll be quiet; come to the
sea-side for your health, and go back when the
season 's over! And you won't make him pay
yellower gold, because, on your way, Tiny
was—"

Here a chorus of wild articulations interrupted
him, for he seemed to have referred to the man
who was hung.

"Good!" he said, when the angry tumult
had a little subsided. "I thought the people of
the North Countree had more fire than that, and
so I find it."

"You may find it to your cost, brother," said
one, in his own tongue. "Now, to waste no
more palaver, what must be done?"

"Waiting. Is that laconic enough? There 's
one witness yet. I must have the old chap
swear to what I learned from him; for if it
should have been just drunken raving, I 'm all
up a tree; poor fellow, it was n't much—"

Here the gypsies, from the clatter, appeared to
be impatient. "Then I shall come for you," he
added, as if waking from a little reverie, "and
you can go in and win."

Other words followed, from which the speaker seemed to gather an unfavorable import.

"You 'll forestall me?" he said. "Try it! that 's all. And you 'll lose the whole. Perhaps he will pay you for silence after you 've told! Do you think I profit by this? Not a haporth. I get the girl, and hers, as I told you, and what 's more, chew a sweet morsel, you know yourselves, a revenge. But it 's late. I 'll go — when your word passes that you 'll bide my time."

Here succeeded a long consultation in that other tongue, interspersed with now and then a bit of English, all which must have been the identical slang wherein Miriam had longed to be a proficient. At last, the stormy voices silenced themselves, and one took up the tale.

"We do as you bid, brother. But hark ye! You fail us, — we donnot fail you. And should we get no share of yon gold, we look to you. And we mun have it though we rob your heart's blood for it! Good night, brother."

The tent curtain lifted, and two or three stooped out into the night; one, an old woman whose voice proclaimed her the recent speaker, with a torch that hissed and spluttered in the rain and flared with the wind. As she held it up, the light fell on the departing guest, and Miriam found him to be, as she had at first surmised, Arundel. The old woman lighted him as he climbed the hollow, till he was lost on the land above, and then returned, sparkling the torch on an evil-looking tatterdemalion who stood with her; on a gypsy girl who held a baby to her breast and peered from the tent with bright black eyes that had the same wild glint, a speck of white fire, that Miriam's owned; and on her own wrinkled yellow face, picturesque rags, and long, torn gray hair. Just as she was disappearing within, the unaccountable Benshee gave a low whinny. The hag cried to her companion, in their own tongue, and turned quickly toward the hedge.

"What'n have we here?" she said, hanging over it, and swinging the torch round the head of the dazzled girl. "Aha! the young Leddy o' Castle Sin Denys! Service to you. A fine night for a gallop, the dew just falling. Ye come such sweet weather for a better fortune? We're none of the elle-folk who dance in the hills and weave fates, ye mun go to them for that. Maybe ye 'd know what makes you one of us? Ye've the wild-fire in your eye, child! Ye'll know soon enough!" Here the hag bent lower, and assuming a leer, extended her palm. "Ye cannot thread the lanes with yellow boys about you. A little charity, dear Leddy," she whined. But at the same instant snatched it away, and hit the Benshee a crack that made her rear upright. "Ye listen at a man's door? Go along with you!" she said, and the beast flew like a ball of fire. Miriam caught the pommel in her shock, and fled fast, hardly knowing which she dreaded most, the fierce gallop in the dark, or the gypsy man breaking over the hedge.

In a mile or two the Benshee relaxed her speed, and soon fell into a trot that she gently ended by standing stubbornly still. It seemed in vain to urge her; Miriam dismounted again, and as well as she could see, led her along in hopes to find some place where she could hitch the bridle, and lie down herself. At last a narrow path opened on the right; she ventured to follow it, and soon found by the slow ascent that she was on the moor. But here she was as good as lost, and after an hour's forlorn wandering, as much from exhaustion as despair she put her arms round the

Benshee's neck and burst into tears. Suddenly the Benshee raised her head, with her pawing feet warned the girl to retire, and by her tremor seemed to recognize some one's approach. Miriam spoke soothingly through her sobbing, but in the next moment caught herself the tramp of hoofs crushing the heath, and clung to the companionable thing for safety. Far, far away, quite at the other end of the moor it seemed to her, she heard a voice call — Miriam! Faint and thin it sounded in her swooning ears; she doubted could she make her reply audible. "Here I am!" she thought she cried like a trumpet; but it was only a murmur, and her head sunk again upon the bent neck of the Benshee. Home, with its fires and lights and comforts, the smiles, the dear voices — one of which she dreamed to have heard just now — was further away than ever, — was lost; she herself might die; all that love, that joy, was lost too. She was sinking on the ground, when an arm caught her waist, strong and tender; passionate lips called her life back to answer them; and lifted a moment in the air, she lay then in Sir Rohan's arms, while mounted on Pharo weary from his day-long search, and leading the Benshee, they trotted slowly and joyfully homeward down the moor.

XVII.

WHETHER OR NO.

MIRIAM lost and found, was dearer now than ever. Dismayed at the chances that might have befallen, he could scarcely endure her out of his sight. Loving, previously, had been like living or breathing; now, it was a positive thing, another existence; and so precious did it seem, that analyzing, he began to entertain a jealousy of it.

He knew very well that he always borrowed tone from the nature that had influenced him last and strongest. Thus when his Ghost was his sole companion, he had been fit for such intimacy; afterward, he had taken St. Denys's genial calm; and now when Miriam, dancing and iridescent as a foam-flake, met and overpowered him with her exuberant life, he was sentient of wearing the same hues in which she beamed. So that, in fact, she unconsciously saw herself mirrored in him, and with a natural self-love was attracted toward the image. An apotheosis of self-love, truly; but then, thought Sir Rohan, what more is any other love? And is not its design and use, perhaps, for the highest development of personality? Those, then, who have loved, — loved in the mad flames that burn away dross and leave the bare edge of self-consciousness welded with that of another, — those may die.

As a corollary to this idea, not long subsequently a strange fantasy seized him. Floating with Miriam in his boat, one sail stretched through light and shade, down a small river that he had not navigated for years, and rocking in mid-channel on the broad oily swells of the receding tide, that, compared to the crisp wavelets nearer shore, surrounded them like fields of calm, he suddenly found himself drifting in a current that ran swiftly out among the breakers at the river's mouth, glimpses of whose white plumes he already caught tossing in glee over their approaching prey. The little boat, once among them, would be staved to atoms, wave after wave dashing against it; the strongest swimmer would only be gored and impaled upon those cruel rocks; while with the effort to free himself, one oar snapped, and he saw it sucked along far in advance. In the midst of his strenuous exertions with the remaining one, he paused to gaze on the unconscious girl, suffering the boat to drift onward, and thinking were it not better both together now to plunge into the vortex of eternity, than that he at some future day, meeting a stronger influence, should cease to reflect her nature, to represent her startling characteristics; should reassume himself, — though still cherishing her tenderly, — and she, finding the pleasing likeness no longer there, should cease to bestow her love upon that which, having held it, was now to her vacant. A thing, he felt, that might be as natural for her, as for a queen to put on and take off the crown.

It was not he that experienced change, but circumstance that conquered him; yet she — change was half her beauty. But while he balanced life and chances, Time was meddling with the weights, and the boat settling downward; and still he gazed at the one whose moments he was numbering, shuddered at the gaunt image of a day destitute of her devotion, and thrilled at the delirious draught of death that it was theirs to quaff in youth should they choose. He knew the wild moment of fear that would snatch her heart away at first; but he also pictured the returning passion when, absorbed in him, she sank down the great gulfs of darkness, while, even should' there be no hereafter, they almost eternized this love by its dying strength, soul closing with soul.

But in this instance, as in others, the instinct for life exceeded the reasoning power, and Sir Rohan, after a struggle, made the shallower water once more, and following the windings of the stream, reached their starting-point at last, in the shades of his unfrequented park, scattering the deer who had trooped to drink in the quiet pools of its lazier flow.

It was not, however, an agreeable conclusion that had forced itself upon him, — that the moment he ceased to present in himself the image of Miriam, she would transfer her love to its next shrine, — nor was it fealty to her. Neither was it pleasant to find himself no relief — no cameo — but merely a vacuum where other and more glowing individualities painted themselves. Yet after all, he believed Death would come to him sooner than loss of love.

In short, it was probably provoking that he had no longer a subject for annoyance.

XVIII.

REDRUTH SURRENDERS HIS ACCOUNTS.

A S Sir Rohan announced his journey and the
length of his stay to Redruth, after giving
direction for certain repairs and decorations, he
added, " When I return, Miss Miriam comes with
me. I shall bring my old house a mistress."

Hardly could he repress his smile at the man's
amazement.

"Dear soul!" he said. "Then we 're to have
a Lady, after all. I knew she never came for
naught!" And for the first time, he dared approach his master on the subject of his conduct in
the cellar the day she went away, admitting his
faults and contrition. But he found that it had
already passed from Sir Rohan's mind.

"We 'll forget that, Redruth," said he. "I
may have spoken too harshly; it was of no con-
sequence."

On entering the housekeeper's room, Mr. Redruth found the table spread for tea, and his wife knitting by the fire with her two maids, to whom magisterially he imparted the news.

"Lady Belvidere!" exclaimed Mrs. Redruth. "Pretty creatur! Well, I knew it all along."

"You knew it?"

"What, but that, driv him to his fever?"

"Drove, my dear."

"Well, drove or driv, it 's all one."

"To think of her coming into this nest of ghosts!" said one of the maids. "The poor, orphanless child."

"But she 's laid them all, Nelly. They have n't walked since she came," replied the other.

"Indeed, she 's not, Nan. They 've left master, maybe, — but I see 'em, when I went in with the tray, the other night, round that brisk man, the solicitor, What's-his-name, that comes from abroad. And the head-piece was standing right behind him, with her hands down, meek as — as anything," concluded Nelly, for want of a better simile.

"Well for sure, Nell, you 're a downright simpleton! That was the statute of Venus," said Nan jeeringly.

"Venice! I guess it is n't that we see every evening, all white and blue, swairthing over the flags out there, that puts me all in a fuz! Nor the Walker! It 's not that we hear, whenever the dark falls, come tramp, tramp, tramp, along the hall, with a low whistle of a laugh anent the very door, and then tramp, tramp, off again, and the swish and trail of her long dress following, till back she come with liker a sob, and sweeps the floor all night till cock-crowing, as if the clouds had got into the house and rained steady. It 's so lonely like near the place."

"Master must 'a done somethin' awful once, or some of his kin," whispered Nan, shiveringly.

"Humph! Miss Miriam may say what she choose. No such thing as bugs round here! It comes just as near as a fourpence to a groat, if it an't one. That 's all."

"Now, Nell, maybe we was fools, and frightened at master's ways, and took silly things for spirits. There 's the gypsies, — who knows? Maybe it was bats, or moonshine, or clothes on the line — "

"There 's no line there, and there warn't a moon, the gypsies had n't come, and we know bats when we see 'em. Besides, May-bees don't fly this time o' year, I 've heard say. If we was fools, then I know who was the biggest one, that summer night when they ran in cold as stone, eyes all starting out and black round about, and mouthing, and looking stupid and brutelike! A body was white as a curd then. I would n't crow before —"

"Hist now, girls!" said Mrs. Redruth, for it was getting dark. "I never see none I could n't explain away myself, nor I don't believe you have. Did you, Redruth?"

"Well," answered Redruth, evasively, "a good many years ago, fifteen — sixteen — eighteen years ago, one dark night, I saw a light on the lawn, where the white camellia-bush is, — and there 's nothing whiter than that when the buds are blown; they are like stars in a sky —"

"But the lights?" queried Nell.

"O, it was only one; but dancing round high and low, now here, now there, dancing like mad. I should have said, if it had been anywhere else, they were thieves with a lantern; but it could n't be that, you know. One would n't need a lantern to pick the blossoms, though they did look a little soiled next day, and the earth was a little loose round the tree; but that might have been the rain, — it rained before light."

"Pshaw, Redruth, it was fireflies! There, we'll quit the matter, and say no more about it!" Whereupon, Mrs. Redruth, snatching her ball from the kitten, proceeded to make tea, and the maids to speculate about the master and his bride.

But after a few moments Redruth rose and left the gossiping conclave. He felt ill, he said to himself, ill and numb, and must take something to send a shiver over him. The old steward's remedies always lay in the cellar, and thither, with a long glass, he betook himself.

Mr. Redruth's family from father to son had, for many generations, held much such a position as he did; and living a somewhat idle and luxurious life, had transmitted to the last weak offshoot of their race, not, indeed, titles and escutcheons, but a certain inheritance not liable to be lessened by superintendence of his master's wines. And if great dynasties run rankly, at last, to insanity, and my lord plumes himself upon his father's gout, — if all hereditary traits imply some honorable distinction,—I do not know why Mr. Redruth might not boast that no ancestor of his had ever died but with palsy. Yet so thoroughly had this family identified themselves with their employers, that it is doubtful if the fact existed among them even as a tradition; they did not tell their children of their own grandfathers, but of their masters'; and though Redruth had often feared this catastrophe for himself, he did not once remember it upon this afternoon. He had, furthermore, an engagement in the neighboring town, in about an hour. Mr. Arundel, who would be there then, had sent for him to swear to the truth of some statement he had made. He did not know what, exactly, but it had troubled and perplexed him greatly during the day, though Sir Rohan's intelligence had excited him in an opposite direction. Moreover, Mr. Redruth was to bring an amaryllis from the town for Miss Miriam, who wanted it in the conservatory, where he had promised her it should be that night; and Mrs. Redruth had ordered a new bonnet — lavender and straw — which he was to obtain; and he believed he would consult a physician, while . there, on the subject of this faintness.

As Mr. Redruth locked the cellar door and hung the key in its place, the conservatory attracted him, as, once before, it had attracted Miriam; and quite forgetting the long glass still in his hand, he entered it, and seated himself carefully in the chair of Madeira wood. It was just after sunset; the honeysuckles, scarlet and yellow with berries, were still brilliant as the vivid light could make them, where they climbed the house-wall opposite, and the open roof admitted the cool evening breeze. He did not feel much better here, and resolved to wait a short time before meeting his engagements, while he looked about on the enchantments evoked by his master's fancy, and breathed the exhalations stealing insidiously round him. The light retreated along the wall, ceased sparkling in the glasses of the aerides; the orchids — so full of life in form that he wondered to see them silent — lost one by one their gay hues; the darkness gathered down the alleys and stole upward, leaving nothing in distinctness but the always vague figures of the fountain; heavy perfumes of the nocturnal flowers began to roll through the dusk, and a nightingale to chant his melancholy songs on a spray without.   The breeze fell, a young moon lay low in the sky, and on the floor of the still air strange new scents evolved themselves and danced gently along.   The charm of the hour was perfect.

The myrtle, collecting the dew on its dense masses, faintly impregnated and shook it from white stars glittering in the shade ; the heliotropes drooped purpler, darker, richer, with their most exquisite of atmospheres ; the ophrys, hanging on the cheek of a nectarine like a bee, married that sweetness with its own ; and the odorous jasmine trailed in golden threads over the tempting purple of a ripened redolent fig.   The epidendrum, too, woke into life with the night, and tossed him its fragrance, and, still lingering along the year, rose and lily and violet and passion-flower all turned and blew their gales toward him.

But to these a monarch waved his sceptre. Just above Mr. Redruth's head hung one of the gilded galleries, and over it in riotous profusion the luxuriant vines of a night-blooming cereus suspended its bursting buds.   Already its dark brown sheathing parted ; already the great star within rivalled Hesper in yellow brightness ; already the long snowy petals, sailing calmly back, enhanced its glory, and the multitudinous silky stamens tumbled out in a cataract on the wind of an untold sweetness; opening wider every moment and burdening the whole air with his imperial presence, while by slower culmination others followed in his train. Mr. Redruth watched it for a while in silence; the nightingale still sung, the moon cast a soft lustre through the panes upon the spreading wonder, the floating lilies, the great agave beside him. Flowering once in a hundred years, as the superstition ran, why did the anniversary of this agave come upon this night? Why, sitting there like an old necromancer bound in his own chains, did it draw the little breaths in among its strong leaves, and emit them sickly sweet? — why did a strange stir and intelligence rustle all its sides? — why but that the spell was loosened, and it flowered to-night. With the blossom dies the stem. Swift as when the sun falls into the west the clouds flout their joyous folds, the arrow of fulfilment struck its heart, and it answered with the weird grand blossom, again flinging magic over the world. But cereus and agave were watched with equal silence by Mr.

Redruth ; the solicited events of centuries transpired unnoticed beside him. He felt ill, he thought, and stupid ; how could he reach town in this plight ? And what would Mr. Arundel do then ? And there was the bonnet and the amaryllis ; could he but gain an apothecary, he might be better. The time when he had told Miriam the story of Fanchon crept over his memory ; he half smiled at her false prophecy, but he remembered also, though faintly, that he had drank one day with Arundel in the cellar. What had he said to him ? What had that conversation been ? Let it be as it might, he could not recall it, — but what did Marc Arundel want with his oath to-night ?

O Mr. Redruth ! the lotus floated in its tank within your reach, the nepenthe lifted its brimming pitcher to your lips, the mandragora grew not far away — eat them, and forget !

Things wavered oddly in a kind of haze before Mr. Redruth's eyes ; he trembled excessively. There was Miss Miriam's amaryllis to be got. He must make an effort ; and he essayed to rise. It was Atlas with the world on his shoulder ; efforts were vain, — he did not stir a line. If he could only stand, he thought, he might walk. The place grew dark, and warm as it was, his teeth chattered, he fell back in the chair, still grasping the glass in his hanging hand. The moon shot a fiery tip upon the flowery pendulums in the dome, then withdrew from aloe and cactus, and left all the tropical wealth in a starlit gloom; but Mr. Redruth did not observe it, since it had been dark some time with him. His mind became confused; a doubt crossed it if his stewardship had been faithful, a stinging certainty of evil goaded it. Could that man harm his master? The veriest trifles buzzed round him; he was afraid to disappoint Mr. Arundel, he was sorry to disappoint Miss Miriam.

Strange scenes from his youth long forgotten, now rose before him: the proud hour when he first signed his name as Sir Rohan's steward; his marriage-day; the night his son was born. His wife, not as now with cap and spectacles, but young, blue-eyed, and smiling, seemed to sit by his side and hold his hand, while dim shadows of childhood and age held their revels before him. Past and present bore themselves unusually. Tasting the wild honey that, a truant boy, he had sucked from the bugloss horns, he drowned in it the flavor of his flask. The cheek he had kissed forty years ago still blushed in his remembrance, but the words spoken yesterday, it might be, sounded faint and far ; and feeblest, yet most persistent idea of all, was himself tearing his master's house in ruins about his head.

Another hour chimed. He had become torpid, the odd sensation was extending to his mind, he felt too weak to catch at life slipping by.

What strange things were moving now ? What face with its malignant mirth flashed on him ? He had thought Mr. Arundel would be displeased. And that sad reproachful one, was it his Master ? And were these, proud of duty never neglected, the stern old stewards dead and gone ? But who was this, awful and white, that ruffled his hair and would have made his flesh crawl, fleshless it-self, touching him with so chill a finger, smiling from those cloudy eyes, assuring him silently that he had done well ? In the noiseless tramp of what host was he marching ? What was this darkness around, this light, this freedom, opening to him ? And what were all the phantoms hurrying by, with him in their midst, and sweeping out, out, from the place ? The flowers might have cowered beneath a presence weightier than they, while the poisonous growths hailed their lord with bold censers and blistering dew, then have risen shaking a sweeter air from their cups, because they were alone again. The nightingale ceased singing in the thorns; the epiphytes fluttered forward to stare at the sleeper; the pallid gleams from some window now and then filled the conservatory with a ghastly light, and shone upon the old man trembling no more, but stiff and white as marble in his chair.

There was no physician who could help his case. Marc Arundel must come for the oath, since all engagements were broken. Mr. Redruth would not go into town that night.

Meanwhile, as Death throned himself here, Life was crowned in the house beyond, and the moments rounded in joy.

Miriam had been riding again with Sir Rohan, and returned, laden with wild fruits like Pomona, was making the night merry with her masquerading. Dancing down the vistas of the rooms, her riding-skirt gathered over her arm, laughing, talking, silent, she still transmuted his long hours by the simple fact of her companionship. And he, as gay, unconsciously inspired the very gladness that created his own. At length as midnight drew near, she had flown from his grasp, and pausing half-way up, dropped him a good-night song, and flown on again.

Sir Rohan moved and went out to close the green-house, delaying within to inhale the cool delicious fragrance. The oranges hung their lamps, dwarfed and golden through the soft gloom, near at hand; stately callas rose waxen-white and spotless, half-guessed, on the other side; and loose southern vines played with his hair and distilled the air around him. The clear sweet singing of a distant nocturne poured a brief melody through the quiet. He fancied he could see the rare scents, passionate, tender, and exhaustless, rolling in globes like smoke from the dropping tubes and shivering sprays.

But after a time the enjoyment became mingled with another feeling, he recognized something foreign in the place; and though he could not detect it, he would have said that the other end of the conservatory was filled with a misty brightness. He looked about him with a singular thought, for it appeared, at the moment, that everything he wrote or wrought, be it in pigments or in flowers, spelled but one word — the Ghost.

While thus thinking, Miriam's step broke the stillness, and she entered, with a lamp, from the chiller air, trailing her gown behind her, the plume of her riding-cap — a branch of the scarlet berries still clinging to it — mingling with her hair, and her face reflecting the brilliance of the scene.

"Mr. Redruth told me I should find my amaryllis here to-night," she said, bringing the frosty, out-door smell with her. "I had nearly forgotten. Where do you think he has put it? Among the lilies?" and seeking it, she walked slowly forward.

"Do you see the cereus?" she asked, at a distance, in a blaze of exultation. "It is a midnight sun, a whole constellation rather. And O, Sir Rohan! the century is capped, the agave is blown!"

Turning slowly with the uplifted lamp, her eye fell, the sparkle faded, her face grew pale again and borrowed the quiet beneath it.

"But what is this?" she cried through sudden tears.

Coming for her amaryllis, she had found the Lily of Annunciation. For the light fell upon Redruth silent as a stone, the white hair waving round his brow scarcely less gray, by contrast stiller; the hand hanging over the chair, still grasping the stem of his glass, while the bowl lay shattered on the floor; the face open-eyed, shrunken, and upturned with the mute, patient appeal of the dead; the alabaster vase still there, the flame within burned out; and the whole cold figure bathed in the richest odors of the world's bright belt, the breath of tangled jungle, brake, and forest, and wrapped in all the gorgeous beauty of the tropics.

XIX.

THE FACE IN THE FLASH.

A WEEK crept through the hushed house, and the funeral of Mr. Redruth was held with every honor, a provision settled upon his widow, and his son installed in his place. Shocked, but not deeply touched, — which would have been improbable, — Miriam's elastic spirits soon regained their equilibrium, and she employed herself to divert Sir Rohan's mind, and dissipate the shadow. She was yet too young and free to own the harvests of sorrow; nor did she know, if this had been a sorrow admitting such end, how to follow in the wild, and lead up to clearer heights; she would seek, instead, to bring one where he stood before. But Sir Rohan needed little of either treatment.

It had been scarcely affection so much as custom that bound him to the old steward, and one shrinks at the sudden sundering of any tie. With all his love for his master, Redruth had never been able to endear himself sufficiently to produce a real grief at his loss; for through fear of offence, he had refused those opportunities which, well used, would have been friendship. The quality we call moral courage is necessary to finished success, and poor Redruth's life had been a failure. Still Sir Rohan felt that he, also, had owed a duty which he had rejected, and he hoped, proportionately with that neglect, to meet his responsibility for the next. He was moved by the old man's affection and sincerity, no less than by his weakness, and he knew it would have been monstrous for him to blame a living being. Thus it did not take long to heal the wound, and having been much delayed, the time was once more appointed for their departure. St. Denys assisted his friend in such instruction as the new steward required, and again the hours slipped by too happily for counting, each one like a drop from the fabled elixir of life.

One only discord jarred upon this period. At the close of a certain day which had fled, like the days of the Blessed Gods, on the vans of inextinguishable laughter, a milder mood fell, one of deep quiet and satisfaction. A perfect space where each, aware of the great love in either's thought, preserves silence regarding it, and glances only on indifferent things. Sir Rohan stood at an open casement, folding Miriam in his arms, and saying little where a lingering kiss or closer pressure brimmed the lapse of happy thought. He did not dream of the surrender St. Denys had made in giving her to him. She was all his own. The past lay veiled and blank behind him, to be redeemed by a future that could multiply nothing but virtue; with such blessedness, the seed of that future, into what blossom would it burst!

A dry thunder-cloud had swept over the sky, and still tinged with the vanished light, was loftily heaping its cyclopean cumuli in the likeness of rolling petals, as if assuming shape from some huge magnolia growing unseen in the lost Atlantis. In its base silent lightnings pavilioned themselves, now and then leaping to earth with a rosy flare, and giving to all things, as the night grew deeper, a somewhat weird semblance.

Remaining thus, Sir Rohan remembered the sudden consternation that smote him when first he knew of the Ghost; the awe and heavy fear, annihilating doubt and following him like a second shadow; the stolidity in which he steeled himself till the edge of his terrors was blunted thereat; the keen watchfulness of intervening years harassed by her influence that bred only a ceaseless pain which he learned to endure; the frantic spasms of that season which had fevered him. He remembered all those hours, and compared them with this where he stood calm and whole, throbbing only with joy, and possessing the cordial of his transudation, sovereign, sweet, and inexhaustible. He wondered if without the past he could have measured the present; he chafed only that these moments were not immortal, or that together they might not slip the knot of life and wander free through fields of eternity too narrow to drain such love.

In the swift gleams he looked down at Miriam, her face on his arm, her lids fallen, glowing, dreaming, smiling, finding heaven with him as he with her; and in a stiller, intenser love he bent above her till she raised the languid splendor of her eyes and returned that passionate inspection.

Other flashes shot across them there, but if the

sky had shrivelled up, so that it left these two they would have been regardless; and Miriam in Sir Rohan's embrace at the open casement, her eyes dropping in the old bewitching way as the long succeeding kiss died into peace, did not see the object that, when Sir Rohan raised his head, in a more vivid sheet struck his sight and faded in the darkness rushing back. It was the head and shoulders of a man leaning one arm upon a horse's neck, and turned toward them. Was it some nightmare, or one of those allies of the Ghost, man and beast, staring at him out of the shadow? Was it that eldritch vision of Marc Arundel, that had so persecuted him with her other malicious enginery? Or was it the real face of Marc Arundel, white and ghastly in the lightning, and full of rancorous hate?

Whatever it might have been, it was withdrawn at the next flash; but notwithstanding, Sir Rohan's tranquillity was at an end,—swimming in a sea of rapture, he had suddenly touched shore.

But when morning again poured light into night, and Miriam met him, fresh and gay as a new creation, he forgot the face and its terrors, and again relinquished himself to the spell.

A flock of pigeons — mufflers, rufflers, fantails, and tumblers — came fluttering and pitchpoling down from the roofs and gables into the old garden, catching the sunshine in a thousand dainty irises, while they were at breakfast.

"Paphian doves?" asked St. Denys mischievously, tossing them some crumbs.

"And so you must have your fling at them!" retorted Miriam.

"At them? By no means. They don't do all the billing and cooing in the house."

"A noise that annoys some folks."

"Love is so pathetic to a third, you find, St. Denys."

"Especially to a minor third," assented St. Denys.

"Not so pathetic as sympathetic," Miriam subjoined. "I tremble lest your example incite papa to match it."

"O no," said St. Denys. "I'm content to match you."

"How brilliant you are!" said Sir Rohan. "Have you drugged the coffee?"

"Your untouched cup looks as if it were a drug. No; but I *made* it! There, papa, poor man, that caps the climax! Shrug your shoulder and remember nature's not to be conquered; vines that twist from right to left can't be made to twist from left to right. The duckling takes to water, — or, what is worse, coffee, — and the pursuer takes a ducking!"

"Miriam, have some mercy!" answered the horrified listener. "You grow worse as you grow older."

"And you don't fancy my bad-in-age! I shall make a gooseberry fool next, or put my ill-breeding into a tart, that I may be reproved accordingly."

"Certainly, I have spoiled you."

"Which is not my treatment of the coffee. I wanted some *café noir*, and, besides, Sir Rohan takes no breakfast, and who knows the magical effects of the potent berry? Confess that it needed oriental hands to brew, and an acquaintance with continental kitchens prior to one with Mrs. Redruth's. All a part of my gypsydom. Ah, you should have taken better care of me; here I graduate, a cook. But why should n't one make nectar? Look at this clear stream, pactolian, yellow as amber and aromatic as Arabia!"

"Aurum potabile," annotated Sir Rohan.

"Rendered shabbily, gold makes the pot —— Now indeed you 're horrified! You don't want me to display further knowledge of the cuisine. Never mind, papa, I won't."

"O," groaned St. Denys. "Must I repeat every day how vulgar it is — "

"Well? How vulgarities what?"

"Incorrigible child!" said Sir Rohan. "Nobody less severe than a pundit from the Punjaub will punish you properly for making such a Punchinello of yourself."

"Et tu Brute!" she returned, poising her fragrant cup.

"Similia similibus."

"And have you come over into Macedonia? But with what a philippic! A conjunction which calls to mind Philippi, which calls to mind the ghost that came to Brutus, which calls to mind, like a chapter in Numbers, a little odd dream I dreamed last night, papa. I thought I was standing at a window, being as small as children are when they cry for the moon, and looking up I was trying to make out the face in its desolate circle, when very clearly and distinctly it became Marc's;

upon which I was frightened, and after the absurd conduct of dreams tried to get down, nobody knowing how I got up, wherewith he began to sing, — the idea, now, of Marc's singing! — sing the last line of that little Kentish song I used to go to sleep by, —

'Wait till I come to thee!'

And I woke up with the great silent flash skimming over the sky from some distant ship's gun, I suppose, hailing a pilot for the channel, or something.   But was.n't it hateful?"

"Very.   But the moon is made of green cheese, you know, which produces indigestion, which produces nightmare, after your manner of induction and a certain luncheon of yestreen."

"Dear me, papa, I don't know whose quibbles are worse."

"What are you going to do, child? What is that basket for, and those napkins? and are you the whole commissariat for an army, with such a battery of bread and butter; or playing Charlotte to nobody's Werter?"

"My amazed papa, what an inquiring disposition! How am I to answer such a mouthful of questions ? Did you ever hear of a picnic ? but off at Abbey ruins, or mineral springs, or ultramontane forests ? Well, I — I, too, shall have a picnic, to-day ; but at lesser ruins, — a *fête champêtre* under aged lichen-painted walls, at the foot of this dear old garden ; by the choked spring that gurgles and sputters and sings and frolics to itself, whose water drunk from hollow leaves shall afford us infinite hilarity ; and you and Sir Rohan are to be my guests, and I accept no excuse, and your only roof is to be blue sky till said roof is gray as twilight, and we will make one veritable long Autumn day too short to hold us. Here is the first chicken that peeped in May, — he plays Werter well enough ; — and here is the tart I spoke of ; and here is a bottle of poison for you, and one of cream for me ; and see these brown pears, which Midas rex has fingered, and these Hamburg grapes, great Cleopatrian pearls and amethysts. Come !

The sweet sad autumn days will we
Make gay with blithe carousin',
Till Mirth's most merry companie
Shall seek our hearts to house in !"

And therewith, to roulade and capriccio, the

imperious Miss Miriam swept the helpless gentle-men through the casement whose threshold re-mained uncrossed till sunset, while every now and then chimes of gayest laughter and snatches of sweetest singing pealed hurriedly up the alleys and startled the pale chrysanthemums and wither-ing autumn flowers on their sad stems; uncared-for rusty blossoms, wan and rapt as a Greek chorus, who looked at each other with melancholy sur-prise and then drooped heavily again, as if they were long ago in the secret, and refused to listen to this last artifice of fate, the echo of a fragmen-tary happiness as brief as shallow.

XX.

THE CLANG OF HOOFS.

AT length their stay drew toward its close; the last day was fading, and Sir Rohan, having given his final orders, was idly pacing the hall, and longing for Miriam. He had no impatience now, for every hour answered to itself, too full of happiness to be hastened.

Miriam, whose voice woke the morning, carolling from her open window, and every now and then filled the dreary walls again with a glad purling, came singing down the stairs; and then, hanging on his arm as he continued his walk, finished the strain.

> Somewhere the long grass over lonely graves
> > Sobs in the rain.
> Somewhere the wild wind vainly o'er them raves
> > Who cease from pain.
> Somewhere, thro' weary years, one weeps, whose salt slow tears
> > Fall for refrain.

"I wonder," she said, after a moment's silence, "why always, when we are happiest, we choose the saddest songs."

"Perhaps," he replied, "to forestall calamity; to deceive Fate with a counterfeit."

"For a charm against Sorrow, you mean?"

"Sorrow! Sorrow! My darling, forget there is such a word!"

"You will never let me feel it," she responded.

"The wind shall not blow upon you!" he said, with fervency, followed by a laugh.

"And you take the windward side, Ungallant? No, no," she added, "if they were charms, all people might be gay, since who couldn't string a necklace of such amulets? I am more inclined to fancy my happiness a cuckoo who pushes the sad little songs from the nest."

"Vile comparison! Is it so false and fickle?"

"That, sir, will be as you please."

"Ah, sweet!" he said. "You know there is no heaven too high for me to sphere you there. That is, provided one had the ordering of the planets."

"Thank you, but earth is very well. Do you

know, Sir Rohan," she continued, naively, "I think you love me too much."

"Miriam!"

"Yes. There! there! Don't look at me so! Was I very wrong to say it?"

"The Easterns worshipped the sun, source of fire, scatterer of night. Have n't I good precedent for my adoration?"

"But I mean that if I should die, I think you would die too."

"Why not?"

"My dear! What do I wear this crown of laurel for?"

"Because you are a Queen, perhaps."

"Not at all. Because when my Love returns to his Art, I believe he wreathes himself with the same immortal boughs; but should he die, what laurel for him?"

"He would not need it then."

"One takes such even into death."

"How sweet a scent your crown has, when bruised!"

"It is poison, nevertheless," she rejoined.

"Why wear it, then?"

"Why?—For an emblem. There is poison in so strong love." .

"Your lecture is charming, your lips perfect. You may convert a Pariah, but never a Brahmin, never a High-Priest. Miriam, should you leave me, my love would grow praying for your return, and every word you speak makes you dearer!"

"I see," she exclaimed, as they entered the drawing-room, and sat together by St. Denys, "I see, clearly, my authority is to be absolute. So I enjoin my first behest."

"Yes, Miriam. Give me a command," he said, bending forward with his eyes upon her.

"You are never, never," she replied, archly, holding her finger before him, "to paint when I am away!"

"Bathos, pathos, and immutable as Athos," he interposed.

"No! that's too much," she continued, heedless of the remark. "We'll add a codicil to our will; not for a long, long while, that is. You shall dream no more dreams."

"Jealous?"

"Not I," she said, with a melodramatic air. "I scorn it. I'll be jealous of a real rival."

"A woman's love, sir, is an absorption," said St. Denys, glancing over his paper. "A sponge, you must learn, that wipes out every one else. Her love is to have no one loved but herself."

"O papa, what a libel! It must be one's self, and not one's lover, one loves when jealous."

"Right, little dame! I see, Rohan, by the news, Arundel contests his borough. What next?"

"Perfect love," said Miriam, still meditating, "implies perfect trust. And we have that, dear," she whispered.

Sir Rohan did not reply, but always clasping her, remained in thought. Slowly again his eyes re-sought hers, the fond exulting smile wreathing his lips as he felt the quickening throbs of her heart at his returning gaze.

"It is a singular thing, this joy," said he. "It makes me tremble; it seems unnatural. I have heard of people of great faith as suddenly feeling their spirituality wonderfully increased, and of others who experienced unaccountable mirthfulness, or happiness, or strength. But Death or some great suffering always supervened," he added with a shudder.

"I wonder why," said Miriam.

"Perhaps the soul," said St. Denys, "always

goes a little faster than life, a little beyond the fact; and so, having beat out and reached its mortal bars, surges back and flows with a double current over the mood of the hour."

The light was slowly dying, and they fell into silence, the delicious silence of passion, more affluent than endearments. It was only broken by the distant clang of hoofs.

At first far off, the quick sharp strokes struck nearer and nearer, like a clock measuring off the time. Here they clattered over a stony causeway, and now were muffled intermittently as the flail of a thresher. On the soft soil of the avenue the sound ferried the silence, like the fleet dip of an oar against the thole. They all sat listening, while it broke their dream; each beat fell distinct as a knell, and no one stirred till it was close upon them.

"It is Arundel," said Miriam then, starting to her feet. "I don't want to see him! Papa, do you mind entertaining him? And we will go out through the dining-room into that garden. I like that dim old garden, and the night begins to fall."

"Don't keep Sir Rohan out too long," returned

St. Denys, as she was disappearing. "Remember he still needs strength, Marc says."

Sir Rohan hesitated a moment. A singular idea of honor had restrained him from mentioning Arundel's murderous attempt, and this was leaving St. Denys at his mercy.

"You are apprehensive of mischief?" asked St. Denys. "You are Marc's neighbor, know his tricks, and would put me on my guard? Miriam told you, I believe, of some game presented us the morning we left here. That was well enough, had it not been bagged in the wood, while the shot pierced my coach, — an impossible way of killing two birds with one stone. He was as much surprised as anybody, probably. Don't fear for me, Rohan: I can take care of Marc; he is poor material for a villain. Besides he may have some business with me relative to Miriam; he has hinted as much."

Miriam ran back at Sir Rohan's delay.

"Papa, is it too cruel to tire you with staying here alone?" she said, putting her arms round his neck, and hiding her blushing cheek. "But I can't help showing him how happy I am, and I would hardly like to, you know."

He parted her dropping hair, and raising the head, gently kissed her forehead before she danced away again.

In after life, when Miriam, free from the rapid vehement tumult of her youth, led St. Denys down the slopes of a calm old age, in a world of quiet peace where neither old sorrows nor future joys obtruded, she was glad that on this night, in the midst of her delights, at the high tide of her happiness, she had not forgotten him.

XXI.

THE GHOST.

IT was nearly two hours later, when Miriam and Sir Rohan approached the house from the shore and paused at the foot of the lawn, near the white camellia-bush where he had seen her crowned with azalias. As they left the strand, a dun glare shone upon the wild sky, and the waves, so shortly since gray and dimly foam-capped, tossed like fanged serpents in the fiery light of their enchantress who, gathering as a magnet great vapors round her, rolled veiled and angry her glimmering rack up the great obscurity.

They paused now, because Arundel was leaving the door. He observed them, however, and drew near, with an extinguished cigar in his hand.

If a voice had whispered by his ear, "Be still.

Do not murder pity; do not destroy remembrance. Take mercy for a staff. You hate him? But see! that swift blood ebbs in hectics; these frosts work like fire; he is weaker to-day than yesterday; his disease consumes him surely; this deceitful decline delivers him to death. Can you not suffer Miriam to mourn a lover? Must you needs poison grief; make tears a sin; turn joy to disgust; stab the memory of love? Take mercy,—you are free so soon—" Had such a voice whispered, it would have been hushed in the imperious "Speak now!" of his will; because the last was destiny.

"I have been giving St. Denys the heads of that story I promised you, Miss Miriam," said he, after wishing them good evening. "And, if you like, you shall have it as well, since I may not be able to come again immediately."

Miriam glanced at Sir Rohan to see if he were protected from the damp. But he wore a cloak, and it was not a cold evening.

"Go on," she replied, with a nod. "We attend."

"It's not a long story," he said, walking to and fro before them. "O, by the way! Some time since, it occurred to me I might be of service to you in the line of my profession, by elucidating your mystery, Miss Miriam, if I had any clew. I intimated as much to St. Denys, who asked you what was that last whisper of your old nurse. And you said, he tells me — "

"That the ring my dying mother wore was hid beneath the seventh stone in the court-yard of the Tower," Miriam replied quickly, not choosing to hear the words from him.

"Exactly so. That the ring your mother wore, when dying, was buried in a book beneath the seventh stone from the gateway of the Tower. I wished to ascertain if I were quite correct. However, that's not my story.

"You must know," continued Arundel, stooping to pluck a blade of grass, "that the way in which I learned these facts — for they are true, Miss Miriam — has in it some dash of the supernatural. I first received a suspicion from certain ways and actions of a person whom I met; and putting together one thing and another, — remembering old county scandal; questioning somebody who had reason to be acquainted with the matter; detecting a likeness; and as I became more in-

terested, visiting the various localities and obtaining further and satisfactory information from the
original sources,—I soon made out a complete
case. But through it all, I have felt as if some
one were directing me; the right thing turned up
at the right time, so that not a moment has been
lost, and I could almost swear that I have been
assisted by some extraordinary and inexplicable
agency."

"O, charming," said Miriam, "a ghost in it!"

"Well, to begin. It appears that several years
ago,—before you were born, and I was but a
child myself,—two boys left school for the University. No matter for dates or names, just yet;
—facts hold good for John as for Peter. They
were warm friends, notwithstanding a slight difference in their years; for one, the elder was a
quiet cheerful boy, and was attracted, perhaps,
by the recklessness and brilliance of the other.
This other had a species of heroism about him,
—so it was called,—a flashing, uncertain element,
but no more resembling the real thing than a
will-o'-the-wisp resembles that solid red heart of
a burning back-log. That is to say, he would go
through fire and water to do some famous deed,

but I doubt much if he 'd have held an umbrella over an old woman with a shabby bonnet. Positively, I think he was a sorry fellow. However, the bigger boy saved him many a flogging, and he, in return, rendered him some important service, besides correcting his Greek exercises and writing his Latin verses. And so, fast friends, they left, as I said, for the University. The younger had been an orphan two or three years when they took their degrees, and the other was now, also, to receive possession of his estate ; to which, accordingly, having been put through the mill, they went down together; and in the press of business that met the heir, it is not at all strange that he was obliged to leave his friend much alone.

"One of the tenants on this estate was a woman between fifty and sixty in age, who held a tolerably good reputation, though more than once accused of too great intimacy with the gypsies and strolling women ; some thought she had come out from them. Still she was honest, and paid her rent, but had not much to say to her neighbors, who called her, on the whole, odd. She was a widow, and lived alone with a grand-daughter, a pretty girl, — no, something more than pretty, —

far too elegant and graceful for the peasants she herded with. Wandering round the region, in the absences of the other, the younger friend, as may be supposed, frequently met this girl. He was a likely-looking youth himself, — was rich, and a gentleman. She was beautiful, impassioned, yielding, — in short, they fell in love. Finally, the gentleman drew his visit to a close, left his unsuspecting friend, returned home for a day or two, and then went to a place he had in quite another part of the country.

"At the same time, the girl disappeared. Her grandmother concealed her surprise, and gave out that she was visiting in a distant town. Nobody believed her, but then nobody said so. Yet when the gentleman entered his residence at the North, he was accompanied by a lady, who has been described to me as the sweetest impersonation of beauty that ever crossed threshold. She was dressed, I am told, with great richness, and wore her splendor as an inheritance, but scarcely seemed to be his wife. They held no communication with any one, employed only such servants as were indispensable, and were totally wrapped in the pleasure of each other; they were never

29 *

found apart, and appeared to be insensible of the existence of others. Sometimes in a skiff they were seen rowing up the stream; sometimes the farmer heard a rash bold galloping, and they dashed by like a flash, with their gay laughs chasing behind; sometimes, by moon or star-light, they climbed the old Tower together and watched the prospect. It was a life of rich merriment and exultation, that, half repressed, burst into bright coruscations fanned by gusty glee,—a life bathed with delight and youth, he rejoicing in the blaze of her beauty, she revelling in adoration. I hope I'm not growing sentimental, Miss Miriam."

"You speak with unction, sir," she replied. "And then?"

"Why, nothing then, or soon. The sweetness cloyed. From a passion, I believe, the lover made it a study; but the intricate psychology baffled or wearied,—he became indifferent. They were met no more together; he rode all day among the hills, alone; she was seldom seen at all. Her beauty began to fall away,—eye and cheek were hollow, lips were pale. But latterly, before her unhappiness began, she had once or twice spoken with a cottager; the little children tumbling in her path had received a smile, already somewhat sad; kind donations, constant charities, were felt by the neighboring poor. Their hearts instinctively warmed to the lady, — who was to be pitied if happy, how much more if not! — and it was no great while before the keen eyes of these good farmwomen detected the cause of her change. But one evening, at about this time, she entered the nearest habitation, and asked that the son might be allowed to go to a distant place she mentioned, with a certain message, and she gave him a roll of gold pieces to deliver and pay his way. They noticed that she wore but one ring, a brilliant thing, on the hand where should have been the marriage ring. Of course he went with expedition, and when he returned the grandame came with him. When they met, said my informant, the lady only fell on her neck and wept, and went away without a word. Perhaps she hoped to regain her fair face and happiness when her child was born.

"So time went on, and the poor lady sat sighing her youth away in the dark room of the Tower. You are cold, Miss Miriam?"

Miriam had shivered as the moon, running out

on the skirts of a long cloud, sparkled at some glittering object Arundel held.

"O no," she said. "Go on."

Her hood had dropped upon her shoulder; she stood attending with a pitying air, a creature all radiance, and bliss, and blushing life, turning every now and then her flaming eyes and tender smile upon Sir Rohan.

With the narration, Sir Rohan had more than once started and flung away her hand, but as quickly seized it again, though his own was corpse-cold, and bent his burning glance on her alone, while it proceeded, for it seemed to him that his Ghost stood victorious with her hosts behind Arundel. His cap had fallen back, and the hair upon his brow was damp; his cloak, too, was hanging loosely, but in bronze-like, motionless folds; his eyes gleamed like caverns pouring forth floods of light; his face grew paler at every breath in the flying light of the chill November moon. And as the wild palpitations of his heart died out, the shadow of a statue was not more rigid than he.

"It is not long," said Arundel, again.

"One day toward sunset, the lover came into this dark room where the wretched lady sat. She had been looking listlessly at the illuminations of a manuscript, which, he had often told her, a monk, rather given to poetry than more orthodox scripture, had spent his lifetime in decorating. This monk had been a contemporary of Spenser, and an ancestor of the lover's; and so when, through some pique, he went into a cloister on the continent, he had taken his friend's book too. I have seen it since myself, Sir Rohan. A curious thing: on one side of the parchment, the verses copied fair, in garlands of flowers and leaves, with bright-feathered birds among the vines; on the other, the pictures, in Armenian blue, vermilion, and gilding. Here, —

> ' A troupe of Faunes and Satyres far away
> Within the wood were dauncing in a rownd.'

" There, teaching that ' rude, mishapen, monstrous rablement,' the fairest Una sat, ' straunge lady, in so straunge habiliment.' There, too, the image of that man of hell, that calls himself Despayre, sitting on the ground of his dark, doleful, dreary den, with hollow eyes and gaunt cheeks half hid by griesly locks; the one whose subtile tongue like dropping honey melteth into the

heart, you know, and who counsels the Red Cross
Knight : —

> ' Is not short payne well borne, that bringes long ease,
> 　And layes the soule to sleepe in quiet grave ?
> 　Sleepe after toyle, port after stormie seas,
> Ease after warre, death after life, does greatly please,' —

the Knight listening ' as he were charméd with in-
chaunted rimes,' while the carle cries, —

> ' Death is the end of woes : Die soone, O Faries sonne ! '

" Again, the gateway of the Bowre of Bliss, —

> ' Archt over head with an embracing vine,
> 　Whose bounches hanging downe seemd to entice
> 　All passers-by to taste their lushious wine,
> 　And did themselves into their hands incline,
> 　As freely offering to be gatheréd ;
> 　Some deepe empurpled as the hyacine,
> 　Some as the rubine laughing sweetely red,
> Some like faire emerandes, not yet well ripenéd :
> 　And them emongst some were of burnisht gold,
> 　So made by art to beautify the rest,
> 　Which did themselves emongst the leaves enfold.'

Or yet the damsel bathing in the fountain, as she
loosens the golden knot of hair over ivory shoulders, and

> ' Withall she langhéd, and she blusht withall,
> 　That blushing to her laughter gave more grace,
> 　And laughter to her blushing.'

"Here the face of Belphœbe shone out, where 'upon her eyelids many graces sate.' And yonder, the Masque of Cupid fills space after space with splendid emblazonry; and still further on, Colin Clout ('Who knows not Colin Clout?') pipes to his Lovely Lass circled by the

'Hundred naked maidens lily white
All raungéd in a ring, and dauncing in delight.'

A real work of art, Miss Miriam, though strange tasks for a monk. I have given it to St. Denys."

"I shall see it, then. But what has this book to do with the lady?"

"I had quite forgotten. The lady had it in her weary hand, but was not thinking of it. She must have been a sad picture herself, with her heartache. Perhaps he remembered, at the instant, what she was, not a year before, and contrasted the laughing, joyous siren he had met, with the sad woman, faded and forlorn, sacrificed for him. So he spoke tenderly, and called her to walk by the river-bank on which the Tower stood. She obeyed, but with a heavy step and slow movement, — all her light alacrity lost; besides, she was not well; and he hastened her sharply. They were standing on the brink, the book still in her hand, when, it may be, encouraged by so faint a glimpse of her old sunshine, she summoned heart, and told him the secret he had never guessed.

"It was a too legible writing of his sins. Harsh words followed,—a blow, perhaps,—I will not say, —for whether fallen, or dashed aside, in a moment more she was sweeping down the tide, with a small penknife, that he always carried, fixed in her bosom. As for him, he re-entered the Tower, paid and dismissed the servants, locked the door, and rushed away. Nor has that door been opened since."

Arundel, in his cruel dalliance, paused again to look at his auditors, ere resuming.

While he listened, almost divining each word before its utterance, Sir Rohan had seemed to perceive a fiery vapor rising from the earth and flowing, like a wall, around himself and Miriam ; but she, unconscious and intent, looked only on the ground.

"And the lady ? " she asked.

"Yes, you are interested, I see. The lady was not drowned ;—don't start—for her hair had caught in a floating branch, and the current landed her some half-mile further down, where she was found by the farmer and his son, and taken to the cottage. And the stab proved to be merely a scratch. Revived with difficulty, she spoke in broken sentences with her grandame now and then, chiefly of these occurrences; took her lover's ring from her finger, directing it to be restored; and lived only long enough to give birth to a child, whose father never knew of its existence; a daughter, whom the woman carried down to Kent, where it was adopted by the gentleman of whom I have already spoken. By St. Denys."

"Marc!" cried Miriam, springing forward. But Sir Rohan's grasp was on her arm like iron.

"A moment, Miss Miriam. The grandame did not obey the lady's direction respecting the ring, but concealed it; and after turning over one or two stones, I found it, together with the knife, whose point was rusted with a brown stain. I found it in that mouldy book beneath the seventh stone from the gateway. You shall see it directly. There is only one word more.

"I have fancied the silent old woman driving night and day, with the dreadful burden lying in the cart behind her. For before going to Kent she took the dead lady and carried her the long journey to the other place of the lover. There were always plenty to assist her. He was not there, however; but she buried her by night at the foot of a camellia-bush, and left her vengeance with it. You are standing on the spot, Sir Rohan!"

So saying, Arundel took a taper from a box in his pocket, and kindling it at his boot, held the ring beneath the little light, toward Miriam.

It was a broad gold hoop, of old workmanship, supporting a violet composed of amethysts and azure enamel; in its centre lay a large, sparkling diamond engraven with a singular device. Some lapidary, in a narrow home of European cities, had perhaps spent his prime upon the precious toil, cutting it by dawn and sunset, and retouching it at starlight. This antique intaglio presented a female figure holding in one hand a distaff, the flax from which, as she had spun it out, she had sportively wound about her. But the filament had snatched itself from her hand while she laughed, and had writhed round in the frightful contortions of a serpent, drawing, each moment, a longer length from the distaff to coil again on her neck and uplifted arm, while raising its head and glittering eyes with a curve, the foamy fangs flickered in her face. The terrible expression of her powerless despair was carved upon the playfulness that had had no time to pass away; both stood distinct, like a palimpsest exposed to fire. Round the ring this legend ran:

O Deus meus vindex!

Illum in istac die atrociter reminiscere.

Miriam did not observe this at once,—she was too greatly bewildered. She saw only a ring in the brief flash of the expiring taper. Suddenly it was dropped into her hand, and Arundel strode toward the house. But it rolled away unregarded in the moments of awful silence that ensued, while Miriam's wild eyes searched for refuge in the wreck.

The grasp left her hand only to fasten on her shoulder, and Sir Rohan compelled her gaze.

"We are standing on your mother's grave," he said in a hoarse voice torn by fragments from a shattered breast. "You are my child. Look at me. Miriam! Miriam! I am your father."

A dreadful noise was in his ears. Like a sword the Ghost struck in a blinding blade of light through his eyes. All the blood in his pulses sung across his brain; and he fell prostrate at her feet.

A space, Miriam stood lost. Then drawing back, she touched him curiously with her foot, in doubt, disgust. It was one of those instants that comprehend eternity; the next, she threw herself on the ground beside him, lifting his head on her bosom, and pouring forth wild prayers and cries and tears. Regardless of Arundel dashing away, of St. Denys hastening down, of all the world, she held him.

But vain to him was joy or grief. Cry or prayer he could not hear. Tears might not move him now, nor that long kiss reinspire life. It was a corpse within her arms.

Sir Rohan was dead of his Ghost.

THE END.

LIST OF BOOKS

PUBLISHED BY

J. E. TILTON & COMPANY,

161 Washington Street, Boston.

J. E. TILTON.   S. W. TILTON

ESCHATOLOGY; OR, THE SCRIPTURE DOCTRINE OF THE COMING OF THE LORD, THE JUDGMENT AND THE RESURRECTION. BY SAMUEL LEE. No book has appeared for a long time which has so universally excited the attention of our ablest thinkers and theologians. Fine cloth.

Price $1.00.

THE RECTORY OF MORELAND; OR, MY DUTY. This Religious Novel is one of the most interesting books ever issued; elevated in style and character, and is already the most popular fiction of its kind. Beautifully printed on tinted paper.

Price $1.00.

LIFE'S MORNING; OR, COUNSELS AND ENCOURAGEMENTS TO YOUTHFUL CHRISTIANS. A most timely and acceptable book for the young disciple. Tinted paper, gilt edges, and a new style of binding.

Price $1.00.

FADING FLOWERS. By the author of "Light on the Dark River," "The Broken Bud," etc. A beautiful collection of original and selected poetry, printed on tinted paper and in a highly ornamented style.

THE ROMAN QUESTION. By EDMOND ABOUT. Translated by Mrs. ANNIE T. WOOD, and edited with an Introduction by Rev. E. N. KIRK, D. D. The Boston Correct Edition. This is the last and most brilliant book from this popular French author, and this translation has met with unprecedented success throughout the country.

Price 60 cents.

GERMAINE. By EDMOND ABOUT, author of "The Roman
Question." Translated by MISS MARY L. BOOTH. Two years
ago, Putnam's Magazine characterized ABOUT as "*among the most
read and best paid French writers in light literature.*" Germaine is
his best novel.

Price $1.00.

LECTURES ON THEOLOGY. By REV. BENNET TYLER,
D. D., late President and Professor of Theology in the Theologi-
cal Institute of Connecticut. With a Memoir, by Rev. NAHUM
GALE, D. D. An indispensable volume to every clergyman and
student in theology. One vol. 8vo. Fine Portrait.

Price $1.50.

OLD SOUTH CHAPEL PRAYER MEETING. Its
Origin and History, with Interesting Narratives and Remarkable
Instances of Conversion in Answer to Prayer. This book is
read wherever the celebrated Prayer Meeting of which it treats is
known.

Price 50 cents.

**THE FRIENDS OF CHRIST IN THE NEW TES-
TAMENT.** Thirteen Discourses, by NEHEMIAH ADAMS,
D. D., Pastor of the Essex Street Church, Boston. A book well
known to every Christian family.

Price $1.00.

CHRIST A FRIEND. Thirteen Discourses, by NEHEMIAH
ADAMS, D. D., Pastor of the Essex Street Church, Boston. A
fitting companion to "The Friends of Christ."

Price $1.00.

AGNES AND THE LITTLE KEY; OR, BEREAVED PAR-
ENTS INSTRUCTED AND COMFORTED. "The record of an earthly
sorrow gradually gilded and finally glorified by a heavenly hope
and faith."

Price 75 cents.

CATHARINE. By the author of "Agnes and the Little Key."
The most beautiful book from the pen of this gifted author.

Price 75 cents.

WELLS OF BACA. By the author of " Morning and Night Watches." A book familiar to every mourner. Price 25 cents

THE MOTHERS OF THE BIBLE. By Mrs. S. G. ASHTON. With an Introduction by Rev. A. L. STONE. A book too well known to need praise. Price 75 cents.

THE LIGHT-HEARTED GIRL. By Rev. JOSEPH ALDEN, D. D. A beautiful juvenile. Illustrated. Price 34 cents.

BIOGRAPHY OF SELF-TAUGHT MEN. With an Introduction by Rev. B. B. EDWARDS. This has received the highest commendations as a valuable book for the young. Price 88 cents.

JACK AND HARRY. By MARY HOWITT. Beautifully printed on tinted paper, and elegantly illustrated. Price $1.00.

THE LOST LAMB. By Rev. JOSEPH ALDEN, D.D. A favorite juvenile by a popular author. Price 34 cents.

FOURTEEN PET GOSLINGS. A popular juvenile, handsomely illustrated. Price 38 cents.

THE CARDINAL FLOWER. By Rev. JOSEPH ALDEN, D. D. A favorite book with all children. Price 34 cents.

SIR ROHAN'S GHOST. A Romance.

DANDY JACK. A beautifully illustrated juvenile.

FAIRY STORIES FROM ELF LAND. Profusely illustrated by Billings. Price 75 cents.

THE BURIAL OF THE FIRST BORN. By Rev. JOSEPH ALDEN, D.D. A suitable companion to the previous volumes by the same author. Illustrated. Price 34 cents.

ART RECREATIONS. Being a complete guide to ornamental work. Profusely illustrated. Price $1.50.

BERTHA AND HER BAPTISM. By the author of "Agnes and the Little Key." A book in which the whole subject of Infant Baptism is treated in a most interesting manner.

Price 85 cents.

THE COMMUNION SABBATH. By NEHEMIAH ADAMS, D. D. A volume which treats of the privileges and characteristics of the Communion Service in a manner worthy of the sacred theme.

Price $1.00.

SERMON AND ADDRESS ON THE DEATH OF THE HON. RUFUS CHOATE. By NEHEMIAH ADAMS, D. D. Flexible cloth, tinted paper.

Price 25 cents.

DISCOURSES. By Rev. E. N. KIRK, D. D. With a fine Portrait. A valuable collection of Sermons from the pen of one of our most popular divines.

Price $1.12.

LESSONS AT THE CROSS. By SAMUEL HOPKINS. With an Introduction by Rev. GEO. W. BLAGDEN, D. D. A book rich in Christian experience, and which has already passed through several editions.

Price 75 cents.

SONGS IN THE NIGHT; OR, HYMNS FOR THE SICK AND SUFFERING. With an Introduction by Rev. A. C. THOMPSON. This book has proved itself peculiarly adapted to the wants of the sick room.

Price 75 cents.

SABBATH TALKS WITH LITTLE CHILDREN ABOUT JESUS. A charming book to interest and instruct the youthful mind.

Price 38 cents.

SABBATH TALKS WITH LITTLE CHILDREN ON THE PSALMS OF DAVID. A delightful companion to "Sabbath Talks about Jesus."

Price 38 cents.